Joyce Windsor was born in Kent and, on leaving school, went to work for the Inland Revenue, subsequently passing the examinations necessary for promotion within the service. Moving to Liverpool, she became part of a fascinating circle, living next door to Fritz Spiegl and just around the corner from Beryl Bainbridge. A shortage of money in no way impeded the determined party-givers of that era and, as a devotee of the Liverpool Philharmonic Orchestra, she was delighted to meet the people like Efrem Kurtz and François Poulenc.

She then moved south, first to Putney, then Dorset. In 1982 her husband died and she retreated to the Isle of Wight 'to die', but by chance hit upon a flourishing and companionable community of writers. Thus began one of the happiest periods of her life, which culminated in the publication of her first novel, *A Mislaid Magic*. The sequel to *A Mislaid Magic*, *After the Unicorn*, is also published by Black Swan.

Also by Joyce Windsor

AFTER THE UNICORN

and published by Black Swan

A Mislaid Magic

Joyce Windsor

BLACK SWAN

A MISLAID MAGIC
A BLACK SWAN BOOK : 0 552 99591 6

First publication in Great Britain

PRINTING HISTORY
Black Swan edition published 1994
Black Swan edition reissued 1996

Set in 11pt Linotype Melior by
County Typesetters, Margate Kent.

Black Swan Books are published by Transworld Publishers Ltd,
61–63 Uxbridge Road, London W5 5SA,
in Australia by Transworld Publishers (Australia) Pty Ltd,
15–25 Helles Avenue, Moorebank, NSW 2170,
and in New Zealand by Transworld Publishers (NZ) Ltd,
3 William Pickering Drive, Albany, Auckland.

Printed and bound in Great Britain by
Cox & Wyman Ltd, Reading, Berkshire.

To Tessa Krailing
with grateful love

Chapter One

From across the room my sister Claudia mouths something at me. Heads, legs, arms and bosoms get in the way for relatives are pouring in on us from all points of the compass. They anticipate a cultural feast that isn't going to happen. The Third Gunville Arts Festival, of June 1937, is off, null, void, the deadest of dead ducks. Naturally they want explanations.

The room is stifling. As I try to eel a way through to open another window and find out what Claudia wants I feel a nip on my bottom. Without turning round I say, 'Hallo, Uncle Henry, is Aunt Phyllida with you?'

'Oh, it's you, Amy. Sorry.'

He is disappointed, confirming that his attention is nothing more than a reflex induced by a female backside in motion. Although I am eighteen I seem to be low on sexual attraction or, as Claudia asserts, a case of arrested development. She claims to have been regularly pinched black-and-blue by Henry since she was fourteen.

'What did you say?' I ask her.

'Can't you get rid of this mob? Tell them that Father's at death's door or something.'

'They're not even listening to each other, let alone me.'

Our family excels at confusion. We seem over-endowed with insensitive, self-centred cousins and aunts and uncles. Signs of impending trouble pass them by.

'Can nobody tell me why the festival has been

cancelled so suddenly?' That is Grandmother Mottesfont. Her voice lows plaintively like a foghorn when she is put out. 'And where is Soapy Sonia?'

Soapy is a barely private adjective for our stepmother, mine and my brother Valentine's, and Portia's and Claudia's. She is the hostess, except that she is missing. The room seethes with various resentments for the only thing about her that the family wholeheartedly approves of is that she established the five-yearly Gunville festivals in the first place.

Without much hope of getting through to anyone I say, 'I know the why but not the where.'

'Do stop muttering, Amy, I can't hear myself think,' my grandmother says irritably.

It's a fiction of hers that I am an incorrigible chatterbox, a typical Mottesfont misjudgement. I am Amity Charlotte Augusta Savernake, youngest daughter of the Earl of Osmington. Most people shorten my name to Amy. In my paranoid moments (like now) I feel that I'm not thought worth the effort of three syllables, though usually I don't mind.

Both my sisters are blonde and beautiful in a somewhat sharp-nosed, chilly, English fashion, and I am small, brownish and unremarkable, so I am rarely noticed. I look on. People behave as though I were deaf, dumb and blind, if not downright half-witted.

Across the buzz of speculation Claudia's voice cuts with vicious calm. 'That woman's a raving lunatic. I can't get any sense out of her about my London Ball. If she makes a mess of it I'll choke her.'

As she is usually too indolent to rage the statement commands near-silence. She is twenty and should have been presented at Court last year. But it was 1936 and King George died in the January so the Court was in mourning. In her lazy fashion Claudia was furious with him. ('Why couldn't the wretched man hang on for just a few more months,' et cetera, et cetera.)

Any hope of getting Edward as a guest waned when

rumours began of something pretty steamy going on in the passion line. Pictures of Wallis Simpson eventually appeared in the newspapers. 'He's abdicating for that hag?' Claudia asked unbelievingly, and gave up our ex-monarch as an idiot.

'You need not worry, Claudia,' Grandmother tells her. 'I've kept my eye on everything. But I should very much like to be told what is happening. I hear it suggested that your father is bringing Nurse Hughes back after all these years.'

A momentary joy floods through me as I wrestle with this piece of news. Dear, loving, laughing Gwennie Hughes. She cried when Father sent her away and swore to write. I received one postcard from Cardiff and afterwards nothing. That must have been twelve years ago, for I was six and, so they told me, too old for a nanny and the nursery.

It was Soapy's doing, I imagine. She was my governess then and later she married my father. I believe now that she intercepted my letters, though at the time I broke my heart over Gwennie's defection and determined never to love anyone again, ever. A child is powerless, and broken promises can wound deeply.

Yet despite everything I can't help rather pitying Sonia. There's something touching about her. Although not the least bit naïve or simple she could not disguise her innocent delight at becoming a countess and having lots of money at her disposal. She even expressed pride in Gunville Place, the family seat, though it is a hideous and inconvenient Victorian monstrosity that ought to be pulled down at once.

Besides, she is absolutely luscious to look at. Imagine a gorgeous ice-cream sundae, full of fruits and syrup and smothered with mounds of whipped cream; that's Sonia. One can see men watering at the mouth and absolutely pining for a taste.

The daughter of a poor baronet, she desperately

wanted Father and tied herself in knots to catch him. Then, quite soon, she was the cause of the accident that changed him from a romantic war-hero into a burdensome invalid. Sonia isn't lucky and she is no good at all with suffering. Life has to be 'nice' – her word.

One gift she gave us that makes me eternally grateful – David, our half-brother. We all adore him, even Father, who with the rest of us is reticent and detached. Davy is nine years old now and a darling, my dearest companion and friend though he's only half my age. His skin is purest pale olive and his eyes are huge and toffee-brown between long, curling lashes. His hair curls too, all over his head. It is almost black but striped faintly with dark gold.

Sonia has taken him away with her. They left two days ago with mountains of luggage and without farewells in the second-best motor car and, incredible though it seems, my sisters failed to notice the finality of their departure. I feel desolate. Claudia is irritated but unconcerned.

Portia is furious at the breach of manners that has left her to deal with agitated musicians and actors. 'I can only suppose that Sonia's erratic behaviour is due to her age. I trust she will very soon come to her senses.'

She couldn't just say it's the menopause or the change of life like anyone else. Portia is engaged to a duke's son and very grand nowadays.

An elderly cousin gives tongue. 'We have travelled all the way from Norfolk for this festival and I cannot see why it shouldn't take place. I thought Sonia had Hughes dismissed because of her Welsh accent and allowing one of the children to refer to Osmington as Da. Said it was common.'

'Common is such a very common word,' Grandmother snaps. 'That woman's too damned genteel for me. She doesn't ring true. If a horse piddles she tells the girls to avert their eyes. Indispensible functions

10

offend her and she thoroughly disliked Nanny. Jealous if I'm any judge because Hughes made Gervase laugh.'

Her long-held opinion of Sonia's gentility may need revision. She's in for a shock. We are on the brink of an awful scandal and she isn't going to like it one bit.

Gervase is, of course, my father, the Earl of Osmington. Gwennie treated him like an exact contemporary though he is years the older. She told him bizarre anecdotes about her village in Wales, a place of love-crazed butchers, undertakers who gambled for corpses, and hell-fire preachers with a weakness for women.

Claudia, now thoroughly bored, says, 'David's never had a nanny so why do we need one now unless she's to look after Father? Isn't Gwennie trained or something?'

'Fully, I believe, but what of Sonia? Are we to expect more histrionics over a nurse?' Grandmother gives a moan and a couple of tears squeeze out of her eyes. 'Oh, if only your mother had not died so soon. I mourn for her every day of my life.'

She particularly resents Sonia for Mother was her only daughter. I mourn too, though at the time I didn't know my loss. It is almost impossible for children of such a family as ours to love their parents properly – we see so little of them. Nannies and nursery-maids take their place.

Naturally the family assumes that I was too young to be touched by Mother's death and that I don't remember her. The family is wrong. I've told no-one what happened to me on the day when Doctor Newton broke the news that Mother was dying.

She did something quite strange. The choice she made was brave and personal and frightening to me. For a while I tried to reject a memory I was too young to digest, but I think now that perhaps Mother understood and cared for me more than I realized.

I sit there and wonder what on earth to do with all these people. Claudia blinks and grins at me. 'Not at all like our lovely festival, is it? Perhaps it was Rudi and the pursuit of sex that made it fun.'

I smile back. 'Our' festival was ten years ago, the first, and full of event and excitement. Rudi, the greatest fixer of all time, would never have allowed the present shambles, but he is several thousand miles away wallowing in glamour.

Portia, looking serious and responsible, appears, standing with the housekeeper in the doorway. She discreetly counts heads. Her incisive voice cuts through the babble. 'I'm so sorry for the confusion. A cold luncheon will be served in the small dining-room in ten minutes.'

Claudia drifts towards her. Cheerful murmurs as the assorted guests collect wraps and handbags and make towards the food. 'Beautiful girls, Portia and Claudia,' Uncle Henry booms to my aunt. Then seeing me right beside him, he coughs and adds, 'And Amy of course—'

'Has rather nice eyes,' I say, finishing the sentence for him.

Mother died in 1924. I was just five years old. It was winter and she had influenza very badly but she wouldn't let the doctor be called. 'If he comes I shall refuse to see him,' she said to her maid. 'And I want the window open.'

'But it's snowing hard, my Lady.'

'Cold and clean. Go on, open it please.'

The maid did so and ran from the room leaving the door ajar. I knew from the look of fright on her face that she had decided to have the doctor sent for after all.

I was where I had no right to be, a runaway from the nursery. Our parents' wing of the house was forbidden to us children unless we were specially invited there. So I sat on a padded window-seat, hidden behind thick velvet curtains and watched the snow fall. It gave me a pleasantly dizzy feeling. The flakes drove diagonally, got muddled together as the wind blew them upwards, and touched the ground in scuffly little clouds.

Mother coughed painfully. Then she sighed and the sound made me both uncomfortable and curious. There was no-one in sight. I slid through the door and stood looking at her for a little while. A huge fire burned in the grate with a nursery guard in front of it and a steam kettle belching on a hob. The room smelt of medicine and cologne. A freezing draught from the open window bent the jet of steam into a curve and frayed the end into little wisps.

She leaned back against the pillows but her eyes were open and she stared as though the wall were not there at all. Already I had begun to believe myself invisible. Keeping very still I watched her watch nothing but I was wearing a holland pinafore and as I breathed it squeaked.

Suddenly she stretched out a hand and said gently, 'You can come here to me, Amy, if you want to. Don't be afraid.'

'No, Mamma.'

'Stay here where it's warm.'

She tucked me under the eiderdown and got out of bed. Gunville Place stands on a high ridge of Dorset downland overlooking the Vale of Blackmoor and from October until March the rooms were icy caverns. At night we all wrapped ourselves in flannel. Mother was wearing an old-fashioned, long-sleeved night-gown fastened up to the chin with pearl buttons. With painful slowness she took it off. She had never let her hair be bobbed and it fell from a big tortoiseshell slide past her waist like the mane of a palomino pony. Naked she walked across to the open window and stood there with the icy air blowing on to her. Against the stark whiteness outside her skin looked warm, a figurine of palest gold.

I could hear the breath rasping painfully in her

chest. She was behaving in a crazy, dangerous way but I was far too well disciplined to protest. Adults were always right. It was not for children to argue or criticize or make a big fuss. A sensation came over me of imminent sadness and change and in a small voice I asked, 'Why?'

Mother stood on. Flakes of snow scattered in over her and made a drift on the inside window-sill. Great shudders began to shake her. Her voice was husky but loud. 'You are still uncorrupted by life and I want you to hear this from me so that you know the truth. Quite soon, Amy, I'm going to die. I'm choosing my own way. I will not, I refuse absolutely, to wait and die of cancer.'

'What's that word, cancer?'

Her poor face seemed to shrink over the cheek-bones and pain-lines ran down to the corners of her mouth. She turned to me. 'Here, on my breast,' she said.

The flesh of it was misshapen and dark and the nipple sunk in like a withered black fruit. And I understood then why she didn't want the doctor to see.

'I put off doing anything about it for too long. At first I was busy, then I was afraid. Men hate women to be ill and a sick wife is only a burden to a man like your father. He needs an efficient organizer and hostess.'

'Please don't die,' I begged desperately. 'Can't Doctor Newton make you better? He made me better when I had the croup.'

She seemed to have forgotten that I was there. Sitting down heavily on the edge of the bed she talked on as if to herself. 'It's not the dying that's hard, though I hunger to live, it's this awful jealousy of those who will take what's mine, the thought of everything going on without me.'

I put an arm around her neck. She was burning with fever but her face was cold. 'Do you like Nanny Hughes?' she asked in a rasping whisper.

'Yes I do, Mamma.'

14

I inherited my previous nurse from my brother and sisters, and she never tired of telling me that I must always be quiet and good because I was a dreadful disappointment to my parents. After Portia and Claudia they hoped for a second son. So from the beginning I got it wrong and then my looks were against me too. Once she told the nursery-maid that I was a plain little mite and the least-loved child. 'A throwback, that's what she is.'

For days I worried. I imagined a tiny, useless fish hooked by mistake and then thrown back in the water. She retired, and Gwennie had been with me for over a year. On the day she arrived we sort of flew together like magnets; a case of instant love.

'And what do you think of Miss Rollands?'

That was Sonia, sometimes secretary to Father, sometimes my governess. One by one the others were escaping. Twelve-year-old Valentine was at Eton, and Portia boarded at a new girls' school near Sherborne. Claudia didn't want to be educated. When she was bored – and this happened often – she wandered off and went riding or cubbing with the grooms, or simply sat in her room chopping her hair about in fantastic styles and playing 'Alexander's Ragtime Band' on the gramophone.

After a careful look to make sure I was meant to tell the truth, I said, 'She's silly, and not nice to animals. She wanted all the stable-kittens drowned, can you believe that, Mamma? Poor little things. And when Portia's puppy jumped up and laddered her rotten old silk stockings she kicked it – *hard*.'

Gwennie had the kindest heart for everyone. Her father was a vet and she hated cruelty to any creature, even bats, which gave me the horrors. 'An anxious poor thing,' she said, when she heard the tale, 'artificial silk, eleven-three-farthings the pair at Gamages, there's sad.' Her voice mourned for the poverty-stricken Sonia, then brisked up to add, 'And if she does that again to a dog I'll fetch out the bones warm from her legs.'

That interested Claudia. 'How will you do it? Can I watch?'

'A figure of speech only,' said Gwennie, grinning at her disappointment.

'I wish you and Miss Rollands could like each other better,' Mother said. 'Darling, there's not much time. The maid's frightened and they'll have sent for Doctor Newton by now. Just one thing, but so important. You'll be told that my death is a happy release, well, it isn't, so don't believe them. Life is magical and hard to leave until dignity goes.' She hugged me to her and kissed me on the cheek. 'I don't worry so much about the others, they are true Savernakes, healthy, tough, ordinary children. But the mind is a private, sacred place and you must keep yours free from their interference. Sonia Rollands will try to change you. Don't let her. Promise me.'

I was not sure what she meant but I promised. 'Why will she try to change me?'

'When I'm dead she will marry your father.'

'No,' I said, feeling angry and desolate and having no words for the anxieties in my heart. How could Mother die and leave us to that woman? I would not believe it. 'She mustn't. We don't want her, none of us do. Don't, oh, don't.'

Doctor Newton's new Ford rattled up the driveway. Mother pulled the covers to her chin. 'Go now, darling. Heaven bless you.'

Returning to my hiding-place behind the curtains I heard the doctor pass by. For the time I hated everyone and everything. I was lost in this nasty adult world and not even a proper Savernake. The mind that I was to keep free from interference presented me with troublesome images. My little white mouse had died. It lay at the bottom of its cage, stiff and ugly and useless. Could my mother look like that?

Voices murmured in her room. Then the doctor shouted, 'A year ago I could have helped you, now it's too late. Why didn't you come to me at once?'

Where Mother got the strength from I don't know but she shouted too, and angrily. 'To be cut about and maimed and then to die? This way is better.'

'You are a foolish, obstinate woman and you have pneumonia, as I dare say you intended.' Then a long silence. 'If ever I'm in a comparable situation may I have the courage to do the same.'

Mother gave a sound between a laugh and a sob. 'They call pneumonia the old people's friend, don't they? Will it be friendly to me?'

'My dear lady!'

'You won't fight me? I shall die easily, you swear?'

'What would I fight with? The weapons of my profession are pitiful enough, and when they are used up only kindness is left.'

Soft footsteps sounded. Someone crept along the corridor and Gwennie whispered, 'Amy, are you there?'

I ran to her and clasped her round the knees. Tears dripped down my face and my nose badly wanted blowing. Out of habit I did my crying silently. Picking me up she said, 'A sad old girl you are, and no wonder. Don't shut it up inside you. It's all right to have a good bawl.'

Bawl was not the word. I sobbed and bellowed on her shoulder and she held me until I fell asleep.

That was the last time I saw my mother. She failed to negotiate the crisis of pneumonia and died ten days later, gently, in her sleep. Valentine and Portia came home. Val stopped Claudia from playing her gramophone until after the funeral. As soon as he went back to Eton the ragtime tunes started up again and I guessed that she was crying and didn't want to be heard.

Chapter Two

It saddened me afterwards to think how little I really missed having a mother. Nursery life carried on as usual. I suppose that Gwennie shielded me from loss as she protected me from Portia's disdain and Claudia's bullying.

One evening at bedtime a surprising thing happened. I was already bathed and in my dressing-gown. Gwennie had drawn my chair to the fender while she warmed milk on the hob. The room felt cosy and sleepy. There was a knock at the door of the night-nursery and Father came in, looking diffident.

Most of the time Sonia ran around him like a puppy-dog. We hardly saw her in the schoolroom. 'Can you read your books for an hour, darlings? So many things to be arranged, and Daddy needs me just now.'

Father was always Father to us, never Daddy. Claudia snorted. She leaned back in her chair and enquired languidly of the ceiling, 'Now let me see, would that be Daddy Rollands? Or Daddy Longlegs, p'raps?'

The cream coating soured a little. 'That isn't clever, it's impertinent, Claudia. When I was seven I spoke when I was spoken to.'

'But, Miss Rollands, you did speak to me, you said darlings, didn't you? And I've finished my book. It was jolly boring.'

I thought for a moment that Sonia would slap her but she took a deep breath and said in a tone so patronizing that I winced, 'Borrow one of Amy's then, some nursery rhymes, perhaps.'

She left before Claudia could draw breath to argue. On the whole Sonia had the best of that exchange. 'Bugger,' Claudia said, and slouched off to her room.

Perhaps in spite of Sonia's attentions Father felt lonely in the evenings. Certainly he scarcely knew his children, except for Valentine, his heir and much more important than the rest of us. He hovered in the doorway until Gwennie said in her pretty sing-song voice, 'Come in, my Lord, where it's warm. Now, Amy, my little one, drink up your milk and Dada here will put you to bed.'

Why didn't I mind that Gwennie referred to him in much the same way as Sonia had done? Because I loved the one and not the other.

'I expect she would rather have you,' Father murmured.

Gwennie shook her head vigorously. 'Not shy, are you, my Lord? No need. I used to prop my eyes open not to fall asleep before my Da came home to kiss me good-night.'

When I had finished the milk, as slowly as I could to prolong the marvel, Father lifted me awkwardly and laid me down in the little bed. 'Good night, Amity.'

'You haven't kissed me.'

'So I haven't.' He bent over and kissed my cheek.

'I want Taffy, please.'

He gave Gwennie a perplexed look.

'Her teddy-bear. I'll fetch it. Tea's brewing if you'll take a cup with me.'

They went through into the day-nursery and I heard their voices and Gwennie's occasional laughter. Then I fell asleep. After that night he came often, right through the summer into autumn. For some months Gwennie was happier than ever, singing snatches of Welsh songs while we were out on our walks and telling me about Merlin and Uther Pendragon and Arthur, the King.

Conscious life began for me when I started to read

and that was so early that it seemed to have been for ever. It puzzled me when Sonia suggested a visit to the nursery and said, 'I can put you to bed and read you a story. *Winnie the Pooh* is a nice book.'

A touch of Claudia got into me. 'No thank you. I read that when I was four. Nanny tells me and my Dada lovely stories and then *he* puts me to bed.'

Two lines appeared at the top of her nose. They looked grey against the white skin and I noticed face-powder in the creases. Claudia told me once in a tone of utter contempt that Sonia painted. I thought at the time she meant the water-colours that hung to dry on a little line in the schoolroom. Sure enough, Sonia's mouth and cheeks were redder than nature, but so pretty that I had to admire them. Her voice sounded stiff. 'And does Nanny teach you to call your father Dada? How very common.'

She turned crossly away and I forgot about her. Then one winter's night Father stayed talking to Gwennie for a long time. When he went I thought I heard her crying. I called out. The nightlight made the room all shadows. She put her head around the door and said steadily, 'Not frightened, is it? Sleep now, old lady.'

The next day I watched for signs of tears but she was the same smiling Gwennie, only perhaps quieter. Father did not visit us that night. Nor did he ever put me to bed again. A year had passed since my mother's death and on the first of February, 1925, a few days after my sixth birthday, his engagement to Sonia was announced.

Poor Soapy, during the months that followed she tried dreadfully hard to please. The triumph showed, of course. I believe she felt that at last she had conquered us. Watched by a dozen pairs of cold, unsentimental eyes, she tripped around, oozing clichés and paying what she thought of as tributes to the dead until I wanted to stop my ears and hear no more. That was the time when she earned her adjective.

She told us that our mother's death was the happy release of a suffering soul, exactly as Mother predicted, and that she prayed to be able to bring the gift of comfort to Father.

As a child Claudia definitely had a coarse streak. Possibly she spent too much time in the stables, learning swear-words and other things. She got really irritated. In Sonia's hearing she muttered, 'If that sodding woman says happy release one more time, I'll slap her across the mouth.'

Sonia chose not to hear. The way in which she managed to rouse people to violence astonished me, as did her inability to see danger signals. To a six-year-old child, Grandmother Mottesfont was utterly terrifying. She was tall, and upright then, and big by any standard. With age she shrank a bit but I suppose she stood about five feet ten in her stockings, her shoulders were massive, and several children or dwarves could have hidden under her bosom.

Grandmother had been likened to Queen Mary and she always wore the same sort of hat called a toque. The effect was of an informal crown made of silk or velvet or grosgrain. She smiled rarely. Her mouth was mostly set in a grim, seamy line like a darn in linen. Yet she had a softer side and she utterly worshipped Mother, her ewe-lamb. Loss left her and Grandpa heart-broken and struggling to contain their grief.

The grandparents' home was in London but at Gunville Place they occupied a private apartment that had become their absolute domain. We never breached the conventions of good manners. But Sonia behaved towards them as though they were her guests and took to dropping in without invitation. She did this one afternoon when they had asked me to have tea with them.

'Good afternoon, Miss Rollands,' Grandmother said.

'Since you are here I will ask for another cup to be brought.'

'No thank you, please don't trouble. Is there anything you need, anything I can have sent up to you?'

In black chiffon – adopted in mourning for Mother and not yet abandoned – she dazzled, and somehow her superb breasts swelled out of the flattening bustband in milky splendour. Even Grandpa had trouble keeping his eyes off them. This did not escape my grandmother's notice but the somewhat weary glare she turned on Sonia lacked its customary power. 'Nothing.'

I sat on Grandpa's lap, listening to his big pocket-watch tick like a racing heartbeat while he fed me snippets of cinnamon toast. It mystified me that Sonia was so insensitive to the atmosphere. How could she not have felt the tension and sorrow? She chattered about Father and how she managed to 'take him out of himself', and then lilted cheerily into that sad room, 'How cosy this is. When Gervase and I are married I hope you will look upon me as another daughter.'

My bereaved grandmother had been patronized enough. A sound like a sob emerged from her capacious lungs. 'Perhaps you mean well,' she said in a low, almost pleading voice. 'I will do you the credit of believing you to be sincere, but such intrusions help no-one, least of all yourself. Please go until we are ready for guests.'

Her eyes glittered, perhaps with tears. As if I were a worm in Sonia's brain I sensed in her the need to bring out every 'suitable' meaningless platitude. Silently I begged her, don't, please, please don't say anything else.

'Believe me, I understand and share in your sorrow,' Sonia said.

Grief can be cruel when affronted. To most minor cuts Sonia's creamy skin seemed impervious. I had thought that only Claudia could regularly manage to drive home the poisoned bodkin. But Grandmother was in pain. 'Miss Rollands, you understand nothing. I trust that poor Gervase never discovers in you your commonplace, vulgar mind and the triviality of your emotions. Now, leave at once and do not return unless you are summoned.'

Sonia flinched. Her eyes, of a pale greenish-hazel and without depth, betrayed every shade of emotion. The clarity went from them. She hung her head like a punished child and the shingled curls trembled on her white forehead. How I wished I could like her and feel sorry, but I couldn't. She walked the whole length of the long drawing-room, knowing that hostile eyes followed her, and fumbled with the door-handle. Perhaps she hoped to be called back.

When the door closed Grandmother said, 'Detestable emollient creature! She reminds me of soft, cheap soap that's been left too long in water.'

'Soapy indeed,' agreed Grandpa hastily, 'but I think the poor girl meant well – thought it was the thing to do, no doubt.'

'How I detest well-meaning, ladylike people. Give me honest vulgarity any day.' And remembering me belatedly, Grandmother said, 'Run along to Nurse now, Amy. It's almost time for your bath.'

'Is Miss Rollands really going to be my Mamma?' I asked her.

'Oh God, oh damnation! There's no escape. We shall be sanitized and slimed to death.'

Grandpa patted her hand. 'There now, my dear, you worry too much. Once she gets securely into Gervase's bed we shall see nothing of her,' he said reasonably.

In the June following her engagement Soapy was due to become the new Countess of Osmington. On a rainy day in April she sent a maid to summon me from the nursery to hear her plans. The message expressly mentioned that Nanny need not trouble but I refused absolutely to go without her.

Sonia wanted her 'darling daughters' – us – to be bridesmaids, together with three of her cousins. Wouldn't that be lovely? Sweet-pea colours as it was to be a summer wedding; the bigger girls in mauve, then blue for the next oldest, and Claudia and Amy, as the littlest ones, in pink.

'No thank you, I feel I should not care for it,' Portia said with the cold haughtiness for which she was to become renowned. Claudia stared silently with such venom on her face that Sonia wilted. 'Amy, you will, I'm sure,' she said. 'We've always been great pals, haven't we?'

Pals – the word made me squirm with embarrass-ment – and with Sonia, I ask you? Feeling a bit sick, I hung on to Gwennie's hand, put my free thumb in my mouth and said nothing.

'Don't suck your thumb, dear, it's common. I'm sur-prised Nanny Hughes doesn't correct you as she should.'

Gwennie laughed softly. She looked particularly pretty that day with dark curls escaping from her white and grey uniform-veil and her blue eyes glinting. 'Oh, we are posh here,' she said. 'Say now, Amy, my lovely one, do you want to wear pink silk and follow Miss Rollands up the church aisle? There's swank for you!'

Between the two women was a tension I did not understand. It felt almost as if the affront to my dead mother extended somehow to Gwennie and I began to be worried and sad. In those days I had one great talent. I could draw illness to me as a witch draws demons and spirits. 'I can't, I'm getting the measles,' I said firmly. And so I did, quite badly.

A month before the wedding day Father again visited the nursery. It was late. I was in bed, feverish and trying not to sleep for fear of the nightmare horrors that waited for me whenever I lost consciousness. A full moon stared through the window.

'I want to talk to you,' Father said to Gwennie. 'How is Amy?'

'Hurting, still, she is, in the head and back. A bad turn, but passing.'

He came and sat beside me with the saddest face. 'I'm disappointed in my girls,' he said. 'Sonia is not, I'm sure, unkind to any of you but you have hurt her feelings, you know.'

Gwennie said, unsmiling, 'Loyalties then, isn't it? Children trust where they choose, and Miss Rollands will want them to be loving her and forgetting their mother. She has need of patience, and something more.'

I could see that her frankness troubled him and I half expected him to react angrily. But of course he was used to nannies and their uncompromising tongues. 'Am I doing wrong then?' he asked dryly. 'A wife is necessary to me. Haven't I tried other ways and been disappointed?'

'There's pretty as a dream she is, and wishing to please you,' Gwennie said hastily, handing him a large white nursery cup of strong tea and sounding uncomfortable.

She stood the biscuit-tin at his elbow. Father selected a ginger-nut and crunched it with enjoyment. 'Why do I never get these downstairs?'

Then she laughed at him. 'Ask, why not, insist, or what's an earl for?'

'When my daughters don't choose to please me, nothing much. They'll be at the church if I have to rope them to the pews.'

'Not Amy,' she said firmly, 'not unless she is quite well. It isn't her fault she has the measles.'

Father looked down at me with rather an odd expression on his face. I gave him a wan smile and closed my eyes. Claudia would pinch me black and blue if I agreed to be Sonia's bridesmaid, but I could hardly tell him that. Yet I was quite sorry to miss the new experience of a wedding.

'But a convenient and extraordinary coincidence, is it not? She's an uncanny child and not like the others at all. We run to bone and Amy's so small. Sometimes I wonder if I'm harbouring a changeling under my roof.'

So all the things my old nanny told me were true. I was an absolute failure, unrecognizable as his daughter. A terrible, lost ache swept over me and a few tears ran down my face.

Gwennie bent over me. 'Hisht you now, my old lady, and sleep. No blame to you, none whatsoever. Changeling is it? I wish I might have ten such. Aren't you a chime-child, and special?'

'What on earth is a chime-child?' Father asked.

'If it's all the same to you, my Lord, you will not say things of Amy to hurt her in her feelings in front of me. Born between Friday midnight and Saturday dawn, that's a chime-child, and gifted with the second-sight perhaps.'

'Are you angry with me?'

'Only sorry. To be so clumsy with children as you are.'

He heaved a deep sigh. 'And with women, it seems. Can we talk now?'

They went away into the day-nursery and I fell asleep only to dream of them and Sonia. 'Impossible, and you know it,' Gwennie said and shook the moon out of the sky with a rattle of curtain-rings. 'Who you marry matters. She will suit the position indeed.'

Sonia hung upside-down and peered through the window. A nightmare put out skeleton hands and snatched at me while I tried to wrestle with it. It said loudly in Father's voice, 'She wants me to dismiss you. I refused.'

'Ah yes then, it's best I go, not dismissed, mind, but resigning. You will tell Amy for I cannot.'

'Oh, Gwennie, please.'

'Give it rest now, you know how it is with me.'

I tried to scream but only a harsh whisper came out. Gwennie heard and came running, and I clung to her, forgetting why I had called.

Father told me as soon as I became convalescent: 'Miss Hughes's mother is sick and she is needed at home, isn't that right, Nanny?'

'If you say so, my Lord.'

'You're telling lies,' I said. 'She mustn't go.'

'Amy, it's time you left the nursery. Sonia has had a lovely room prepared for you, all to yourself. And there are some rabbits waiting for you in the stable.'

The extent of their betrayal and my loss reached me then and I began to scream with grief and anger. 'No, no, no, no. I don't want a lovely room or rabbits, I just want Nanny.'

Did Father really say through the hullabaloo, 'I feel like crying with her,' or did I imagine it?

Gwennie held and hugged me. Her blue eyes overflowed and big tears rolled down her face and got muddled up with mine. 'Be my good old lady then and I'll write to you.' And to Father she said, 'Take her, please, I can't bear to say goodbye.'

My new room turned out to be a round, narrow torture-chamber in one of the pretentious towers that decorate each corner of Gunville Place. No power in earth or heaven could have made it lovely. On the high ceiling were gross swags of swollen plaster fruit and diseased-looking flowers, and the narrow lancet windows excluded most of the light.

Sonia had decked it out in baby-pink muslin. It was horrible. Night after night I wept for Gwennie and wished I were not an earl's daughter. I longed to live in a square white house, with a semi-circular fanlight over the front door. There would be four front steps

27

and iron railings painted black, and rooms that people would like to sit in. Did it exist? For me it did and I began to look for it wherever I went.

And I loathed the rabbits. I wouldn't even name them though Soapy came up with some truly vomit-making suggestions like Fluffy and Buffy. To me they were just her and him. They were black-and-white and the doe had pinky eyes. When the buck was let out of the cage he bit my toe painfully, ruining the new red leather Clark's sandals that Grandmother had given me.

Claudia quite liked them, the rabbits that is – she thought the sandals babyish. Sometimes she came with me when I had to feed them. One day the buck leapt on top of the doe, half-squashing her. 'He's fighting,' I said interestedly. 'Perhaps he'll kill her.'

'He's doing sex, stupid,' Claudia said.

'What's that? What's it for?'

'Don't you know anything? It's to make more rabbits. You'll have dozens.'

The appalling prospect hardened me. I marched off and waylaid Sonia. 'Sod rabbits,' I said, 'you feed them.'

She avoided me for several days. Grandpa Mottesfont told me on the quiet that she complained to Father that I swore at her and that Claudia was a corrupting influence.

'What did he say? Is he angry with me?'

'Not he. He said, "We've given the child dross for gold. I won't tamper with her life again."'

That was my last rebellion. No-one gave me serious thought afterwards or even seemed quite aware of my existence. I battled through the indignities of child-hood alone. Gwennie sent a postcard showing Cardiff Castle. On it she said I was not to forget her for she loved and missed me. She asked to be remembered to Father.

I didn't forget but she must have done for she never

wrote to me again. Upset, I turned to petty crime. I became quite an accomplished thief, starting a fund to buy my white house out of filched pennies and six-pences. Grandpa winked at me one day and offered me a shilling. 'Or would it be more interesting to steal it?' he asked.

So I decided to reform and gave Claudia back her blue celluloid hair-slide and the ring she'd got out of a Christmas cracker. I kept the money since it was for buying a dream and began to keep a secret journal. An aunt had given me a Letts diary for Christmas but the spaces were too small. I fetched a stack of exer-cise books from the schoolroom. My thoughts and emotions were primitive enough but on later reading I shivered a little. A child's observation can be frighten-ingly cold and clinical, and they are all fixed there in round-hand, the family and the friends, and their secrets.

My grandparents more or less made me go to the wedding. 'The servants and workers will be there and we must not let your father down.'

Sonia looked utterly delectable and radiantly happy. Father was, after all, a handsome man as well as being an earl and a tremendous catch. She behaved with a soft, appealing charm that I found hard to resist until I thought of Gwennie.

Valentine, who was a nice boy and kind, made a diplomatic speech. Portia congratulated them coldly but politely and earned a grateful smile from Father. To several guests she announced her intention of becoming a nun. She seemed to be going through a religious experience, or perhaps she only wanted to seem persecuted.

Predictably Claudia idled through the ceremony and reception in a state of torpor. Then eight-and-a-half, she managed to look eighteen. She had slicked her fair hair down under a cloche hat and obtained from

29

somewhere a shiny sort of dress with handkerchief hems. Instead of ignoring me as she usually did at parties, she collected a large plateful of food and sloped off, dragging me with her to her room.

'Doesn't Sonia look nice?' I ventured, forgetting the power of Claudia's fingers.

Sure enough, her sharp nose pointed at me like a beak and she pinched me hard. 'She's sending me to rotten school, rat, and if you don't hate her I'll kill you.'

The threat didn't alarm me. I knew that she was too idle even to swat a fly. 'What happens now?'

'Oh, I expect they'll go away and do sex a lot and Soapy-bitch will smarm about spending piles of money.'

I had a vision of them coming back loaded down with baby rabbits but even my ignorance could not support the idea. 'Will they have some children?'

My voice sounded nervous and Claudia pounced. 'Dozens, and we shall be pushed out, unloved, to work in the fields in rags until we die. You're the smallest so you'll be first.'

'Shall I live in a cottage and not be a lady any more?'

'A peasant in a hovel with rats.'

'Then I don't think I mind very much. I could paint it white and get a terrier to kill all the rats.'

'A traitor to our class!' Disappointed with my reaction, she pinched me again then stretched out on her bed. 'Bugger off, I'm tired.'

Father took Sonia to Europe and they were away for several months. A few postcards came for us from different countries. Claudia tore them up.

The hunting season began soon after they returned. Sonia rode a little. A safe mount we called the rocking-horse was always saddled for her. Basically she was nervous of animals, particularly horses, but she conceived the notion of keeping up with Father during the hunt. She practised gallops in the paddock and tried to jump a low box-hedge that fringed the drive.

My grandparents and I watched from their window as the hedge gradually became demolished. Grandpa snorted. 'The woman has no business near a stable. Why will she ride when she's a blighted menace on horseback?'

'Oh, vanity of course,' said Grandmother. 'Her legs look well in breeches and boots.'

'An avid piece,' Grandfather said unexpectedly, 'sex-ridden about the eyes, but virtuous. What a mixture! She'll wear him out.'

There was a pleased note in his voice. He did not much care for Father, blaming him quite unjustly for the early death of his daughter. I looked up the word avid in the dictionary. It disappointed me rather as it only meant greedy or hungry or desiring keenly, nothing to do with being sex-ridden at all.

When it happened, the accident changed Grandpa's feelings as it changed everything for ever. I hated things to be killed and never rode with the hounds but I loved to see the Hunt meet, and Father in his pink coat and black cap. On Boxing Day morning the weather was clear and frosty – just right. I saw him go down to the stables with Sonia beside him and ran after them. His black hunter and Sonia's rocking-horse stood saddled and ready in the stable yard.

'Not that one,' Sonia said petulantly. 'I tried the young mare last week and I shall ride her.'

The head stableman met Father's eyes and shook his head which seemed to throw Sonia into a temper. She pushed past them into the stall and began to struggle with the harness.

'This is foolish, Sonia, but if you must risk being thrown I'd better help you,' Father said, easing in after her. 'Lead her out, then drop the saddle on her back, don't throw it, and tighten the girths gently.'

I could see how much she wanted to show that she

could manage by herself. She wouldn't wait until they were in the yard. In the stall there was hardly room to move, and the mare, excited by the prospect of exercise, pranced a bit and stepped on Sonia's foot. It hurt her, of course. As Father went forward she yelled and lashed out with her hunting-crop, catching the horse on the nose.

It screamed and reared. In that small space it was frightening and Sonia went out of her head with terror. She hit it again and again. The poor beast tried to back and bolt but Father stood in its way. He struggled to hold it but it slithered on the icy ground and went over on its side, kicking, and he was underneath it.

Sonia shrieked and shrieked. I hauled her out and pushed her across the yard, not caring what happened to her. While they got the mare to her feet and lifted Father on to an improvised stretcher he didn't make a sound though the pain must have been awful. His pelvis and both his legs were crushed. I thought he would die.

Rules were suspended. Every day I stole through the dressing-room into his bedroom and no-one tried to stop me. High screens shielded the bed from draughts. Probably they didn't even notice me sitting there.

After months of operations and agony he recovered a little but the numerous doctors could not give him back a whole body. 'We can do no more,' they said.

'Am I to go through life crippled like this?'

'My Lord, you will walk again supported on sticks. I wish we could work a miracle.'

He gazed sombrely into a future that held nothing. After a while he sighed and said, 'Boring. I thought the War was the worst thing. Poor, poor Sonia.'

Chapter Three

My father treated his servants and the people of our little village of Gunne Magna with a tolerant kindness that made him loved. He was generous with donations of money and practical help. Every organization expected the use of his house and gardens and each was accommodated in its season.

He played host to galas and fêtes, shows and rallies, entertaining among many the Wolf Cubs, the Scouts and Guides, the Pig Fanciers, the Evening Institute, the Ladies' Gardening Club (flowers), the Mens' Gardening Club (vegetables). Horticulture divided naturally and strictly as to sex in our part of Dorset. No man would be seen dead tending a petunia or a hollyhock.

You can imagine then, with the story of the accident losing nothing in the telling, the punishments suggested for Sonia in a place where the role of women had such strict definitions. ''Er needs 'er bum tanned raw, that's what.' 'I'd drop she in the river if I 'ad 'er along of me,' were about the mildest. Our local river is the aptly named Piddle, so the second suggestion was not all that much of a threat.

In her malice against Sonia, Claudia became almost animated. Once a week I was allowed to go down to the post-office shop and spend some of my sixpence pocket money on toffee-apples or golden string-candy made by the post-mistress's mother-in-law. That was my most private pleasure.

I had a choice of routes. The lane was the quickest, and full of interest, but Gunne Magna lies in magic country, about halfway between Bulbarrow and Cerne

33

Abbas. (Legend said that once there was a companion village, Gunne Parva, but that the Cerne Giant squashed it flat under a huge foot on his way to take up residence on his hillside.) So the dawdling way, over the top of the Iron-Age barrow where larks nest, made me aware of ancient presences and produced a delicious quiver of fear.

When Claudia offered to come with me the walk got spoiled a bit. Cold rain danced down, giving the bare branches of the trees the polish of jet, and rooks lumbered through the sky as though they could hardly be bothered. She looked weird stumping along in a shiny yellow mackintosh and a sou'wester with the brim turned down. All that could be seen of her face was the pointed wedge of her nose, reddened with cold. A dewdrop trembled on the end of it.

If I stopped to look at anything she groused, 'Oh, come on, let's do this and get back. It's absolutely *miles*.' So then I ran on in front of her. Plodding at the same slow pace she turned quite spiteful. When she caught up she stuffed a handful of wet gravel down my front and stepped hard on my foot which was cold inside my wellingtons. 'Bloody, bloody show-off!'

'Why do you come with me when you don't enjoy it, Claudia?' I asked despondently.

'For evidence, stupid.'

'What's that? What do you want it for?'

'Shut up and don't ask baby questions. Soapy-bitch is nearly a murderess and I hope Father will send her to prison for years and years. They'll know in the village.'

I did shut up, though I could have told her that Father had no intention of punishing Sonia. But telling would have involved me in answering questions like how did I find out? and did I think I knew everything? and an assault with bony fingers if I failed to explain. Claudia would definitely have been an asset to the Spanish Inquisition.

34

Because I was small and quiet and young, people held private conversations over my head. I almost never repeated what I heard. But when I discovered about Father and Sonia my listening was secret and deliberate.

She came to the bedside as I slid out into the dressing-room, and she was crying. Father said gently, 'What is it, my dear?'

'It's dreadful, it can't be true that you'll always be like this, it can't. Only an accident, that's all. Everyone blames me, I blame myself. Oh, I'm sorry, truly, truly sorry, and I can do nothing.'

'Well, I'm sorry too. Neither of us now will have the kind of life we planned and it has to be faced. Try to stop crying about it.'

In a low, bitter kind of voice Sonia said, 'I wanted a child, I still want one desperately, and you, how can you?'

Father must, I think, have been smiling, though his smiles had no humour in them then. 'The doctors assert that the essential part of me is undamaged. Forgive me, my dear, that I don't immediately press my attentions on you. Perhaps when the pain is less and I learn to walk on sticks without falling I can give you your wish.' I heard the rattle of silver. 'Tea,' he said. 'Now dry your eyes and pour out for us.'

Under cover of the sounds I scooted away. Of course, I speculated about what part of Father was undamaged so that Sonia could have a child. Would Claudia explain about doing sex if I asked her? And especially how it produced babies? I decided that acquiring knowledge was not worth a supercilious look down that sharp nose.

To give Sonia her due, she had a conscience. She did not, even with us children, try to evade blame. Indeed, for a while she heaped it on her own head. But she was one of those fortunates with a short memory for their

35

own faults and sins. Having quickly forgiven herself she then forgot. I think it surprised and peeved her that others remembered and could not forgive.

In the spring of 1926 Claudia went away to Portia's school. I was to follow in a year or so. The staff and village people spoke to Sonia only when it became strictly necessary. We had callers, but they came to see Father and had little to say to her, so she was utterly deprived of amusing gossip and of any opportunity to show off. My grandparents removed to their London home and stayed there. Her life lacked interest.

Having no governess and no lessons, I spent much of the time reading in my favourite hiding-place, a stone seat almost overgrown by an old cedar-tree. One day my father found me there. He had wheeled himself down from the house in his new chair and he looked tired and grey.

'I know this is your private place,' he said, without looking at me, 'but don't worry, I shan't intrude nor let others. Sonia wants to tell you something.'

He never suggested that we should treat her as a mother or call her by a mother or aunt kind of name. What her feelings were I never knew. We all called her Sonia and that was that. 'Can't you tell me?'

'Yes, Amy, I could, but I want there to be some kind of normal relationship between you. Also, I ask you to be kind to her. She's wretched enough.'

'But it was her fault.'

'It would be easier if she had someone else to blame, you know. Do your best.'

I began to wonder about Gwennie, and whether he ever remembered those nursery evenings. They were not so distant in time yet they had the remoteness of dreams, and he had retreated too far from our brief intimacy for me to ask him. Suddenly he stared into my face just as though I had spoken my thoughts aloud. 'You miss her, don't you?' A rush of tears stung my eyes and I nodded. 'I'm sorry, Amy, so sorry,' he said.

What Sonia had to tell me was that the house would soon be overrun by workmen. Father needed a suite of rooms on the ground floor. 'While that's being done the men are to install radiators in the public rooms, and a new boiler. You need clothes. We shall buy them together in London and stay at the Ritz for a month or two.'

I thought about this. Father had not seemed put out to be left to his own devices. It felt strange but married people sometimes behaved in an extraordinary way. Sonia's tight defensive look, as of a castle under siege, began to lift as she talked, and her glowing opulence beamed through. 'The theatre, concerts, lovely shops, think of it, Amy! There's no cultural life in the country and I haven't been to Town for ever so long. Isn't it exciting?'

In a way it was. I had been to London before, but always to stay with the Mottesfont grandparents and be taken to a pantomime. Cocooned in our comfortable country isolation we knew nothing then of labour unrest or the brief, recently ended General Strike or the two million unemployed. Sonia, Countess of Osmington, believed that she had a right to pleasure.

I asked, 'What about Father? He can't stay here with just the servants.'

'Of course not. He'll take a holiday too, to various spas to convalesce.'

'Which spas?'

My tone must have sounded critical or suspicious. Sonia closed up again. 'Well, Bath, I expect, places like that. It was his idea, you know, not mine, he's been stuck here in bed so long. He can't get up to the House yet, and he misses it.'

I had forgotten how much Father enjoyed to sit in the House of Lords. In a way he was important, though a bit less important than he might once have been because the Earls of Osmington adhered to Rome and the Pope rather too long. Long enough at any rate to irritate Queen Elizabeth. Then the current Earl got proscribed from the Court of James the First for unwise comments about the execution of the king's mother, Mary, Queen of Scots.

In the eighteenth century the Osmingtons took to breeding daughters. The earldom lapsed. About the time of Waterloo, a firmly Protestant lady in the direct line of descent produced a son, and then four more, and the title revived.

The thought popped into my head that with our help Father could have come to London too. But Sonia showed so little enthusiasm for his company I concluded that he felt quite glad to get away from her.

The Ritz was super-bliss. Warm bedrooms, warm bathrooms, heavenly food, and the kind of discreet glitter and luxury that Gunville Place, for all its pretentiousness, lacked. Whether I had any more reality for Sonia than a doll or a dog is anyone's guess.

She treated me kindly enough. A city abundant in coal-carts and brewers' drays provided some squirming embarrassments. Incontinent horses seemed to lurk about, waiting to be rude until Sonia appeared. The fluting cry, 'Avert your eyes, Amy,' drew those of grinning passers-by. There is definitely a point where modesty becomes shaming.

We spent days together in Gorringes, fitting me out. Mostly she let me choose though she did inflict on me a droopy pink party-dress that made me feel like strawberry blancmange. She was fond of pink.

I fell deeply in love with a fitted vicuna coat the colour of Cornish cream. It had a brown velvet collar. With it came a round hat to match with velvet streamers tipping over the brim. It made me look elegant and fit to walk beside Sonia.

'Isn't it a bit impractical, Amy? Easily marked, I should think, and very expensive.' She recollected that she now had a fortune at her disposal, coughed, and added, 'Since you will grow out of it quite quickly.'

The assistant recognized my desire and smiled at me. 'There is ample scope for letting down the hems, my Lady, and the cloth cleans beautifully. Lady Amity will be a careful wearer, I'm sure.'

'I will, oh yes,' I agreed fervently, feeling rather a fool. No-one at home ever gave us children our titles, not even Valentine who was Viscount Gunville, and it was taking a bit of getting used to.

Sonia, to her evident pleasure, got the full works everywhere. Bows from the waist, and my Lady this, my Lady that, and 'A cab at once for the Countess of Osmington'. Heads turned. The ripeness of her looks made her doubly difficult to ignore.

I had by then achieved the age of seven. My bedtime also was seven, but at the Ritz Sonia permitted me to stay up for an extra hour so that she need not dine alone.

On the night that brought the first of many strangers into our lives I had begun to nod off over the dessert. 'Go to bed now, Amy,' Sonia said, but before I could get down another voice said over my shoulder, 'Oh what luck, what amazing luck. I haven't spoken to a soul all day, and here you are, my dear Sonia, and heaven-sent.'

Her face bore a curious mixture of expressions – disapprobation, social embarrassment, and also, quite definitely, pleasure. 'Mr Lotts, I'm surprised you dare address me. I never expected to see you again,' she said stiffly. 'Amy, I will take you upstairs myself.'

'You're still angry with me. Don't be, I beg you. Your cousin is the dearest girl in the world but the engagement would never have worked.'

'Certainly not after you were found in bed with her maid. You are an atrociously wicked man,' Sonia snapped with uncommon directness.

Naturally, with the mention of wickedness my

thoughts flew to Claudia and doing sex. Feeling on the brink of true education I turned right round to stare. Mr Lotts looked quite pleasant and ordinary but his blue eyes were unregenerate and very wicked indeed. He focused them intently on Sonia's bust. After lingering there for what seemed an awfully long time, they moved with deliberation to her face. He moistened his lips. Sonia blushed absolutely scarlet.

Infant I was, and without words to express the idea, but I think I recognized at once that I was witnessing a carefully practised piece of male impertinence calculated to flatter and confuse. Vicarious heat burned in my cheeks. I began to edge away from the table but a hand lightly clasped my shoulder. 'I wish I could be virtuous as you are but I'm too weak. Try to forgive, dear Sonia. Now, who is this, or am I not fit to be introduced?'

His voice was soft and rather pleasant, with a hint of a London accent, carefully, though not entirely, suppressed. Sonia seemed hypnotized. 'Ronnie, this is Lady Amity Savernake, my youngest step-daughter.'

'Not Ronnie, if you please, dear, and a Lotts no more. It doesn't quite do. I live now in the world of High Art and Rudi Longmire sounds so much better, don't you think?'

He made me smile though I wasn't sure why. 'Good night, Mr Longmire,' I said.

'Shall we not come with you and put you to bed?'

'No thank you very much. I'm seven, I can put myself to bed. Besides, there's a nice maid if I need help.' And I left them to do whatever they wanted. It will have been something perfectly innocuous. Sonia was far too cautious and, to be fair, far too proper to compromise her reputation for the Rudi Longmires of the world.

But Rudi became our constant companion. He assumed that people liked him and that made him likeable. In his business it was an invaluable asset for he arranged things. He acted as agent, go-between, factor, for any venture related to music or theatre or painting.

If some of the services he provided would not bear public advertisement, he worshipped his artistic gods with passion. It was Rudi who first had the idea of a festival of arts at Gunville Place.

Sonia genuinely loved music. She played the piano rather well and her untrained mezzo-soprano voice had the same melting richness as her looks. With Rudi she did not trouble to disguise her unhappiness and boredom. 'An accident like that might have happened to anybody. Gervase admires so those jolly horse-riding girls and I wanted to fit in though I loathe animals.' A sulky gloom darkened her face. 'In Italy we were at the opera or concerts almost every night and met all sorts of cultured people. Now it's ended almost before it began. Everyone pities Gervase; well, it's awful for me too. Illness upsets me yet I get not a scrap of sympathy.'

Rudi seemed faintly dazed by Sonia's view but he rallied nobly. 'Poor girl, how very unlucky you are, but so rich and comfortable. Can't you be valiant and count your blessings at all? Surely you can go anywhere, do anything you want.'

Absorbed in my book, I heard, though only with half an ear. Sonia lowered her voice almost to a whisper. 'It's not just that. I'm alone among all those Savernakes; I might almost say savages, for Portia is supercilious and Claudia is perfectly ignorant. All she cares about is herself and raucous jazz tunes. Men never understand but, Rudi, you can't know how desperately I long for a child of my own.'

'But I do understand, Sonia. An ally in the enemy camp. Is it so much of an impossibility? Aren't there four evidences of fertility already? Or perhaps a lusty groom to help the matter along.'

The line of conversation had suddenly become promising. I watched them from behind my lashes and saw that Sonia wore her most angrily genteel expression. 'That's a disgusting suggestion, Ronnie – Rudi, I mean. Trust you to descend to the depths. You're not at all a nice man and I shan't talk to you ever again.'

I must have made a small movement for Rudi gave me an interested look. 'Of course you will, and I have the perfect idea for you. You're dreadfully tense and that isn't conducive to – er – fecundity. Diversion, pleasure, of a cultural nature of course, would provide the necessary relaxation.'

'Well, I know that. Haven't I complained that there is none at Gunville Place?'

'But it can be brought to you, a festival of music – no, better still, of all the arts – staged at Gunville. It would be a sensation. And aren't you lucky after all, Sonia? I can arrange everything, performers, musicians, tradesmen, the lot.'

A kind of electric excitement passed between them. She said, 'Could you truly do it? Would anyone come all that way? I should have to consult with Gervase, of course.'

'Surely you've learned by now, dearest girl, that everyone loves a lord, and a countess too. Throw in a high-class bun-fight as well and the world will flock to your door. Think of it, the Summer – no, Midsummer is much better and speaks of enchantments – Festival of Arts, under the patronage of the Earl and Countess of Osmington. Concerts, theatre, exhibitions, picnics, all alfresco if we are lucky. And you the radiant star.' Rudi descended to earth and added in a prosaic tone, 'Lots to arrange if we are to hold it next year.'

'But surely all that will cost a terrible amount of money?'

'Of course, and those who have it shall pay. I don't

lack wealthy friends, you know, and I've no conscience about helping them to spend their fortunes.'

'Who, for instance?' she asked in a sceptical tone.

'John Eppingham, the industrialist, for one, and also
Pan Metkin.'

Sonia's eyes opened very wide and she leaned
forward, staring into Rudi's face. 'You can't mean
Pandel Metkin of Metkin Fine Arts, surely?'

'I can and do. We are old chums from my Paris days
after the war. He's the sweetest, most gentle man
imaginable and about the fourth richest in the world.
Beautiful things make him weep. He'll adore to meet
you.'

'But doesn't he – isn't he – haven't I heard rumours?
He isn't married, is he?'

She got dreadfully tied up with whatever was
troubling her, and Rudi smiled. 'Try not to worry
about it. After all it's his business entirely and, as I
said, he's a dear man, and generous, and that's all that
need matter.'

With apparent absentmindedness he began to stroke
Sonia's arm. She shook him off. 'Don't, I hate that kind
of thing. It's awfully common in public and people are
looking.'

'Well, of course I *am* common and you are amazingly cold. Yet together we can arrange magic.'

He smiled his nicest most disarming smile but Sonia
was lost in thought and not watching, so it was wasted.
Rudi was nothing if not a perpetual optimist. Virtue
baffled him.

He shrugged, and plunged into a discussion of
plans. 'Shakespeare, of course; the *Dream* is the
obvious one but several others come to mind: say six
principals and local recruitment for minor parts. A
good provincial orchestra, four or five voices. I have
the very artist for scenery and costume design.'

I wanted my lunch but nothing happened except
Rudi talking. I think I must have dozed because all of a

sudden the lounge seemed to fill with actors and clowns and dancing women. A princely figure glittering white with frost bent over me. 'Wake up, Amy, it's lunchtime,' Sonia said.

Rudi may well have been the all-time opportunist, and a cad, and utterly sex-mad, but he was a wonderful companion to me. 'I'm not at all sure that I should let Amy go out with you alone,' Sonia said. She had an appointment with her dressmaker.

'I'm not a good man, as you keep reminding me, dear, but I cherish children, especially Amy, and you can trust me as you would trust yourself.'

Later I asked him, 'Why do you especially cherish me, Rudi? Most people don't.'

'I know, but most people are rather stupid. I suspect that you see and hear a great deal more than they realize. Your eyes and ears may be of immense service to me when Sonia's festival takes place and I intend that you shall be my right-hand girl. Also, Amy, your company rests and refreshes me.'

He took me to a matinée of Noel Coward's *Hay Fever*, my first grown-up play, and to a revue. And he made no secret of his poverty-stricken beginnings. 'I've adored the theatre, any kind at all, since I was a ragged kid. I was always desperate to get a few coppers for a ticket.'

'How did you get them?' I was interested because of my house-fund which seemed slow to grow.

'I went around with my eyes on the ground, hoping to find a penny or even a ha'penny. Sometimes a drunk dropped a handful of change in the dark, and then it might be sixpence or more. That was largesse from heaven for I could buy a bag of sweets as well.'

'Suppose you couldn't find any?'

'Then, Amy dear, I'm afraid that sometimes I stole it.'

As a reformed thief myself I could scarcely condemn

and I shocked him by giggling. He taught me the Charleston and the foxtrot and one evening we fairly twinkled down a deserted street behind Drury Lane Theatre, doing the bunny-hug and singing at the tops of our voices.

Perhaps I liked Rudi only because he was such fun. He wasn't exactly handsome but he had a nice long humorous face and neat thick brown hair. I know I loved a little bit the child, hungry for glamour, who searched the dirty pavements for pennies to open the door of his particular heaven.

And why did he bother with me really? Well, lady-killing must take a lot of energy. I think sometimes he quite enjoyed not having to pretend to be anyone but plain Ronnie Lotts, and being a boy again.

We still had more than a month of luxury to go when Sonia received a telephone call. She came to me in a tearing rage with something of pleasure in it. 'That was the headmistress of your sisters' school. Claudia has been expelled.'

I had recently begun to read the novels of Angela Brazil and thus I knew that expulsion was a terrible disgrace. One never felt sorry for Claudia, but it must have caused awkwardness for Portia, the prospective nun. 'What did she do? What will happen to her?' I asked.

Angela provided no information as to the later careers of such outcasts. I was deeply interested, and also curious to know what crime Claudia had committed.

'They actually wanted me to go down there and collect her. I said that the Place is still shut up and that I will not have her staying here with us.' Sonia crossed to the dressing-table, sat down and stared at her immaculate face. She patted her hair complacently. It was an unusual reddish-black, almost the colour of dark cherries. 'She will be brought to London by a mistress and taken to your grandparents' house. I shall send a note round at once. Claudia has a vulgar tongue, a coarse mind, and undesirable habits.'

And she offered no more information than that. For the full story I should have to wait until I got Claudia alone. If, as I suspected, she felt pleased with her freedom, a few weeks with Grandmother Mottesfont would quench her complacency.

Once a week I was taken to my grandparents' house for an afternoon visit. When my grandmother was present the strain of it caused my eyebrows to lift, and my scalp became sore, just as though a hand was pulling me up by the hair. Alone with Grandpa was better. He gave me the heavy photograph albums to look at and explained who was who.

I came upon a sepia picture of a statuesque young lady in Grecian robes, leaning against an inadequate pillar. Rather uncertainly I asked, 'Who's that lady, Grandpa?'

The uncertainty arose because I was not sure whether he could be trusted to tell the truth. A plump person in long skirts and a curious hat whom I had taken to be a lady, turned out to be, according to Grandpa, the Bishop of Buxton.

Grandpa leaned forward, smiling. 'A fine figure of a woman, wasn't she? That's your grandmother just before we became engaged to be married. Did you know – well, of course, how could you? – she loved the stage and wanted very much to become an actress.'

'Are you sure that's her?'

'You don't recognize her? She hasn't changed so much.'

I passed over the awful fib. 'Didn't she go on the stage, then?'

'Her mother had hysterics for two hours without stopping when she found out, and her father locked her in her room on a bread-and-water diet. So she married me.'

'What's his derricks?'

'Hysterics. They consist of laughing and crying at the same time. The noise is atrocious. Promise me, Amy, never to indulge in hysteria.'

'All right, Grandpa, I won't.' I turned the page and pointed to a group of uncomfortably dressed children of mixed sex. 'Who are those?' But his eyes had closed and a quiet, rhythmic breathing stirred the ends of his moustache. He slept.

I imagined Claudia in disgrace, possibly locked in as Grandmother once had been, and on a prison diet. But I had forgotten that she was the favourite. I found her swanning around the house like an ageing witch-queen, terrifying the maids out of their wits. She told me that the grandparents had gone to an agency to try to engage a temporary governess. 'They'd better not find one,' she said. 'Education's useless to someone as clever as me. You can't imagine how boringly pious Portia is these days, and almost utterly without enter-prise.'

'I don't think you're clever,' I said unwisely. 'Sonia says you have a coarse mind.'

She glared menacingly. 'Come here.'

But in Rudi's company I had gained confidence. 'No, and if you ever pinch me again I shall pinch back double.'

Her confident face became thoughtful. 'I like that coat. Can I have it?'

'No you can't. You always want everything of mine and I'm tired of it. Grandmother likes you the best, ask her to buy you one.'

'You're an outsized rat, Amy Savernake. Bugger off.' I winced at hearing such a word uttered in Grand-mother's drawing-room. Claudia smiled and suddenly looked rather pretty and nice. 'That was partly what got me expelled,' she said, 'that and smoking in the lavs and not studying much, and asking disgusting questions.'

Pleased with my small victory I lured her from the house to St James's Park and told her all about the coming festival. 'It's going to be lovely and I shall be stuck in school.'

'Not in Portia's you won't. The old crone swore she'd never accept another Savernake.' A morose look clouded her pale blue eyes and I realized that she was a bit ashamed after all. 'It was utterly humiliating, Amy. I was called out at Assembly and made to stand by myself. The Head said, "Take note, young ladies, that Lady Claudia Louise Imogen Savernake has disgraced her family name and proved herself unfit to be a member of this school. She will be leaving in a few days' time and until then no-one is to speak to her. Is that understood?" All the little sheep went baa of course, except for Portia.'

'What did she do?'

'Quite a brave sort of thing. She's rather splendid at times. She walked out of her place, stood beside me and demanded to be expelled too.' Claudia kicked a stone listlessly and drooped against the railings. 'They didn't want to lose her and in the end she was talked out of it but she insisted on staying with me until I left.'

Portia always did the admirable thing quite naturally but I was ready to bet that she jawed the culprit worse than anyone. It may well be thought that I didn't like Claudia. But in a way I loved her enormously and hated to see her cast down. Just then I could have kissed her. Because of her I never did have to go to school, and when the festival came we were both in the thick of it.

Chapter Four

'I must speak to the Earl myself,' Rudi said on my last day in London. 'He may loathe the idea of having his estate taken over, and I'm not sure that I altogether trust to Sonia's sense of fair play. What do you think?'

He spoke quietly as we were in the Tate Gallery inspecting the oblong babies and those white-faced men who wore high black hats even in the house. It was August and Sonia found the heat enervating. Work at the Place was finished and Father installed in his new rooms. There was no reason to stay on in Town.

I swung on Rudi's arm while I wondered how much of Sonia's virtue came from not being very secure. She had boasted rather a lot in a quiet, persistent way to the friends she entertained at the Ritz and got some sour looks when her back was turned.

'Grandmother says she meddles, and sometimes she sneaks. I bet she's told her cousin about meeting you. The one whose maid you ruined,' I explained helpfully, in case Sonia had a lot of cousins.

'Dash it, Amy, can't you forget you heard about that? Honestly, I didn't ruin the girl. I know I'm a fool over women, but I don't want you to know, if you see what I mean.'

I did see. All of us hid something, even from ourselves, and only wanted people to see the good bits of us. Suddenly the stray thought popped into my head that Father was hiding a regret that he had married Sonia. I buried it at the back of my mind and said, 'It doesn't matter to me a bit, Rudi, truly it doesn't, but

49

can I say what I wish you wouldn't do? You won't be cross, will you?'

'Fire away.'

'Please don't do that look at Sonia when Father's there.'

'What look?'

I attempted what must have been a close but obscene parody of the stare I remembered from our first meeting. He blushed absolutely scarlet. 'Oh, Amy, don't! What an ass I am; I didn't expect you to notice and now I feel awful. It's a sort of private joke – I can't explain to you – and I only practise on Sonia. It doesn't mean anything, believe me.' He stared mournfully at a fat-faced, complacent lady who oddly resembled my grandmother and was surrounded by cowed children. 'She and her cousin are ice-maidens who look like houris, poor dears.'

Immediately his upset communicated itself to me. After all it was a grown-up's thing and not my business, and I didn't know what houris were. 'I'm sorry if I hurt your feelings, Rudi, I truly am.'

His mouth curled neatly into a really attractive smile. 'You're a dear girl, and I'm a wicked wretch,' he said. 'I see that I had better be frank with the Earl and tell him all about my past and how I came to know Sonia. He may throw me out but I hope he won't. A festival at a grand house is so new and exciting, and how Sonia adores the Place! It must rival the streets of Paradise.'

I gaped. 'No it doesn't, Rudi. It's awful.'

'Familiarity certainly breeds contempt in you. It can't be that bad.'

'Just wait till you see it.'

Rudi appeared to be unhaunted by fear of disillusion or disappointment, trusting to his persuasive charm. 'In a couple of weeks I hope to. I've written to your father and asked if I can bring Cyril Fox with me. He's the best stage artist in the business and he'll know what can work and what can't.'

Mercifully a lot of trees hid most of the frontage of Gunville Place. Tall glass doors now opened on to the terrace at the back and there was a ramp for Father's wheelchair. He could come and go as he pleased.

The effect, among a prodigality of turrets, and silly little bits of crenellation, and fretwork eaves, and scutcheons, and scrolls, was to give a leering glitter to the house. It peered malevolently at me through thick spectacles. An unsuccessful effort had been made to restore the Portland facing-stone to its whiteness and it sported a leprous patching of dirty greys. I thought of my white house and mentally replaced an ornamental balustrade around the roof with a plain one.

Earlier Places had burned down. As I stared at our dank mausoleum I wished for a pantomime wizard to make it disappear. It exercised a dimming effect on me. I quite expected Rudi to have forgotten our friendship and I was disproportionately grateful when he asked for me within minutes of his arrival.

Mr Fox looked nothing like a Cyril or an artist. Under a dark, shabby business suit he wore a singlet and neither shirt nor tie, but the brim of his trilby hat had a jaunty curl to it. The muscles of his shoulders and arms dragged his jacket sleeves halfway up to his elbows.

He nodded to me and stared at the house. For a moment he was silent, then he said, 'Jesus F. Christ, what is it? Don't tell me people actually live in that.'

Rudi said, 'It's bound to be better inside.'

'Worse,' I muttered quietly.

Cyril proved himself an artist after all. 'Don't ask me to transform this into a street in Verona,' he said, almost in tears. 'My wonderful sets; I won't do it, I won't. I might as well lay a beautiful rose on a dog-turd as put up a Tudor balcony here.'

'*Pas devant la jeune fille*,' Rudi said hastily.

Portia, who was learning French at school, told

Claudia, who told me, that any phrase of that kind meant that our ears or the servants' were being protected from something unsuitable. It was kind of Rudi but a bit superfluous with Claudia around.

Cyril brushed any notion of delicacy aside. 'I've been thrown out of more elegant whore-houses,' he mourned.

Rudi laid a consoling arm across the bulging shoulders. 'There'll be somewhere, a large room perhaps, there's bound to be. Think, Amy, where would you stage *Romeo and Juliet*?'

Which one was that? My acquaintance with Shakespeare was limited to the reading of Lamb's *Tales*, and to be truthful I had not found them very inspiriting. Everyone seemed to die in the end. But I was flattered to be asked, and the pride of it and Cyril's mention of a balcony recalled to mind one of the coloured pictures. 'Is that the bit about the dying lovers? If so, there's a place I like, though it's nothing more than an old tithe-barn. Grandmother told me that travelling shows used to be done there in bygone days.'

'How old is it?'

'At least three hundred years.'

'Big?'

'Huge, with a gallery on two sides and double doors at each end.'

Rudi swung me off my feet. 'Amy, I love you. Take us to it.'

The bleached oak beams and the old bricks of the barn enraptured Cyril. 'Leave me,' he cried. 'Look at those doors, floor to roof. Perfect, Rudi, a natural theatre.'

'Dressing-rooms?'

Cyril dragged a tiny pad from his pocket and began making faint pencil squiggles. He wasn't interested. 'Oh, a tent somewhere, anything.'

When Rudi went in to talk to my father I longed to listen but I didn't want to be caught. The spas seemed to have helped a bit. As soon as I got back from London Father made a point of asking whether I had enjoyed my experiences.

'Yes, thank you,' I replied. 'Did you like the places you went to?'

'They were restful.' He hesitated for a moment and looked at me as though he were summing me up. 'Amy, I met' – and at that point Sonia drifted into the room – 'some interesting people,' he finished. I had a feeling that he really meant to say something else.

'Oh, you're here, Amy,' Sonia said. 'Run along, I want to talk to Daddy.'

She still wasn't cured of the Daddy gush. Sadly I realized that I was noticed only to be sent away. I wondered what it would be like to have someone say, 'Come in and stay; don't go.' In London I used to hope that one day I would see Gwennie coming along the street towards me. I imagined her delight and mine. But it was only a daydream and a silly one. Nursery life had gone, and she and I could never be the way we were. Yet I couldn't stop looking for her.

Sonia had ruined my chance for a proper talk with Father. I knew that his containment would admit of no later questioning. And I knew too that if he set his face against a festival that would be the end of it.

We were still suffering the mild shock of Claudia, who got a tremendous ticking-off from Father and mooned around like a tragic actress with the back of a hand pressed to her brow. She had acquired some new gramophone records. From behind her door came a tinny voice yelling, 'Everybody's doing it, doing it, doing it,' until I had it on the brain. In my dreams I saw bears dance in ragtime.

Sonia declined to speak to her at all. This proved fairly unnoticeable. At the best of times she scarcely bothered with our part of the house.

The advent of Rudi diverted Claudia from her

solitary brooding. She kept an eye on him from afar though she declined to emerge and meet him. 'Are you sure he's a ravisher of virgins?' she asked. Her knowledge of sex had come along nicely during her brief association with schoolgirls. 'He looks utterly harmless and rather sweet.'

'I didn't say that about virgins, I only said he did something in bed to Sonia's cousin's maid. And he *is* sweet in a way, but you aren't,' I said disparagingly. 'He'd hardly want to do anything rude with you unless you wash more. Your hair looks as though it's full of nits and your fingernails are filthy.'

She seemed gratified. 'Sackcloth and ashes – penance you know, like the RCs. It makes life entirely easy.' Then collecting herself she stamped on my foot. I kicked out at her but she dodged and sneered. 'Serves you right for being a pious, sneaky rat. Let's waylay your precious Rudi.'

'He's with Father and I'd rather not have him see what a mess you are.'

'I bet he's sent packing.'

She was quite wrong. He and Father emerged into the September garden laughing together; it was obvious that they liked each other. We watched and listened in the shelter of a clump of the spotty laurel with which Gunville Place abounded. I heard Rudi's voice echoing the streets of South London. 'I'm a bit of a mountebank, my Lord, but I can make something brilliant of this, something for us all to remember. And Pandel Metkin will definitely help finance it. He knows I can get a guinea's worth out of every pound.'

'Give Sonia an interest and I shan't grudge you money.' Rudi must have confessed about her deceived cousin for Father added, 'One stipulation, Mr Long-mire, you will respect the conventions of the house, please, and watch what you are about with the maid-servants. Most of them are Dorset girls and country revenge can be primitive. If a farmer chooses to take

54

a hay-prong to you, don't ask me to interfere.'

Rudi shuddered. 'My Lord, I promise to give no cause for complaint. I shan't have time for transient pleasures and I would die rather than spoil a marvellous event.'

'I told you so,' I said to Claudia smugly. 'And do stop hanging over my shoulder. You niff.'

'Outcasts always do.'

'No they don't. You're trying to annoy Sonia and she hasn't even noticed. It's silly.'

She pulled a leaf off the laurel, scratched her name on it with a fingernail and put it down the front of her dress so that the writing would turn brown. 'Why silly?'

'Because you're quite pretty really, and you could probably be in a play if Rudi likes you.'

'Bugger you and your Rudi,' she said venomously. There was a bit of a silence then, 'How long do I have to wait to be grown up? Sometimes I could howl and scream. I want my mother to talk to instead of old Soapy-bitch.'

Tears ran down her face, leaving clean tracks in the grime. I couldn't think of anything to say so I took her hand and she squeezed mine back fiercely. We sat on under our bush but heard nothing more of interest. Eventually I hauled her to her feet.

'What do you think you're doing?' she snarled.

'Just come on. You're going to have a bath or everyone will know you've been crying.'

She ground her teeth. 'I haven't, rat, and if you breathe a word I'll pull out your toenails one by one.'

'All right,' I said, 'but do it when you're clean. Did I tell you that Soapy wants a baby because Portia's supercilious and you're perfectly ignorant?'

'No, you jolly well didn't.' For a moment Claudia seemed to half believe in the scene she drew for me at Sonia's wedding. 'She'll try to push us out, you'll see.'

'Father won't let her.'

'We must watch for signs. Smocks is the first thing, they get fat round the middle and wear smocks. She might be having one already.'

I thought of all the lovely clothes Sonia had bought in London. 'No, she can't be or she wouldn't go on so, and her dresses are sort of wispy and short.'

'What about her stomach? Did you see her in a negligent or anything?'

'It isn't called that, it's neglijay, but I did and she's flat except for her busts sticking out.'

The unswerving attention we gave to her middle whenever we encountered Sonia unnerved her rather. 'Why are you staring in that ridiculous fashion?' she demanded at last.

'You wear ever such pretty dresses,' I improvised hurriedly. 'We were just saying, weren't we, Claudia, what pretty dresses Sonia wears?'

'Um,' Claudia muttered.

'Really? You surprise me.' Sonia sounded cool and unconvinced. 'Haven't you learned yet that staring is vulgar? And only badly brought-up children make personal remarks to their elders.'

Claudia smiled in the superior way that never failed to aggravate. 'Thank you for explaining that to us. D'you think you'll ever have a baby of your own to bring up nicely?'

Sonia smacked her face and burst into tears, thus sealing the bond of loathing between them. I felt sorry for them both. And it caused me deeper distress to realize that I had brought the confrontation about.

I dragged Claudia away. 'I'll never tell you anything again,' I said.

Claudia swelled with triumph. 'I knew I could make her hit me one day.' She was pleased, my wretched sister, actually pleased.

I expected a dull winter, imagining that everything would somehow be created in London and then transported suddenly to Gunville. And it wasn't a bit like that. In the grounds we constantly tripped over strangers, trailing tape-measures. They cut lines in the turf to represent marquees and temporary buildings, and other men lopped trees and shrubs and erected a skeletal foundation in the park that would be a stand for distinguished guests. The gardeners foamed at the mouth with rage and complained to Father daily.

Rudi came down often. The grubby caterpillar that was Claudia underwent a metamorphosis. She celebrated her tenth birthday in the autumn of 1926. The presence of strangers seemed to make her aware that adolescence lurked around the next corner.

She left her blond hair alone other than washing it a lot with Amami shampoo, and defied fashion by allowing it to grow to her shoulders where it curled gently. The beginnings of her cool beauty began to appear.

For several reasons Christmas of that year had an unexpected magic. Rudi came and even Claudia roused herself from lethargy and found him an amusing companion. Associating him with the Ritz, I had felt no curiosity about his home. He lived not in chic luxury but in a one-roomed flat in Camden Town, and though I expect he sometimes entertained a lady he must often have been lonely.

Valentine spent the holiday skiing with friends in Switzerland, but Portia was home from school and we did all the usual things. Father thought it smacked of feudalism to hold a party for the village children at the Place. 'Their parents terrify them into silence and make an ordeal of it,' he said. 'It's far better for you to be their guests.'

A tree was put up in the village hall and our servants did the spread, helped by their many relations from Gunne Magna. Father could no longer dress up and give out the presents so Rudi volunteered. He insisted on helping to choose what was given. With his flair for drama he made the best Santa Claus we ever had. The little kids climbed all over him, batting him in the eye with china dolls and getting clockwork cars and fire-engines tangled in his whiskers.

He held back my present, saying it would spoil a surprise, and I must wait. I was pleased that he did. Father gave me a black and silver bicycle. 'Rudi has promised to teach you to ride it,' he said.

In my delayed parcel were a bell, and a basket to go on the front. 'You had better sew garters into your dresses to keep the skirts down,' Sonia said primly.

Of course I never did. Although I was nearly eight my knees and thighs were not such as would tempt even the most hardened lecher, being lean, and scratched from climbing trees and fences.

Our present to Rudi was a silk dressing-gown and a pair of cuff-links. He went pink with pleasure. 'Silk and gold – absolutely decadent and just like Noel Coward in *The Vortex*! I could never have afforded them for myself.'

He gave to Claudia a vanity-case like actresses carry. In front of Sonia she was always guarded and cool. She thanked him primly but I could see that she loved it and was waiting until she got him alone to tell him so. In my parcel were books, *A Midsummer Night's Dream* and *Romeo and Juliet* in a bowdlerized edition, and a beautiful plush Bonzo dog.

'He's the real present,' Rudi explained, 'but I couldn't help noticing that you've read no Shake-speare. We're doing both those plays at the festival and you'll get much more out of them by reading them first. We might try them together, aloud, doing the parts, you know.'

'Not in front of people,' I said in a panic, hugging Bonzo to my flat chest. 'I'd die.'

'Just us, I swear. And I must show you what Sonia and I have decided on for the music. The acoustics in the ballroom are rather good and we thought of

58

operatic excerpts, perhaps even a complete opera, as well as orchestral and chamber concerts. Absolutely all I lack is a theme for the cast entertainment.'

'What's that?' I asked.

Sonia waved a languid hand and looked superior. 'It's the tradition when a season ends to hold a farewell party for the cast and invited friends, Amy, that's all.'

I betted that she had only just found that out from Rudi for she seemed to sense vulgarity in the idea. But he cried, 'All? My dear Sonia, it's of enormous importance to sweep up the triumphs and failures and joys and despair so that the least of the performers goes away happy. We must think hard and come up with a really good idea.'

Nothing occurred to anyone since we were having breakfast which was scarcely a good time for ideas. Outside snow fell thickly so I couldn't try out my bicycle. Father went back to his rooms and Sonia drifted after him. Portia practically ignored Claudia and me. She couldn't wait to get back to school where she was happiest.

She received and gave her presents without enthusiasm. When I tried to kiss her she said, 'Get off my foot, Amy, please, and do stop snuffling. You sound as if you have adenoids.'

I tended to breathe a bit heavily through my mouth when I was excited or nervous. The combination of Christmas and Portia induced both emotions but I resented being told this by a sister even if she was thirteen. 'Stop being a beast to Amy, will you?' Claudia muttered without looking up from her plate.

She scowled fearsomely and didn't see my pleased look. I think she felt at a disadvantage with me for being caught doing something nice. Swinging her feet, she kicked Portia's shin.

'Ow!' Portia momentarily lost her dignity. Icicles formed in her pale-blue eyes. 'Don't do that, and don't dare speak to me either. I'm Captain of Hockey and best student for the third term running, and all I ever get asked by new girls is if I'm the sister of the girl who got expelled. I'm never going to live you down and it's not fair.'

Claudia yawned and began to nod off over her scrambled egg. We all sat like stones. The joy of the day seemed about to fade but I wouldn't let it. Emboldened by support, I said, 'Nag if you want to, Portia, but I'm going to have a happy, happy Christmas. Come out with us.'

To my surprise she got quite cross. She stood up. 'I never nag and it's snowing. Father should do something about you two, you're running wild and making unsuitable friends.' This was a dig at Rudi. She had dismissed him with a single look. I knew she wouldn't dare say anything to Father who was just as capable of squashing her as she was of squashing us. 'Don't make a noise outside my room, please. I have some holiday work to do.'

On Christmas Day! Could anyone believe it, or wonder why I never managed to get close to Portia? She was just naturally boring.

In the afternoon the snow stopped. I grabbed Claudia before she could disappear with the new gramophone that Father had given her. 'Rudi and I are going tobogganing – you too.'

'Madwoman, I need my rest and I've got some lovely records.'

'Oh, do come, Claudia dear, and don't be so elderly,' Rudi urged, shivering though he stood directly in front of the fire. 'It will warm us all up and you'll have nothing to do but sit down and be pushed.'

She looked up into his face and I saw a gentle smile curl her lips. My sister, proof against discipline and good manners and reminders of her station, was not proof against Rudi's trusting friendliness. 'Wait,' she said and strolled away, returning wrapped in a heavy boy's sweater several sizes too large for her –

Valentine's I suppose – and a woolly cap and scarf. She put a mittened hand in Rudi's. 'Come along. Amy, you run ahead.'

That time I didn't mind at all being sent away. She could thank him properly without betraying any of her heart or her hidden longings to Sonia or to me. Bulbarrow Hill stood high, white and inviting against the skyline. I lugged the toboggan to the top and launched myself into space, arriving at the bottom in time for Rudi to take it up again.

On Boxing Day and at the Servants' Ball Rudi truly came into his own. Usually we were allowed a peep at the ballroom and the buffet before the guests, invited from as far away as Blandford and Wimborne, arrived. Father could no longer open the Ball by leading the housekeeper on to the floor, handing her on to the butler, then retiring. Sonia knew better than to appear. But Rudi had a proper invitation and that was a great honour.

I couldn't sleep and lay listening to the distant music – a real dance-band – and sudden bursts of laughter as doors opened and closed. Very late, when our part of the house had been silent for a long time, I heard the soft crunch of footsteps in the snow outside my corner turret and Rudi's voice. A woman laughed softly. I got out of bed and clambered on to the window-seat to peer out. Frost patterns almost obscured the narrow slit of window. I huffed on it and cleared a little patch with the corner of my dressing-gown.

Below me Rudi's sleek brown head bent over a fair one. I could see a dark dress spangled with sequins move close to him as they kissed. Wondering who the girl was, I lifted the bottom sash and leaned out. He had kept his promise to Father. The girl, or rather woman for she was a bit elderly and bleached her hair with peroxide, I knew to be foreign and lady's maid to a manufacturer's widow. She ranked rather low among those servants with titled employers; they are dreadful snobs.

The pair wandered off glued together and disappeared into the house. From a window farther along came a low hiss. Claudia waved a hand and began to whistle 'Mademoiselle from Armentiers'. She said, 'I bet they're ravishing each other like mad. The French are known for it – they're fast.'

Another few crumbs of information for my store. I put down the window, went back to bed and thought that the servants seemed to have more fun than us. Trust Rudi to get a share of it!

He stayed with us for several weeks and made good his promise to teach me to ride my bicycle. He proved the very best kind of education, not just for me but for Claudia and, I suspect, Sonia also. Life's vicissitudes, he maintained, were for overcoming. He thought it a betrayal of the gods to be so surfeited with sorrow that pleasures and joys went untasted. The marvellous thing was that he looked at us and actually saw us.

As soon as the snow disappeared from the lanes he borrowed a bike from the stable boy. 'We shall ride into Blandford and go to the pictures,' he said. 'Mae Murray in *The Merry Widow* – returning by popular request it says in the paper – and a Charlie Chaplin.'

Claudia, who also had a bicycle, showed interest and then she must have thought of the effort involved. 'Not me, it's too far.'

'Yes you will, for I have an idea about you, my child.'

'What idea?'

'First the films, and since I know you to be lazy but athletic, you shall ride behind me on the step.'

It was all of eight miles from Gunville Place to Blandford Forum and I expected Claudia to reject his offer with scorn. 'I'd rather go on the crossbar,' she said after a moment's thought. Wonders will never cease!

I forgot to bother about what Rudi had on his mind in the rare treat of sitting in the rather smelly darkness of the Picture Palace. Dutifully I laughed at Chaplin though I didn't find him as funny as I expected. Claudia's gaze was fixed unswervingly on the screen. She seemed rapt, her nose forward like a blackboard pointer and her mouth slightly open.

It was her first experience of the cinema and only my third. In London Rudi had taken me to see Lionel Barrymore in *Moby Dick*. It had terrified me. To make up he had insisted on combing the suburbs for a cinema showing Rudolph Valentino in *The Sheik*, a film I had heard of. He had eventually tracked it down at Sydenham in the shadow of a gasometer.

How did we manage to be so entirely seduced by a silent version of a musical play with just a pianist to thump out the Lehar tunes? I emerged into daylight with a headache and eyes that rejected reality.

'What did you think of Mae Murray?' Rudi asked Claudia, all innocence. 'Sonia might play that part rather well, don't you think?'

Claudia snorted. 'She's a boring blob, fat too.'

And having delivered herself of that spiteful libel she began to waltz along the pavement, fluttering an imaginary fan and reproducing the glamorous Mae to the life.

'There, I knew it!' Rudi sounded triumphant. 'Come on, let's get back. I want you to read for me, Claudia.'

'Read? What for?'

'The part of Puck in the *Dream*. You'll be perfect if you can just stay awake long enough to learn the lines.'

'I don't want to. I thought you were getting actors from the Rep.'

'Heaven forbid that I denigrate the people of Dorset, but I've looked and there isn't a sprite or a fairy among them.'

She scowled. 'Ask Sonia if you think she's so clever.'

'Did I say clever? Gorgeous, yes, not fat as you so unkindly suggest, but too – er – pneumatic is the best word, I think.'

All at once I realized that Claudia, the idle, the spiteful, the unhappy, truly wanted to play the part. She had backed herself into a corner. I didn't bother urging her to change her mind. She would either pretend not to hear or do the opposite just to keep me in what she deemed to be my place. In her philosophy the youngest sibling was born to be trodden on. My recent resistance, for which she blamed Rudi's partiality, already caused her enough irritation.

She walked away from us and I tugged at Rudi's arm. 'She'll go on saying no while I'm here,' I whispered. 'Get her alone and ask her as a favour, tell her that if she doesn't you'll ask me. She's dying to do it really.'

Rudi smiled and hugged me. 'You know, Amy, this festival wouldn't be much fun without you. You're the best of good luck. It's going to be a wonderful, wonderful time.'

My face expanded into a pleased grin. No-one had ever thought me fun or found me lucky before and I quite forgot to look for Gwennie or my white house. The cold little street in Blandford shone glamorous with make-believe. I felt glad to my bones that Rudi had come into our lives.

Chapter Five

Claudia put up a fight against Rudi but he persuaded her in the end. I wanted very much to hear her read but as I slid into her room she hissed at me, 'Filthy sneak and spy, get out, and don't listen at the keyhole,' pushed me back through the door and shut it in my face.

'I wish you wouldn't call names,' I protested.

She knew perfectly well that I never listened at keyholes, not really, and I certainly didn't sneak. I hung about outside until Rudi came out alone. He was smiling and pleased. 'That girl can act,' he told me. 'We fought dreadfully.'

'But she'll do it, the part?'

'Oh yes. Claudia needs something, a success that's all her own. I'd dearly like to know what she really wants of life and how to give it to her, but this may help. So much pent-up boredom and unhappiness is unbearable to watch. I pointed out that becoming a prize bitch won't drive Sonia away, however much she strives. She bit me, look.' He held out his hand and there were Claudia's toothmarks on his wrist. 'I slapped her, of course.'

'You didn't!'

'Oh yes I did. She doesn't respect forbearance and nor do I. And she called me all kinds of names I won't repeat. Where on earth does she pick up such language?'

'From the farm boys I expect; she has them in thrall, they're terrified of her. But are you sure she won't back out?'

'Absolutely sure.' Rudi looked sly. 'I happened to mention that Sonia wants you girls sent away while the festival's on. It's true, too. *She* is the Countess and patron, but none too sure of herself. A bevy of step-children might well be cramping to her style.'

I felt awful, but Rudi, seeing my stricken face, said, 'Oh dear, Amy, I've worried you now. It's all right, the Earl refused to hear of it.'

Sonia was livid when she found out about Claudia. She tore into Rudi like a yapping terrier, quite forgetting to be detached and dignified. 'That beastly, foul-minded child! How could you even think of letting her loose on an audience? She'll disgrace us all.'

In some ways Sonia took an almost realistic view of herself and those about her. 'I meant to suggest myself for a part, Hermia or Helena perhaps, but I won't step on to the same stage as Claudia. You can't know what she's like, quite spiteful and wicked. Somehow she would contrive to make me look ridiculous and if you're a match for her I certainly am not.'

'Dearest Sonia,' Rudi said, at his smoothest and most sympathetic, 'would you not be wasted in a tiny part when there's so much that only you can do? You have a voice and I mean to use it to the full.'

'How? There are to be professionals, I thought.'

'I hadn't dared broach it, but as you know, we're doing *Figaro*, and I need a Cherubino. What an utterly, utterly delicious boy you'll make while remaining so very much a woman.'

Odd how one instinctively applied foody adjectives to Sonia. I thought Rudi was laying it on too thick for any woman to swallow. Not at all. Her full white throat arched, and a contented sigh heaved up from her unfashionably resplendent bust. From the maids I learned that she spent a fortune on the latest thing in flatteners, to no avail. It would have been a pity anyway. She wasn't a flat kind of woman.

Rudi saw me watching him and changed what might

have been a leer into respectful homage. Sonia hadn't noticed anyway. 'But I'm a mezzo and that's a soprano part,' she said.

'Just now you shrieked well above high C. I believe your range is greater than you know, quite enough for Cherubino. I'd like you to take a few lessons. The teacher I have in mind will extend you and he'll come down at a word. What do you say?'

She bridled. 'Well, Rudi, I'm sure I didn't know I was so loud and vulgar, and I apologize. But I suppose I could try. It might not work.'

'Then I'll get the part scored for a mezzo.'

'That definitely wouldn't work. Four soprano voices; the entire balance will go wrong if you suddenly bring in a mezzo.'

It was decent of Sonia to care enough for music not to let the opera be spoilt on her account. I knew positively that the idea of casting her as Cherubino had only just come into Rudi's head. Later, when I saw the opera, I realized that Sonia's voice was pretty good. I doubt whether it would have mattered had she croaked like a raven for in costume she was surpassingly lovely, and there were consequences that could never have been guessed at.

Perhaps the events afterwards would have happened anyway, and the opera had nothing to do with it. Did Sonia herself ever truly understand how peculiar the circumstances were? Probably not. She had a way of extracting from any situation what it pleased her to know and ignoring the rest.

By the Sunday before my birthday most of the snow had gone. We were in the garden, Claudia, Rudi and I, kicking down the remains of our snowman. Sunday used to be the most awful day of the week until Rudi came because of Sonia's zeal to do the right thing, especially if it got us away from the house.

There was church, of course. Then last winter after

Father's accident she enrolled Claudia and me in the Sunday School. I had a docile readiness to become pious. Dozens of village children were there, including some of the worst boys. On the wall hung a picture of Jesus, reassuringly clean and English-looking in a long gown: he embraced some equally clean children of different continents and colours.

'Are all those big boys religious then?' I asked a little girl sitting next to me.

She gave me a scornful look. 'They come for the treat a'course.'

Once a year those scholars who attended regularly and behaved were taken to Weymouth for the day by charabanc. They looked forward to the occasion all year. Claudia must have been responsible for a few disappointed hopes. The situation was tailor-made for surreptitious bullying and some of the girls endured much rather than jeopardize their treat. My sister was made of sterner stuff.

We knew the teacher by sight. Her father had the dairy farm that supplied our milk. She threw the heavy brassbound churns around as though they were made of feathers.

'Someone give out the texts,' she said, leafing over the pages of a hymn-book.

A boy at the end of a row darted out and grabbed some small coloured pictures. Then one-handed and with a speed clearly attained by practice he dropped his trousers and lifted his shirt.

'That boy's showing his winkle,' Claudia shrilled indignantly, pointing an accusing finger.

He froze in mid-recovery, rumpled and unbuttoned. The texts slipped slowly from his grasp and scattered on the floor. The teacher pounced on him. She shook him vigorously, dislodging his trousers again. 'Dirty article, outside with you,' she said. Grasping his collar she helped him to the door and hurled him through. 'Right. We'll sing "Gentle Jesus, meek and mild".'

The boy sitting behind Claudia grabbed a fistful of her hair. 'That's my bruvver,' he said. 'I'll get you outside.'

She dislodged him with a swinging elbow in his ribs. Nettled, he waited until we stood up to sing, and put a sharp tin-tack underneath her.

'Bloody hell,' she said loudly and fell on him. Pushing him to the ground she seized his ears and began beating his head up and down on the dusty wooden floor. Naturally I went to help though it wasn't really necessary. The fight that followed involved half the class.

Trailing homewards Claudia said, 'We've done Sunday School then.' She had the air of one asking where the next entertainment might be found.

'Your nose is bleeding a bit. Does it hurt?'

She wiped it with the back of her hand and inspected the red smear with interest. 'Noble gore,' she said. 'My head is bloody but unbowed.'

'I'm not going back there.'

I had gone right off Gentle Jesus and felt he had probably gone off me as well.

So there we were, jumping up and down on hard lumps of snow while I tried to persuade Claudia to come for a walk. I didn't notice the approach of Great-aunt Hildegarde until she was almost upon us.

The speed with which Gunne Magna and every village within a radius of twenty miles got wind of the coming revels ought not to have surprised me. Our tiny branch telephone switchboard was under the control of the post-mistress. Required only to connect calls to the Dorchester exhange, where her sister and accomplice worked, she listened without shame and as one divinely appointed. ('Leave the line open, my dear.')

Rudi spent hours on the telephone, reserving trunk-calls to London and Liverpool and Norwich and Salisbury, practically every city in the country. Several times he spoke to Pandel Metkin in Paris and once to a singer in Rome. For the sisters every day must have been a gala.

But I had forgotten Aunt Hildegarde. She lived quite near us at Sturminster Newton and she had religion in a big way. The family said that she was Low. This sounded as though they constantly found her down in the gutter. What they meant was that she favoured chapel rather than the High – or even the Broad – side of C of E.

Amiably she trundled towards us like a steamroller made of pillows. Her wiry black and grey hair pushed her hat to the back of her head. There was something funny about her shoulders because her dresses were always up in front with several inches of pink celanese petticoat showing. Claudia said she bought all her clothes at jumble-sales.

Clutched in her hands was a small parcel, my birthday present and her excuse for visiting. I knew what it would be, a pair of hand-knitted gloves to go with the nine other pairs reposing unworn in my dressing-table drawer. Hildegarde always gave gloves. Her knitting left much to be desired as she dropped stitches without noticing.

'More sodding gloves,' Claudia muttered to Rudi. 'Why doesn't she give proper presents? She's as rich as creosote and the foreign missions get it all.'

'I think you mean Croesus, and where are you off to?'

She slid away, rapidly for her, and didn't answer, as our visitor got within hailing distance. Hildegarde waved her parcel. 'Ah, there you are, dear, and here's a little something for your birthday. Don't open it until the day, will you?' No temptation there! 'Why has Claudia vanished in such a hurry?'

'She needs the lavatory,' I said hastily, unable to give the true reason which concerned the more embarrassing manifestations of Aunt Hildegarde's Lowness.

She was much more acute than she looked. 'Rather a mistake to go away from the house, I should have thought.' But Rudi, her true target, stood innocently smiling at her. 'Now you must be Mr Longmire. This evil you propose will be fought. Entertainment is the Devil's Snare and the theatre an antechamber to Hell!'

'But Aunt Hildegarde, it's to be Shakespeare,' I said.

She beamed myopically at Rudi. 'Please don't take this personally; you seem like a nice young man. But I am on the Lord's side. Dorset, you see, is a place of curious and wicked survivals, and neurotic in a way that no stranger can comprehend. They must be wiped out. "Onward, forward, shout aloud, Hosannah," as the hymnal says.'

'Er, madam,' Rudi began.

'Call me Aunt Hildegarde, dear, everyone does.'

'Thank you, Aunt Hildegarde.' Rudi smiled back at her, knowing an old love when he saw one, but worried all the same. 'There'll be no violence, will there? I really couldn't bear it.'

'Certainly not. Perhaps an egg thrown or flour if a convert gets carried away, though I am definitely against it. Mainly picketing, placards, prayer, but most effective at times.'

'Won't you come to the house and discuss it over a glass of sherry?'

'I'm an abstainer, dear, Band of Hope, you know. "My drink is water bright".' The mild blue of her eyes held Rudi's gaze for a long moment. 'Unloosing what has been pent up for many centuries is no wise thing to do, and I hope, dear, that you will be very, very careful, especially of Amy. I love the child. Now, she and I are going to church and I think you had better come with us.'

I very much did not want to go to our church with Great-aunt Hildegarde. 'I'm rather busy today, Aunt.'

'Never too busy for Jesus, dear.'

We were trapped. Aunt Hildegarde varied the

hymns with sudden shouts of 'Hallelujah' or 'Praise the Lord' and after the rest of us had sat down she remained standing and 'testified'. Apparently in chapels this was quite the thing, but our vicar wasn't used to it.

Cringing with mortification I tugged at her skirt. 'Sit down, Auntie, *please*.'

Rudi, trying to ingratiate himself and avoid a riot at his festival, muttered, 'Well said,' and 'Amen,' until I could have hit him. When at last I got them out he said to me, 'She's a lamb but a little disconcerting. I can't have religious protests going on in front of distinguished guests, and things thrown. I must do something; tell me, what?'

'Don't ask me,' I said irritably. 'She's cracked and sometimes I think you are too.'

'She's your aunt, try to concentrate.'

'No she's not, she's Father's aunt. This Band of Hope and water bright business.'

'A fraud, a secret toper?' Rudi asked eagerly.

'Not exactly, but she loves scrumpy, real local farm cider out of the barrel; apple-juice, she calls it, and she may think it's non-alcoholic for all I know. It makes her a bit tipsy.'

'But does it make her overlook Jesus?'

I smiled. 'It's rumoured that she once called a visiting missionary a boring, long-winded old poop, but I don't know whether it's true.'

'Well, well; well, well, well.' He had an admiring look on his face. 'I do hope she did.'

'Rudi, surely you're not thinking of undermining poor old Hildegarde.'

'Undermining? Not at all. Elevating perhaps, self-expression. I thought there must be more to her than hallelujahs.'

Having no relations to speak of Rudi could not have known what a seething stew of passions he would arouse among the Savernakes, Mottesfonts, and collateral branches. Great-aunt Hildegarde was only the first bubble to reach the surface.

What concerned him more than her chapel hooligans was the prospect of going back to Town without having found a theme for the farewell party. 'Everything's been done already, Amy. I want it to be something glamorous and memorable, a romance we can all live up to. Perhaps London will inspire me.'

As only he knew what he was searching for I was dumb. Until he came our lives were dull and characterless beyond belief. Inspiration did not, I thought, lie at Gunville Place.

The grandparents Mottesfont had not been seen in Dorset since Father married Sonia. Knowing my grandmother's animosity, it came as a surprise to find the maids turning out the deserted apartment.

In one of my compulsory fortnightly letters I had mentioned Rudi's presence. Could it be that they had heard of the ruined honour of Sonia's cousin's maid and wanted to ensure that Claudia and I were not in moral danger?

The more I thought, the less likely it seemed. Our relations could never be accused of undue worry about each others' welfare. And stark realism compelled me to accept that not even the prurient Sonia would think of me as a target for passionate and improper advances. Claudia could be trusted to look after her own morals.

But something fishy was afoot. On the day after their arrival Grandmother asked to see Rudi. As his unshakeable shadow and protector I couldn't let the poor lamb go alone to the slaughter. I took him into the presence. He shied slightly at the sight of her statuesque figure advancing on him with smothering bosom and hand outstretched.

'Hallo, Grandmother,' I whispered, expecting to be told to run along.

Such was her preoccupation that she looked clean

through me. Rudi made a gallant sort of half-bow and announced his name. She was tremendously gracious, enquiring about the festival and the musical entertainments, and where the art shows were to be held, and had he thought of lectures by eminent writers? Rudi chattered on with growing puzzlement.

'And what plays, Mr Longmire? Something old and something new, perhaps?' she asked archly.

'Shakespeare of course, Lady Mottesfont; the *Dream*, and *Romeo and Juliet*; then a revue especially arranged for us, a sort of pot-pourri of songs and sketches.'

'Mrs Mottesfont please; we have no title nor need one,' Grandmother said with ferocious *bonhomie*. 'You know, it was always my intention to go on the stage but my parents forbade it. Acting was not then thought to be a respectable occupation for a young girl.'

'A loss to the profession I'm sure.' Rudi edged towards the door, collecting me like a spare coat as he passed by. 'And so kind of you to take an interest. If you will excuse me now.'

Grandmother swept away from him to the window, her face suffused with angry colour. 'Then good day to you, Mr Longmire.'

And all at once he realized. 'Oh my word, Amy, she wants a part,' he hissed under his breath, and recovering splendidly he turned back and with a lovely show of humility said, 'If you won't think it an impertinence – but dare I ask it of you?'

'Ask what?' Grandmother sounded deeply huffed.

'Juliet's nurse and Lady Capulet, not yet cast, you see. Since you are so nearly a professional, would you, could you be so wonderfully kind as to read the parts for me?'

She did quite a good piece of acting then and there. 'Well, I'm not sure that the family would find it appropriate, Mr Longmire. Insufferable sticks, some of them.'

'An impertinence on my part, and I mustn't press you or impose.' Rudi was a miracle of respectful eagerness. 'I go back to London tomorrow, you see, and return in April so there's not much time. Will you do it?'

'Yes,' Grandmother said baldly. 'When?'

'This afternoon, in the small drawing-room?'

A graceful inclination of the head. Grandfather raised his eyebrows at me over the top of his *Times* and lowered a lid in a broad wink. I slid out before I disgraced myself by laughing.

'With a lightning movement she lay on her face, raised her elbows on the tiger's head, and supported her chin in her hands,' I read. 'Perfectly straight out her body was, the twisted purple drapery outlining her perfect shape, and flowing in graceful lines beyond – like a serpent's tail. The velvet pillows fell scattered at one side. "Paul – what do you know of lovers – or love?" she said. "My baby Paul!"'

Sympathetically I too turned on my face. My ears were stuffed with cotton-wool against Claudia's gramophone. Rudi was putting Grandmother through her paces. I was alone. My Christmas books lay pristine and unopened.

We were supposed to share a maid, Claudia and I. It worked out that Claudia, who never bent to pick up a sock from the floor if she could help it, hogged ninety per cent of poor old Ivy's time and energy. I got the frugal remaining tenth.

Ivy could not, in fact, have been much more than thirty-five but she complained a lot and had an elderly soul. She grew up in Birmingham. Her residence in Dorset she owed to a certain family raffishness, and most of her wages went to keep her deserted and penniless mother.

In middle-age her father ran away to live in company with a gipsy woman. They occupied a tent in a lane

outside the walls of Dorchester under the wistful sur-
veillance of Ivy's mother, who hoped one day to win
back her man to the domestic hearth.

'Mum come of a respectable family, like,' Ivy confided
in her flat accent that sounded as if she were about to
cry even when she wasn't. 'They thought she threw
herself away on our Dad, didn't aspire, as you might
say. Love's rubbish when you come to think about it.'

Romance had never entered her life in the flesh and
she had small reason to trust men. But her passion for
sixpenny novelettes transcended her cynicism.
'They're a smashing read, and they take me out of
meself,' she confided. 'I'll give you a lend of them but I
want them back.'

Ivy must have been a democrat of the truest sort.
Because I gave her very little trouble she counted me a
friend. I'm certain it never crossed her mind that her
choice of reading might be unsuitable for a child of a
different background, and only just turned eight. So
under my bed and safe from prying eyes was stacked a
pile of concentrated and irresistible tosh from which I
extracted almost as much pleasure as Ivy.

Deeply absorbed in Elinor Glyn's *Three Weeks* I
snaked away on a tiger-skin with the lady. 'A rage of
passion was racing through Paul; his incoherent
thoughts were that he did not want to talk – only to kiss
her – to devour her – to strangle her with love if
necessary. He bit the rose.'

I had flicked over the pages of *Romeo and Juliet* and
failed to make out what on earth they were on about.
Nobody ever seemed to say what they meant. Pallid
stuff!

I read on. 'But Paul's young, strong arms held her
close, she could not struggle or move. Then she
laughed a laugh of pure glad joy. "Beautiful, savage
Paul," she whispered. "Do you love me? Tell me that."

' "Love you!" he said. "Good God! Love you! Madly,
and you know it, darling Queen." '

' "Then," said the lady in a voice in which all the caresses of the world seemed melted, "then, sweet Paul, I shall teach you many things, and among them I shall teach you how—to—Live." '

What, I ask you, did Shakespeare ever write to compare with that?

A frustrating line of dots followed. The rest of the chapter was about a storm and the fire crackling. It annoyed me that Elinor missed out what happened next. I rather wanted to be taught how to Live myself and she might have explained properly.

I had got to the supposed wedding night, though all mention of a ceremony had been carelessly omitted. The lady and Paul were both emoting marvellously when my door flew open. Hastily I stuffed the book under the counterpane and unstopped my ears.

It was Rudi. 'Stiff as a ramrod, dear Amy, but possible. She couldn't quite condescend to playing a nurse – Lady Capulet, yes. What a gorgon! I'm exhausted.' He thumped down on to the bed and lay back with his feet on the pillow. Then he wriggled. 'I'm lying on something.'

I went hot with embarrassment all over when he fished and came up with my novelette. 'Give it to me, please.'

He began to laugh and held it up out of my reach. 'Good Lord, Amy, you're reading steamy stuff. Listen. "Beloved, beloved!" he cried, "let us waste no more precious moments. I want you – I want you – my sweet." '

'Stop making fun of me,' I said crossly. 'You didn't help me with Shakespeare and he does go on so. I can understand almost all of that one except for the dots.'

Rudi flicked the pages over abstractedly. 'Strange how one always laughs at Elinor Glyn yet there's a certain persuasion in her torrid sexuality. Silly and vulgar, of course, but tailor-made for the stage.' He stopped and stared at me as though he had found a diamond-mine. 'Amy Savernake, you are a wonder beyond price. Think of Sonia and jewels and furs and scarves and clinging robes. If only I could find a way to melt her marble exterior what a heroine she'd make.'

I couldn't deny that with all that rounded front she looked the part. Rudi thought her too cold. But I remembered the view of another man. 'Grandpa said once that Sonia's an avid piece but virtuous.'

'Did he now? Do you understand what he meant?'

'No. Everyone goes on about doing sex but they won't tell me what it is.'

I expect I sounded hopeful for Rudi shied and said, 'Oh no, Amy, not me. I'm not going to explain, it's not the thing, you know. Ask your grandmother.'

What an absolutely rotten suggestion! She would chew me into little pieces and spit me out, or have me sent to reform-school to work on a treadmill. I was disappointed in Rudi.

But then he said, 'Or wait until the knowledge comes to you naturally and without tensions. Believe me, sometimes it's better to be innocent.' He laid the novelette in my lap. 'Now, think how simple this story is, and how perfectly it can convert into a play. I shall use it as my main theme and present it for the party, *and* I shall acknowledge your help on the programmes. Claudia will be green!'

'Yes she will, especially if Sonia gets the biggest part. Rudi, I do like you ever so much. It's going to be miserable while you're away.'

'Not at all. I shall telephone and write and give you a great deal to do.'

I'd heard and believed that sort of thing before. But I felt smug. There were wonderful treats to look forward to. I could tell Claudia that the theme for the last day of the festival was determined and that it was to be SEX!

*   *   *

78

I found her painting her lips. Her eyelashes were spiky with mascara and she smelt of face-powder. 'After the way you went on about Sonia!' I said.

She tried to answer and the lipstick smeared down her chin. 'Blast,' she said, 'now I've got to start again. It's a matter of acting and husbands. One has to make up for the stage and it's as well to start thinking out well in advance who to go for. All the theatre women use pounds of make-up and men flock around them so I suppose they like it.'

'Isn't getting married about falling in love then?'

She made a being-sick kind of noise. 'What mush! You're beginning to talk like Soapy.'

I covered a blush by blowing my nose vigorously. 'No I'm not, it's what girls are supposed to do.'

'We're not just girls, stupid, we're ladies, and we have to get it right about money and family, Portia says.' Claudia started again on her mouth.

'Since when have you taken any notice of what Portia says? Even ladies fall in love,' I said, feeling dreadfully sorry for any man that she decided to marry. 'It's in a book I'm reading and Rudi's going to make a play out of it for the cast party.'

'Balls,' Claudia said, looking cross. 'Why would he want to do one of your silly kids' books?'

'It isn't a kids' book, it's about a slinky lady on a tiger-skin and a man called Paul doing sex, so there. And that's going to be the theme. Won't it be fun?'

'If they let us be there it might. Bet you Sonia tries to stop us, and anyway you won't understand it.'

'You've smudged your mouth again. Can I have a go?'

'No, you can't.'

'Don't get angry, Claudia, but Sonia won't stop us. She'll be on the stage. Rudi's putting her in the play to be the lady.'

With her lipstick she drew on the looking-glass a recumbent female form with Sonia's sort of bust and added some ghastly blood-drops. 'I wish he'd get a live tiger; that would really be fun,' she said morosely.

Watching Claudia's half-painted reflection behind the scrawled red I got a sudden and unexpected thrill down my spine. Colours seemed to move and merge in the glass like bright figures in a dance. A mysterious alchemy was at work. For all of us changes were coming, and knowledge, and new emotions. I felt a certainty that just beyond my grasp lay understanding and that the festival would make all puzzling things plain.

Chapter Six

So much was happening that it was all I could do to find time to keep my journal up to date. I trotted after Rudi like a pet dog. While he was away I prowled the house from one focus of interest to another, listening to Sonia practising scales and snatches of Mozart, watching Cyril Fox slap great gobbets of paint on to wood and canvas, and sneaking up on to the outdoor stage and doing a bit of pretending.

Sonia had, in Rudi's words, been tickled pink at the idea of playing the lead in *Three Weeks*. At first he said, 'She's too stately for words, but once I overcome that deadly respectability and get her to writhe nicely she'll be sensational.'

Her looks were absolutely right for a mysterious, unconventional queen, so it seemed an awful pity that she loaded down her life with taboos. They made her unhappy and fretful. At a time when everyone wanted to laugh and relax she became more and more serious and tense.

I gathered from Ivy that Claudia's barbed remark about babies had really hurt her. She threw attacks of temperament and cried a lot, declaring that we all wanted her dead.

'I'm glad I'm not her maid,' Ivy said. 'She's taken to breaking glass and throwing face-powder. It takes hours to clean up. I'd have said she was on the gin, but she don't drink so it must be glands. Women get glands and go broody in spring.'

'Perhaps it's mumps. Claudia's glands went all swollen when she had mumps.'

'The doctor says she oughter drink red wine for her blood, but she don't do it. Or a drop of milk stout's nourishing too.'

Remembering the way Sonia handed off the village women who wanted to show her their infants, I said, 'She doesn't really seem to like children very much so I can't think why she wants one.'

'Glands, like I said.'

Unlike most of her acquaintances who poured down the gin-and-Its as if a drought was coming, Sonia only had a little glass of champagne on birthdays and anniversaries. She didn't smoke cigarettes either, so it wasn't bad habits that were holding things up.

Of course I had discovered when I finished reading *Three Weeks* that the lady made Paul give her a baby though she already had a cruel and beastly husand. Poor old Soapy, babies wherever she turned!

Elinor Glyn failed to make clear the exact way that Paul managed to do the deed. I was tempted to ask Ivy how someone got a baby. She would have told me, I expect. She possessed a wealth of information about awful-sounding things like whitlows and car-buncles and gatherings and yellow jaundice and cardiac hearts and proud flesh. I guessed she would make doing sex sound just as horrid so I held my tongue.

Claudia and I had stopped expecting smocks or other signs but surreptitiously I inspected Sonia and found that although she could not be described as starved she was thinner, with less bust. She nagged a lot too.

Rudi scrupulously kept promises made to children and he telephoned me often which made her waspish. Gunville Place had only two receivers. One was in Father's study and reserved for his private and official business. The other was in the main hallway. If she caught me there she stood and sighed and scowled and asked how long I was going to be until I got nervous and told Rudi I must hang up. Something was eating her without a doubt.

The day Rudi came back to us, life, which seemed to have run down, started up again. Time whistled along like an express train. He must have been really good at his job for the hectic pace didn't seem to trouble him at all. He coped with accommodation, deciding who should stay at the Place, booking hotels, and renting houses and cottages, to the joy and gain of our village neighbours.

The London street-arab, used to living on his wits, thought of Dorset countrymen in terms of simple sons of toil, virgin souls. He couldn't have been more wrong. A dignified, slow-moving, silent breed, they did a persuasive line in innocence. But under placid exteriors shrewd brains were at work. It wasn't that they set out to cheat strangers. They simply had a nose for profit and an ability to drive bargains that would put financiers to shame. No move that Rudi made went unmarked.

He arranged with a Dorchester firm to do the bulk of the catering. 'The special things, smoked salmon, pâté de fois, must come from Fortnum's, and extra wine if needs be. The Earl, bless the man, is rifling his cellar, but he says he's cursed with thirsty relatives.'

Rehearsals were being held in London mostly. Claudia pined to go there with Rudi and she moaned when he refused. 'He says he won't take me unless old Soapy-bitch comes too as I'm a responsibility. I ask you, Amy, what's the use of going if I have her hanging around?'

I thought it sensible of him but I didn't say so. Often I walked down to meet his taxi-cab at the gates and hear how the day had gone. One evening his way was blocked. A broad back shut him off from me and as I approached I heard a familiar voice asking, ''Ow many gartos will you be wanting then? Missis always does they gartos. 'Er needs to know where you be a'putting of 'er stall.'

The assault had begun. There was to be a fête and every country person knew how such things ought to be run to turn an honest penny. Rudi looked non-plussed. 'What's he saying, Amy? I don't understand.'

'Hallo, Sammy,' I said. 'Rudi, this is Mr Bowells. He wants to know where the cake-stall will be and how many gâteaux Mrs Bowells should make.'

'Cake-stall?' he said faintly.

'And the bookays.'

'That's flowers,' I translated.

'Does she do flowers too?'

'Yes, of course. Leave it with us, Sammy, and we'll get it arranged somehow. Mr Longmire has a lot on his mind just now.'

'Righto, Miss Amy, I'll be off down-along then,' he bellowed, making it sound like a threat.

Our farmers tend to speak loudly because of some-times needing to be heard several fields away. Sammy smiled and nodded and departed satisfied.

Rudi watched him go with an unbelieving expression on his face. 'Can his name really be Bowells?'

'Oh yes, it's common around here. And Biles and Piles.'

'How dreadfully intestinal. And I thought that Lotts lacked euphony! Amy, what is all this about gartos and bookays, what am I supposed to do? It's a festival, not a vicarage sale of work. And in the village they hang over fences and stare, and little groups follow me around. Don't they like me being here?'

The basic answer was, they like the smell of money and want as much of it as they can get out of you, but I didn't feel able to destroy his vision of rural simplicity. 'You're auditioning and might hire them,' I said.

'Oh God! I can probably use a few girls as chorus and walk-ons, but none of the men. Just look at their forearms – pure beef. They'll hardly make fairies for Oberon, but I don't much want to be the one to tell them so.'

I took his hand. 'You mustn't worry. They're already thinking of other ways to get something out of us, like Sammy.'

'That's a very cynical remark.'

'Is it, Rudi? I didn't know. I'm sorry, but it's true, you'll see.'

'Can't you put them off?'

'Do we have to? There'll be a bookstall, you said, and London people might quite like to buy country produce – honey and jam and fresh eggs and cakes. Gladys Bowells does heavenly cakes and her goosegog jam always gets prizes.'

All in all it seemed kinder not to mention childrens' handicrafts while he was in a weakened state. I couldn't see him – or anyone in their right mind come to think of it – admiring crocheted wool antimacassars, orange raffia tablemats, or bead whatsits for looping back curtains.

'Goosegog jam,' he murmured, and seemed to fall into a light trance, rousing when I took his hand. 'Let's go in, Amy, my feet are killing me and I'm hungry. Very well then, those things if I must, but not, definitely not, the cast bouquets. Somehow I don't see myself with the courage to offer Marie Dearlove the tribute of a bunch of garden flowers.'

Miss Dearlove was his up-and-coming star (Juliet and Titania), not quite top-rank but heading that way, and afflicted with vanity and chronic bad temper. There was no sense in getting him in a stew. He didn't seem to have much sales-resistance and I should just have to protect him from the pressing tactics of the villagers.

But the family was trapped. We should all feel obliged to buy tight bunches of border-pinks and sweet-williams with a smile and cries of, 'How lovely!' or, 'You really do have green fingers, Gladys.'

I saw my meagre house-fund shrinking further. The red velvet curtains I had almost decided on would have to go. In my mind's eye I replaced them with black and white striped mattress-ticking at fivepence ha'penny a broad yard. Trimmed with braid in bright blue they looked rather elegant. My dreams were becoming economical!

In the first week of May the workmen hammered the last nails into the stand and turned their attention to the marquees. Driven on by the shuddering distaste of Cyril Fox, Rudi decided to do something about the house.

'Who built it anyway?' he asked. 'A man like the Earl deserves better than Frankenstein's castle and a wife as impossibly self-centred as Sonia.'

I wondered whether he knew the cause of her unrest. Perhaps she felt jealous. Father had come out of his shell a lot recently, and looked perpetually amused. The young actresses, even then settling into lodgings and boarding-houses, made a great fuss of him, partly because of his rank but also because he treated them with unfailing courtesy. Gravely he discussed with them their hopes and fears and, encouraged, they talked to him about their boys and their mums and dads. Somehow they found an ease with him that we, his children, envied.

I said to Rudi, 'My great-grandfather's best friend designed it and no-one liked to tell him it was awful.'

'The kindest thing is to cover up as much as possible.'

So Cyril Fox painted a huge banner that read 'Midsummer Festival of Arts Gunville Place 1927 – 14th June to 22nd June'. Men went on to the roof and hung it so that it hid the stupid crenellations. The style seemed a bit sketchy and odd but it made a lovely splash of colour. I thought that some of the female relations might not altogether approve as it also showed a lot of ladies with no clothes to speak of. Rudi said they were muses and classical so that made it all right.

He hired an army of nursery-men who cost his wealthy friend a fortune. Apparently Mr Metkin was very sensitive to beauty and Rudi thought that he would consider the expense worthwhile. I certainly did. The result turned out to be absolutely gorgeous. Creepers fell green and gold and bronze from the balconies, and pots and boxes of flowers stood on parapets and in niches, their colours enhanced by the grey of the stone. Slender palm-trees reared their heads on the terrace. Spotty laurels bit the dust in dozens and rose-bushes in full bloom took their place.

Under a benevolent sun excitement fizzed up and spilled over the countryside. The ancient sleepers under the rich earth of Dorset turned in their slumbers. Men not known for imagination reckoned that they saw the ghosts of wild fair men silhouetted against the night sky.

Then a dead may-tree threw out fresh leaves and flowered within the week. Sammy Bowells said contemptuously, 'Women's foolishness. Un weren't never dead. Ate up a bit by er-mine moth, un were.'

Sensible explanations weren't wanted. The local white witch absentmindedly put a love-potion in her pig's mash and sent it mad. She got cross with herself. The pig was fattening up nicely for sale. She had to stuff it with valerian and other sedatives to get a good price at Sturminster Newton market.

Gunne Magna became touched with madness altogether. Two girls were molested in the woods. Someone grabbed the first from behind and caressed her in a familiar way that she deeply resented. She was strongly built. 'I clouted 'e one,' she said, 'and 'im ran for it.'

The second girl heard a low, hoarse call and turning her head saw a naked man advancing on her. She found difficulty in describing him. Although he showed her a great deal that she didn't much want to see his face was obscured. On his head he wore an ooser, an ancient bull-mask.

When she ran he tried to follow her. It must have been difficult to see properly through the eye-holes in the mask. A lot of bramble bushes trailed over the ground and he tripped and fell into one, to the maiden's acute amusement.

The vicar's wife, our amateur local historian, went into transports when she heard. 'How I wish I'd been there,' she said to the post-mistress. 'I've searched years for a genuine Dorset ooser. The only authentic survival disappeared in the last century. It's the Horned God cult, you know, pre-Roman, and I'm furious to have missed it.'

She shocked the post-mistress. 'Not a word of sympathy for they girls. Thrilled she was. If he had catched her she wouldn't have noticed nothing but that mask, no matter what else he'd got.'

Claudia expressed deep and bloodthirsty interest. 'If he bled we could get the hounds out after him. They'd tear him to pieces. Or perhaps the village would hang him on the old gibbet.'

'Not if he was in pieces they wouldn't, and I don't think it's allowed.'

' "Troop home to churchyards: damned spirits all," ' she chanted. 'You're turning into a know-all rat, Amy Savernake, and it's boring.'

I knew she was saying some of her lines at me. 'And you're a great show-off just because you're in a play,' I said, weakly resisting.

She glanced around for something to throw at me but her impulse to action didn't last. 'I'm resting for my public,' said Claudia, the budding actress, with insufferable condescension. 'That's what we stage people do in between roles.'

'You'll be simply MARVELLOUS at that, darling,' I cried with exaggerated sincerity, aping Marie Dearlove.

She blew a raspberry which was a noise considered vulgar even in theatrical circles. 'I hope the Ooser gets you,' she said.

I ran errands for Rudi and for Cyril Fox, who drank beer by the gallon when he was working and never ever appeared to get drunk. He sweated a lot and ruined several singlets a day.

For me it was a time of ecstatic happiness. When the carrier delivered the programmes Rudi showed them to me. 'One for the festival proper, here. And this one is for the last day; it has to be separate because it's private and I have to watch copyrights. Take a look at them.'

And there my name was in big gold print. ' "Organizer and Festival Manager, Rudi Longmire. Assistant to Mr Longmire, Lady Amity Savernake," ' I read aloud.

'Now the cast entertainment.'

Again I appeared, almost at the top, under '*Three Weeks*, by Elinor Glyn, a Dramatized Version'; 'Special Adviser, Lady Amity Savernake'. I hugged myself with glee. 'Oh, Rudi, you're lovely to me, you really are. I'm so excited. Only twelve days to go. Will you be ready?'

He put an arm round me and said, 'Amy, if ever I meet an absolute dear like you of the right age I shall certainly marry her.' I went beetroot red with shyness. 'And yes, we shall be ready, and I've had a telegram from Pan Metkin to say that he arrives tomorrow.'

A crumb of foreknowledge sent shivers down my back. Rudi had talked so much about this legendary figure. His wealth and the beautiful objects with which he surrounded himself made him a kind of Caliph out of the Arabian Nights. The power of romance stretched out a finger and touched me.

It had taken for ever to find a house fit for him to rent. Even then he had sent carpets and cases of silver and china and pictures to embellish it. The hugest motor car I ever saw had been shipped over from Paris.

He couldn't also be kind as Rudi said, not with all that luxury.

When I remember the moment that I first saw Pandel Metkin I see us inside a beautiful shimmering soap-bubble, cut off from all things real and dull. A small biplane, a rare sight then, flew low over the house and I went on to the terrace to watch it. It landed in our park. Two men in bulky leather jackets got out and walked up to the house, pulling off their flying-helmets as they came.

The sun shone full in my eyes. Beside me stood Rudi with Claudia; Sonia had just come out through the glass doors. 'Here they are, Pan and Jimmy,' Rudi said.

Impossible to mistake which was which. The name, Pan, conjured up an elderly, sharp-faced, goatish creature. The reality drove the breath out of me. My eyes skipped rapidly over the fair good looks of Jimmy. Pandel was dark. His hair curled closely to his head, his smile made the heart ache with its perfection, and the symmetry of his features conjured up all kinds of comparisons that I immediately rejected.

Rudolph Valentino in *The Sheik* was a crow, and Lionel Barrymore might as well drop dead. Once, at a time when I got frightened of the dark, Gwennie told me I had a guardian angel. She taught me to say the rhyme, 'Matthew, Mark, Luke and John, bless the bed that I lie on.'

'Can't I choose my own angel?' I asked her.

'Why not, my lovely?'

I chose the Archangel Gabriel. Somewhere I must have come across a picture of the Annunciation and only half remembered it. My angel had dark curls touched with gold and big, kind, dark eyes.

So, put feathery wings behind Pandel Metkin's curly head, replace the flying-suit with robes of purest white, and there he was, about to tell Mary that she would bear a child. A nonsensical image. As well that Sonia couldn't see inside my head.

We all stood like statues. In the heat of the June day, Pandel stopped at the bottom of the steps and stared and stared at Sonia. She looked utterly delectable. Her two-piece of heavy white silk clung a little to her hips and stopped at the knee, showing off the elegance of her legs. At her neck and wrists and ears gleamed the pallid watery blue of huge aquamarines. The stones caught light and cooled it like a long iced drink.

Her eyes, the greenish colour of shallow water, were trapped by the intensity of Pan's velvety-dark gaze. Excluded from that meeting of beauty with beauty, we could only watch them and admire. I thought wildly of Paul and the lady, and passion on a tiger-skin, and the Annunciation. I breathed heavily through my mouth in the way so deplored by Portia.

Pan and Sonia together made a radiant picture. Yet somewhere lay unreality. A shade of feeling that I had become used to noticing in men was absent. They are beautiful, I thought, and absolutely *not* made for each other. I had no idea why; the reasons came later.

How long we stood there silently gaping I don't know. We must have looked weird. Rudi moved and spoke. 'Pan dear, and Jimmy, come and meet Sonia, Countess of Osmington, and Lady Claudia Savernake, and Lady Amity Savernake.'

'Glorious,' Mr Metkin murmured, obviously meaning Sonia.

Then everything became fairly ordinary again except for me thinking fiercely that the festival would alter everything, alter us. Exotic airs transmuted the familiar Dorset landscape. The power of ancient wizards stirred strongly under the hills and I heard faint echoes of their voices.

Rudi, who on the surface seemed so ordinary, belonged to them. He was the genie out of the lamp. Aladdin in pantomime wished and his wishes were

91

granted. China suddenly changed to Africa, rags turned to splendour and dull safety became a glittering romance.

Just so had Rudi appeared, to grant us all our dearest dreams. He flew us from Gunville Place to a land of sun and burning sands, spice-scented and brilliant and full of marvels.

In her days as our governess, Sonia often read to us from a book called *Eyes and No-Eyes*. On walks we were supposed to look around and discover about natural things, though I got the distinct impression that on the whole she rather disapproved of Nature, feeling that it was vulgar.

She would have no truck at all with burial-mounds or the grassed-over remains of old, old towns or any other kind of antiquity. Once she took Claudia and me to a lecture on them given by Rachel Moot, the vicar's wife who wanted to meet the Ooser. Sonia expected to hear about Merrie England and the Good Old Days. Dates were never her strong point. Before the end she dragged us out. 'That woman ought to be stopped,' she said.

I'm sure she thought ancient rites totally disgusting, what with virgins sacrificed on altars or being raped and pillaged. Virgins certainly seemed to have a thoroughly rotten time of it.

The walks were short and never a great success. Claudia declined to be interested in the prettiness of wild-flowers and berries. Mostly she elected to be a 'No-Eyes' unless the chance of an embarrassing question arose like, 'Why is that sparrow jumping on that other sparrow's back, Miss Rollands?' She knew that we would be hurried back home unenlightened.

We didn't go as far as Cerne Abbas. Passing through the village in a motor car, Sonia might instruct me to admire the abbey. ('Look to the left, Amy!') Claudia would usually be asleep. Yet that doesn't altogether explain how I managed scarcely to notice the huge figure cut into the chalk of Giant's Hill.

I knew vaguely that it was there, only three or four miles away. Claudia never spoke of it. If she'd had any idea she couldn't have resisted showing off about it, particularly if she upset Sonia. But then I always suspected that my sister's knowledge was more sketchy than she let on.

Enlightenment came in part by way of Rachel Moot. We were in Pandel's lovely motor car with the top down, clutching at our hats to stop them blowing away. Jimmy, his friend, drove us, and there as we swooped round a bend rose the hill and the Giant. In the middle of the road, gazing up at him, stood a lady wearing Land Army britches and leaning on a bicycle. It was Mrs Moot.

The car stopped suddenly a yard away from her. 'Great Heavens,' Mr Metkin said, 'do look at the hill, Jimmy, Rudi. It's amazing.'

Sonia made a strangled sound of embarrassment. 'There's a splendid old abbey on the other side of the road, and some dear little stone cottages,' she said hastily.

No-one wanted to look that way. Claudia's questing nose was alert. The vicar's wife leaned over the side of the car and said, 'Absolutely splendid survival, isn't it? Ithyphallic, a fertility figure, of course, and highly thought of.'

'Is it indeed,' Pandel said. 'It surprises me that the English haven't tried to cover up that startling nudity.'

Our national correctness amused him. When he had recovered enough from the initial impact of Sonia to notice Claudia and me he had refused to be addressed as Mr Metkin. 'Pandel, my dear ladies, or Pan, or if you're uncomfortable with those, Uncle Pan. Is it proper to use your titles?'

He had seemed a little disappointed when I said it made us uncomfortable and that we weren't supposed to address adults by their first name. With disarming honesty he had admitted that it thrilled him to mix with aristocrats. 'But,' I had said, 'you're far richer and grander than we are, and ever so much more handsome than anyone I ever met.'

'It will be a pity when you learn to dissemble, Amy,' he had said, smiling. 'Thank you, but none of those can quite make me forget my mongrel blood and the poverty of my youth. Part Jewish, part Cretan, part unknown Middle Eastern, who am I but the sum of my possessions? If I owned the world the doors of your father's clubs would remain closed to me. Rob him of all he owns and he is a nobleman still.'

I couldn't imagine anything more boring than mixing with the pompous lords that Father met in clubs. Pan interested me far more. Squashed between him and Sonia in the back seat of the car I felt that, lapped in the warmth of their bodies, some of their beauty might rub off on to me.

Over the Giant I found myself mildly baffled. I couldn't see very well. Each time Sonia moved her bust pushed my panama hat down over my eyes and she leaned forward, half-obstructing my view. I got the impression that the Giant wasn't actually nude but a bit covered up. I glimpsed below the waist a peculiar arrangement like an ornamental belt or a sort of loincloth.

Rachel groped for a hairpin and stabbed it ferociously into her soft bun of fine, greyish-brown hair. It was always coming down. She put on her lecturing voice. 'Not even the church has dared touch him, you know. Barren women put faith in the phallus still, and legend has it that to sleep in the lap of the Giant ensures many children. Midsummer's Eve is thought to be a particularly favourable time.'

Sonia made a sharp, affronted movement of her head. She disapproved deeply of the vicar for marrying someone of liberal education and free tongue. His wife looked every inch the faded kind of woman fit to run a vicarage and a parish, but she wasn't like that at all really.

For a start she had been a suffragette. Once in Mothers' Meeting she announced, 'Ladies, the happiest day of my life was the General Election of nineteen-eighteen when women were able to vote for the first time.'

Her audience probably felt that she ought to have said, the day I married the vicar. They muttered among themselves and said it was a scandal that she kept wearing trousers when the war had been over for years.

'Can we move on, please?' Sonia said.

'It's a treasure,' Pan said warmly. 'Do you know anything of its history?'

'Certainly. I'm writing a pamphlet. Come to the vicarage some time – Gunne Magna, next to the church – and I'll show you my researches.'

'Please,' Sonia said in a cross voice, 'I should like to go home now.'

Mrs Moot gave a sarcastic smile. Our hasty departure from her lecture had been noted and remembered. 'I won't detain you. Lady Osmington is of a sensitive disposition, I believe. Come any time. Delighted to see you.'

'Cats will scratch,' Rudi murmured. 'That fellow arouses passions and I should like to go too before I die of jealousy!'

Surprised, I wondered if perhaps he had fallen into one of his sudden desires over the vicar's wife to feel so jealous, but the two other men laughed so I supposed he had made a joke.

Poor Sonia had become very quiet. I stole a glance at her and thought she might be crying. Between clenched fists she crumpled her cream glacé-kid gloves into a tight ball. But I didn't dare speak or touch her. She and Pan had stopped noticing me quite quickly and leaned together to talk across me. The reminder that I wasn't just a cushion would have made her irritable. When the rest of us were all so happy, I didn't know why she gloomed, but I couldn't help feeling sorry.

Pan unclasped one of her hands and turned it over. He looked at the palm and then raised it to his lips and kissed it. 'Your hands are exquisite. All will be well,' he said softly.

If he had been English and ordinary he might often have sounded a bit soppy and affected. Instead he got away with it, being so graceful. Sonia neither freed her hand nor smiled. 'Oh, what's the use of wishing?' she said.

The two of them looked gravely at each other as they always did when they were together. But even Claudia couldn't have found sex in those looks. I don't know that Pan Metkin particularly liked Sonia much at first, but she certainly fascinated him. He puzzled me a lot.

Claudia reached home in a state of suppressed excitement, and with a decidedly evil look in her eye. Rudi considered her dispassionately. 'Whatever you are thinking of saying to Amy, you're not to say it, do you understand?'

'But, Rudi—'

'Behave like a lady or be cast into utter darkness where there's only weeping and gnashing of teeth,' he said. 'I've taken considerable trouble to civilize you so practise at all times.'

'What *were* you going to say to me?' I enquired, wondering if I was getting left out again.

'Bloody Rudi seems to know. Ask him,' she said.

'Language like that will get you excluded from all parties,' he said sternly to Claudia. 'And, Amy, if you have any questions about that monstrous Giant please bring them to me first and I'll find the person to answer them.'

'I don't have any. Why should I?'

Claudia gave me a glare of utter contempt. 'God, you're dense,' she said.

So nothing new there. But I did sort of wonder a little what the fuss was about. I meant to pump Claudia when Rudi wasn't around but with so many other things going on I completely forgot.

Chapter Seven

The entry in my journal for Sunday 13 June 1927
covered eight pages. It mostly concerned Sonia's
supper-dance. That day was the eve of the festival and
a kind of prelude to what came after. For the first time
that I remembered Gunville Place was full, which
improved it no end.

Some of Father's noble friends from the House of
Lords occupied the state rooms in the centre of the
house. Dozens of relatives and their maids, valets, and
other oddments packed into the two long wings
and resumed quarrels begun years before and destined
never to end except with death. Free hospitality didn't
make them the least bit grateful. They eyed each other
suspiciously and complained if they thought someone
else had a bigger room. So they were more than ready
to carp.

But they couldn't fault Sonia's dance, or Sonia
herself. I noticed some of the old lords eyeing her like
hungry wolverines and pretending to be fatherly so
that they could pat and stroke her a bit.

Pan told me that Sonia's gown came from Worth in
Paris. Most dresses ended at the knee then. Sonia's
didn't. It clung to her very closely until it reached her
hips and frothed out into a swirl of shot green and gold
silk-chiffon to the ankles. Most of her back was bare.
She wore lots of emeralds and diamonds.

'Such skin as that Fragonard might have painted,'
Pan said. 'How it invites one to touch. There's a quality
in the Lady Osmington's beauty that makes me weep
for joy.'

Jimmy gave a funny kind of smile. 'What you weep over, my dear, you usually want to possess. Is this to be one of your times?'

I didn't know what he meant but Pan must have done. 'Not possess, borrow perhaps. Will you very much mind?'

'When do I ever?'

'Never, Jimmy, and nor do I, that's the secret of our devotion.'

In one way and another the evening supplied a lot of interesting things to write down. Claudia and I almost didn't go. Sonia got hold of me beforehand and said, 'We're great chums, aren't we, Amy? I want you to help me.' Chums, pals, she certainly tried hard. I waited without answering. It never did with her to commit oneself too readily. 'Claudia is not to come to my supper-dance. You know how awful she is and not a bit trustworthy.'

My old dislike of Sonia boiled up and made me want to swear worse than Claudia. When my mother said that she would try to change me I hadn't really understood how it could be done. Sonia's principle, haphazard and imperfectly carried out, was divide and rule. But slanging my sister alienated me and put a mile of distance between us.

'I don't know that. Claudia's not awful at all,' I said.

As usual she swept on without noticing. 'You must tell your father you are worn out with the festival almost here. I'll arrange for lovely trays to be sent up to your rooms.'

Perhaps I didn't always have Claudia's sharpness but I wasn't too dim to realize that Soapy didn't want me at her beastly dance either. 'But, Sonia,' I said, 'that wouldn't be true at all. We don't get tired so easily, and you wouldn't want me to tell lies to Father, would you?'

She ground her teeth slightly. But she could hardly say that was exactly what she wanted. 'Very well, if you're determined to upset me, but this is for grown-ups and you're far too young. I shall insist that you go to bed no later than eight-thirty.'

If Sonia had been straightforward I should have agreed with her that we were too young. I had taken it for granted that we were excluded. It was a shame that she could never resist having a dig at Claudia, so making it a point of honour to cross her.

The dance didn't start until eight. The curfew would be no problem and easy to evade. Then Claudia got moody and said she didn't want to go to any rotten old party. I thought of how I hated wearing the pink blancmange and decided that perhaps I wasn't all that keen either.

'Absolute nonsense,' Rudi said when he heard. 'I shall need you both to dance with, and the first thing is to find the right thing to wear.'

He must have spoken to Father, for we went together into Dorchester and Rudi insisted on having the final say. 'Claudia, you are to look your age, no more, no less, if I have to break your arm,' he said.

He wasn't at all a man who gave an impression of power and yet he controlled Claudia better than anyone. For some reason she cared about his opinion. He even persuaded her to be economical with swear-words, saying they should be saved for occasions when nothing else would do.

She made straight for a droopy black satin number about as grisly as a dress could get, and suitable for a forty-year-old widow. With admirable patience Rudi said, 'By all means have that, Claudia, if you choose to look a freak. But I shall decline to speak one word to you.'

She glowered at him. 'If you try to put me in baby frills, I'll bite you.'

He won, naturally. Magnanimous in victory he allowed a visit to Woolworth's without a murmur. Claudia bought an orange Tangee lipstick and a tiny tube of Velouty de Dixor powder-cream which smelt delicious.

Rudi talked her out of buying a sixpenny bottle of Californian Poppy scent. 'Put that stuff down, unless you want to smell like a charlady,' he said, 'and for God's sake not Devon Violets either. I'll find a chemist and get you a camomile wash for your hair and some good scented soap, they'll be enough.'

So there we were, Claudia matt of complexion in a sophisticated handful of soft, blue-grey silk with a dropped waist and a huge bow where her bottom started, and me inconspicuous in my favourite cream colour. I knew I couldn't compete with anyone at all until I grew up. Probably not even then.

Well, only when it came to dancing. The Ringwood Ragtime Rascals supplied the music. All the Rascals looked a bit elderly, as if they would be glad to get home and have a nice cup of cocoa and soak their feet, but they managed pretty well.

I felt enormously grateful for Rudi's teaching. 'I'll only make a mess of it,' I protested as he took my hand. But he just smiled, and when we did the foxtrot, with *chassées* and kick-steps the way he had taught me, the other dancers cleared the floor for us and clapped like anything. I glowed with bashful pride.

'You dance better than me,' Claudia said in an injured sort of voice.

'Yes, I do, don't I? Rudi taught me in London.'

It didn't happen often that I could crow over her, so meanly I made the most of my little triumph. In the end she had other things to care about. The night had an oddness to it altogether, a suppressed excitement that made the nerves prickle as if the various emotions gave off sparks of electricity.

We went to pay our respects to Father who said, 'I'm putting you two on your honour to go to bed the minute you feel tired. Tomorrow will be a full day and I want you to enjoy it.'

He didn't mention eight-thirty but by then it was already gone nine. I thought what a dear he was and wished we could get closer to him but I'm certain Sonia would have stopped us somehow. A little pang touched me as I remembered him awkwardly putting me to bed when I was small, and the contentment in his voice and Gwennie's, and their laughter. 'I wish,' I said.

'What do you wish, my dear?'

I wished he was well as he used to be, and I wished he hadn't married Sonia, and I wished Gwennie hadn't left me, all sorts of useless things. I bent and kissed him. 'Nothing really, Father, just that life didn't change all the time.'

Claudia dragged me off to the buffet and came back carrying two half-glasses of champagne. 'Drink up,' she commanded.

'You first.'

'No, you, and don't waste it. He won't give me any more. I had to bully him to get these.'

I sipped cautiously. 'Ugh, that's beastly. I don't like it, it's all sour. You try.'

She tilted the glass and swallowed. Her cheeks drew in and her mouth went all puckered. She sneezed. 'An excellent wine,' she said in her most elderly voice, and finished it.

I poured most of mine away into a vase of flowers. But I rather think it might have been the champagne that made Claudia so ready to become fascinated by an older man. Sonia had not confined her invitations to family and friends or the party would have been quite dull. She included actors and actresses and all the musicians of the symphony orchestra, and it was upon one of the clarinettists that Claudia's sudden interest alighted.

All the players were English except for Emil, who was stateless. In several small European countries he had been a spying kind of journalist, digging up nasty things about powerful people. Not unnaturally they had got fed up and thrown him out. 'I am Communist,' he declared to Claudia, 'these fat aristocrats insult the starving workers who make the wealth.'

'All sullen, black-browed passion,' she told me later, 'and munching through the aristocratic caviare and pâté with truffles as if he were laying it in for a famine. He looks awfully ill-natured and depraved and ancient – thirty at least. His manners are worse than mine. I think I'll elope with him.'

As she was only going on for eleven I doubted whether Emil would want that. But it spiced up the festival for her no end. Also Emil caused trouble later on that gave her an excuse to reject him without losing face.

Rudi smooched around with lots of girls. Sonia lanced a frigid eye at him now and then. Her jilted cousin had come for the festival expressly, it seemed, to cut him dead. Perhaps she even had hopes of getting him back, but the competition was keen and the chilling looks she gave him didn't exactly encourage repentance.

I pursued my favourite pastime of watching and listening. The evening weather was glorious and it stayed that way right through the festival. Perhaps the moonlight accounted for the feeling I got that events were beginning that must not be stopped. Fate brooded over Gunville.

An odd night, as I said, and Great-aunt Hildegarde came. In view of her opinions on festivals, that seemed the oddest circumstance of all. Wearing an electric-blue afternoon-dress she ambled around, talking earnestly with Rachel Moot. She beckoned to me.

'Hallo, Aunt Hildegarde, are you enjoying the party?' I asked, preparing to pass on.

She laid a soft hand on my arm. Rachel Moot was in full spate. 'Someone must be lying,' she said. 'The Ooser can't possibly have been seen at Childe Okeford and near King's Stag at virtually the same time. That would make him supernatural.'

'Not necessarily,' Aunt Hildegarde said. She had a softly exasperated expression on her face. 'I beg you, Rachel, let this drop. Leave it to the police. Great harm can come of tampering and someone may be hurt badly.'

'Is it the Ooser again then?' I asked.

Mrs Moot seemed about to tell me but Aunt Hildegarde stopped her. 'Will you be kind enough to fetch me a glass of lemonade please, Rachel.' She waited until we were quite alone. 'Now, Amy, I'm afraid the folly that affects the souls of our dear county may continue for a while yet. It's hard to stop it so I can only warn. I tell you what I have told my young chapel-girls, do *not* go out alone at night.'

'But why me, Aunt Hildegarde?'

'Mention it to Claudia as well. You are virgins, you see.'

Surely rotten times for virgins were long past? 'I honestly don't understand this,' I said, thinking that at last Aunt Hildegarde had gone clean off her rocker.

'Thank you, Rachel. Shall we circulate?' she said as Mrs Moot pressed a glass of iced lemonade into her hand. 'Don't forget, Amy dear, but don't be worried.'

I hadn't been, but I wondered whether I ought to be. Among the vast pots of shrubs and ferns and flowers the Ooser seemed to lurk, and nymphs and satyrs played. It calmed me to see a familiar satyr pass by in the form of Uncle Henry.

His pink face beamed with benevolent lust. Yelps and little screams punctuated his progress around the ballroom as he snapped garters against silk stockings and nipped away at rounded bottoms.

Aunt Phyllida pursued him. 'Hallo, Amy. What on earth is Hildegarde doing here? She hates functions. I see she's wearing her best underslip – lace-trimmed! Did Henry pass this way? I wanted to dance.'

She didn't stop for an answer. But I followed to see what would happen. I liked Aunt Phyllida. She was firm and sensible but a really good sport. Henry must have been a trial to her yet she seemed to understand him and tolerate his peccadilloes. They loved each other.

Henry kept several yards ahead of her and she didn't manage to nail him, perspiring and happy, until he got to the buffet. A knot of young actresses surrounded him. 'Leave the port alone, you old fool, you'll have a stroke,' Aunt Phyllida said loudly.

'Lovely party, Phylly. How about a glass of champagne?'

'A cup of Ovaltine for you and then bed.'

'But, Phylly!'

Some of the girls seemed quite sad to see him go. A chubby little blonde braved Aunt Phyllida's set face, kissed him on the cheek and said, 'Don't be cross with the dear, naughty old thing, it's just his way of being friendly.'

Aunt Phyllida, my father's sister, showed herself a woman of mettle. Not caring to have her husband explained to her, she stepped smartly on the girl's lightly shod foot, eliciting a gasp of pain. 'Oh, was that your toe?' she asked in an uninterested tone. 'You really should get that bunion seen to. Now say good night to the dear, naughty old thing. If his liver plays tricks he'll keep me up all night.'

'But, Phylly!'

'Yes, Henry, what is it?'

'Oh nothing, my dear, nothing at all.'

Later in the evening I noticed Rudi do his sex-mad look at the blonde girl. It seemed to work. She must have told him about Aunt Phyllida. She pointed to her foot and he rubbed it for her and then her leg right up above the knee. When I looked for them again a few minutes later they had disappeared.

*   *   *

The ghostly feeling of invisibility came over me again. Everyone was taken up with someone else. I found a comfortable place behind some assorted shrubbery and settled down to watch. It seemed to me that Sonia and Pandel Metkin had been created to dance together. Fabulous as a prince and princess from a fairy-tale, they lightened the heavy Victorian ballroom with a dreamy grace and splendour.

Those who preferred not to dance sat out on little buttoned velvet seats. Snatches of conversation pierced the general din. I heard Grandpa Mottesfont say, 'Have to give the soapy one full marks for organization and looks.'

'I've never disputed her physical charms, and no doubt Mr Longmire helped a great deal with the arrangements. He's a remarkable young man in spite of his background,' Grandmother replied. 'No pretence of being other than he is which, I suspect, is more than can be said of Mr Metkin.'

'Hm, does he pretend? Perhaps so. The secretary chap or whatever he's called gives the game away rather, but without the Metkin money this might not have happened. As long as they're discreet it hardly matters. And you seem so content, my dear, to be fulfilling your ambition at last.'

'I confess that I am. And of course that sort of thing is common enough in theatrical circles. I believe the young man, Jimmy, was an actor before Mr Metkin, er – took him up.'

I speculated about what might be wrong with Pan. In Ivy's novelettes mysterious strangers often turned out to be blood-sucking vampires or bigamists or wife-murderers. None of these seemed at all probable and before I reached any conclusion I must have dozed for a while.

When I came to, the grandparents were walking away and Pan and Sonia took their place. 'Dear Countess, are you unhappy still?' Pan asked gently.

'No, of course not. I just got a little upset with that wicked Rachel Moot mocking me because I have no children, and going on about the awful Giant, though she knows I don't like that kind of thing.'

'Ah, I see, the Giant, yes.'

'Don't pretend. You were fascinated by it and Rudi was making remarks in front of the children. It's disgusting.'

I saw Pan's beautiful profile as he turned to her and took her hand. 'To our eyes, yes of course, and because you are a lady and incomparably lovely it offends you. My Countess, my dearest Sonia, once upon a time the Giant was a powerful god, and worshipped without shame because fertility was not shameful but earth's greatest good. Does he not still work magic for women who believe in him?'

'Country girls have no sense and precious few morals. I don't believe it's magic at all. It's nothing but a coarse and vulgar joke.'

'I wonder if it is,' Pan said very softly. 'Sometimes I think that wanting something very much and getting it is the greatest magic of all.'

'And getting what you want can also be a big disappointment.' Sonia stood up. 'I expect you would like a glass of champagne, and I must circulate.'

I felt that Sonia had got what she wanted and then destroyed it out of stupid vanity. She pitied herself but not my father. Pan didn't seem to mind that she was shallow and selfish. A beautiful woman painted on canvas had the power to obsess him, so perhaps with flesh and blood it was much the same thing. I wondered why Sonia thought the Giant disgusting. What I saw of it had seemed all right to me.

The noise of music and laughter and the constant shriek of voices reached such a pitch that it began to wear me out. Heard once, the noise of the upper-class English at play is unmistakable. I stood outside that

107

merriment. My sisters, my cousins, were all budding English roses, fair and blue-eyed and decisive of feature. They wore silk and pearls in Town and tweeds in the country. Until they graduated to Chanel after 'coming out' they smelt discreetly and suitably of Houbigant's Quelques Fleurs.

A feeling of utter desolation swept over me. I was the dull plain one, the changeling child, resembling nobody. I began to inch my way to the door.

Grandpa Mottesfont said, 'Still up, Amy? Aren't you tired?'

My eyes filled up with tears. 'I'm going to bed.'

He looked at me kindly and closely. 'You're upset. What is it?'

'Nothing. I'm stupid.'

'That's nonsense. Out with it, my dear.'

In a sudden rush of self-pity I said, 'Why don't I look like any of the family, Grandpa? I'm small and plain and boring, it isn't fair. Even Father said I must be a changeling as I'm so different.'

'Hm, did he, the foolish man.' He took me by the hand and led me to one of the long mirrors that lined the walls. 'Now there's me and there's you. Ignore the moustache.'

'Why, I look like you, don't I?' I said. 'Oh goody, Grandpa, I look like you.'

'Of course you do. Changeling, poppycock! Now kiss me and go to bed at once.'

I gave him a big, smacking kiss. 'I love you, Grandpa. See you in the morning.'

'Bless you, Amy, good night.'

I slipped out on to the terrace for a moment to breathe the cool sweet evening air. The glass doors to Father's apartment stood open. I heard his voice. He spoke softly but a word or two came through to me. 'Not without you. How I wish you could be here. Yes, you know that.'

Tiredness almost overwhelmed me. Fat moths flew white in the darkness, beating at the windows to get at the lights. Bats swooped low in pursuit. I could hear their high squeaking in those days. Shuddering with revulsion I slipped along in the shadow of the wall and bumped into Claudia coming the other way.

'Did he pass you?' she asked.

'Who?'

'A dark man in a cloak.'

'You're raving,' I said. 'No-one passed me.'

'Are you sure?'

'Yes. Have a look inside and do get out of the way.'

She stood her ground holding me by the arm. 'What an awful fag it is pushing through that mob. I don't think I can be bothered, and I expect he's gone by now.'

'Come up to bed then, and stop pinching me.'

'He'll have forgotten me by tomorrow, I know he will. I must tell you, Amy, it's exciting.'

If I hadn't felt so weary I should have been astonished that anything could excite Claudia. As it was I just wanted her to shut up. 'Remind me in the morning,' I said.

She fell into step beside me. Here and there in the garden bushes rustled and there were whispers and stifled laughter. 'Listen to them, all slopping and kissing, and I'm not going to be grown-up ever.'

'You will be one day.'

'No I won't. Oh hell!'

Next day I overslept but it didn't matter. Breakfast was on trays. Ivy plonked mine on the bed and sat down. I could hear distant music. 'Lovely, in't it. "Rose Marie".' She threw back her head and in a piercing, strangulated soprano yelled, 'Yoo-hoo-hoo-hoo-hoooooh-hoo-hoo-ooh-hoo-hoo. It's the Indian Love-call, that, what Red Indians sing.'

'Perhaps it sounds better when they sing it.'

'What's to do with Miss Claudia, then? Up already and dressed quite nice for her, you might say. Sammy Bowells is asking for you.'

'I hope he isn't going to be awkward.'

'Not him. The old devil's in the kitchen supping ale, with a rose the size of a cabbage in his buttonhole. Eat up that egg, mind.'

'I'd better get up too.'

'No rush. They're mostly in bed still, groaning and sending for arsperin and Beecham's pills. Ulcers on the stomach I'd guess. They'll get worse before they get better, after ten days of it. His Lordship says we can see the plays and things when we're off-duty, in't that nice? I'd like to watch Miss Claudia doing her part.'

That came later. Today was an afternoon orchestral concert outside, *Romeo and Juliet* in the barn at eight o'clock, and in between all kinds of other delights.

'Sorry, Ivy,' I said, 'I'm too excited to eat.'

'Thought you might be. I brought some apples. Here, put one in your pocket.'

As I dressed I realized with some surprise that but for miserable Sonia with her hankerings and her awful modesty none of this would be happening. Rudi, all embarrassed about the cousin's maid, had offered her the best consolation he could think of. And by doing so he had given me a magic land.

Sammy Bowells was pleased with the place I found for Gladys's cakes and flowers, right beside the main gate. He brought her up in style on a scrubbed-out cart pulled by a horse in full carnival regalia, ribbons and arches of flowers and bells and brass. 'Us'll do fine, Miss Amy,' he said. ''Ow about a nice penny nosegay to go on that pretty frock, then?'

Resignedly I produced a threepenny bit. 'I'll have a couple of strawberry tarts as well.'

'Got a nice drop of scrumpy under 'ere – 'ome-brew.'

'Too early for me, Sammy. Look, I think you've got some customers.'

Walking up the drive eating a tart and dripping juice down my chin I ran into Rudi. 'I'm too excited to keep still,' he said. 'Stay with me, Amy, for I can't possibly manage without you.'

Dear Rudi, he was certainly a genie, or master of the revels, or lord of misrule. No-one had asked me to stay before; it was always, 'Run along now, Amy'. My heart overflowed with affection for the ragged boy who arranged things and tried as far as possible to give everyone their heart's desire. He tucked my hand into the crook of his arm. The first Gunville Festival of Arts had begun.

Chapter Eight

The oddness of Aunt Hildegarde, and the virgin-threatening Ooser slipped comfortably out of mind as I plunged into the worldly revels. Angela Brazil offered nothing to compare. I drifted through a dozen of Ivy's novelettes rolled into one. The brilliance of the gathering, the sun and the flowers, the slinky silks and expensive scents, awoke the senses even of a small, shy chrysalis like me.

A light ensemble played the newest American tunes – 'What'll I do', and 'All alone', and songs from *Showboat*. On the terrace Sonia held court. She was surrounded by men chattering in French and Italian, and other tongues I couldn't recognize.

Now and then I encountered dark-skinned gentlemen dressed in dazzling white suits or Jesus-type robes. They asked me peculiar things. 'Tell me, Lady Amity, what is the price of a wife in England, the Lady Osmington for example? And is it customary for the bride to bring with her a substantial dowry? And would it be in goods or gold?'

The blankness of my expression must have convinced them that I was half-witted for after waiting in vain for answers, they bowed and moved on – perhaps to make Father an offer for Sonia.

Art, which related not at all to Real Life, moderated the English scorn for effete Latins and other caddish types. 'The foreigners leaven our lump,' Grandpa said. 'Some of the French women couldn't be uglier, by God, but they carry off their clothes so well it takes a while to notice.'

112

'We think it's bad form to be *chic*,' my grandmother said with a sigh. 'How weary I get of the done thing. The old aren't allowed to be eccentric any more; their families quietly lock 'em up and lose the key.'

A transformation scene. The presiding magician whizzed the stage around and ugly old Gunville Place vanished. There on the other side lay Baghdad and the Caliph's palace. I sniffed the air for cinnamon and nutmeg and allspice and clove and ginger-flowers.

At lunchtime Claudia buttonholed me. 'That's him there,' she said.

'Who're you talking about?'

'Emil, my horrible lover, playing the clarinet.'

I emptied my mouth of sandwich (smoked salmon – delicious), almost choking in the process. 'Your what?'

'If you don't stop asking dim questions I'll flatten you. My lover, the man of vice. He's so dreadful he's wonderful. He wants to string up the boorj woisees on lampposts. What are they, do you suppose?'

I had just bitten back the same enquiry. 'Don't know. He's a bit short. And old.'

'No he isn't, he's just right. I'll have to look it up.'

'Ask Rudi, he'll know. Are you really in love?'

'I told you!' Claudia gave me a heavy thump and said hopefully, 'Perhaps he'll want to ruin me, though he says I'm the produce – no, that's wrong. He's got a funny sort of accent, being stateless. Anyway, what it boils down to is that Father and the rest of us are tyrants, feeding off the labours of the something-or-other.'

'He doesn't have sex-ridden eyes or anything, and he's sort of ugly and mouldy-looking,' I said. 'Not like Pan. Or even Rudi when he does his look. And *they* don't call us stupid names.'

'Why do you say like Pan?' she asked, her attention caught. 'What's he done? He's nice to Sonia and other women but I haven't seen him drool at them the way Rudi does.'

'It's just that he's so beautiful – like a film star or someone.' I didn't want to say archangel, Claudia would have sneered. 'Grandmother thinks there's something odd about him, I don't know what.'

The minute the words were out of my mouth I felt sure that I had made a mistake. Claudia would probe. Being the favourite she might well tell on me and ask Grandmother outright, then I would be branded eavesdropper and miserable sneak. But at that moment the ensemble stopped playing. Emil hurried for the buffet-tent with Claudia panting along on his heels.

Thirty minutes before the afternoon symphony concert was due to begin, a wagonette drawn by an ancient horse rolled up the drive. Handling the reins was Great-Aunt Hildegarde. She always drove herself and she would have no truck with the motor car. (The Devil's Chariot, dear!)

Considering that they were on the Lord's work her party overflowed with unexpected jollity. Several chirruping ladies aged seventeen to seventy descended into the arms of burly, red-faced lads. They were followed by a hand-cart, painted red, blue and yellow. It seemed to be the property of a strange-looking youth with rather too much head, who dusted it with a cloth and relinquished the handles reluctantly.

'It will be quite safe, Avon,' Aunt Hildegarde said, 'no-one shall harm it, I promise.'

''Er's special.'

'Yes, dear, I know, and it's good of you to lend it.'

After some effort, the boys unloaded a harmonium from the cart and smirked virtuously when Aunt Hildegarde said, 'Well done, Christian soldiers. Bring the posters, please. I see a nice spot to the right of the stage near that big marquee. A quick chorus of "I am H-A-P-P-Y" and then we'll eat our sandwiches.'

I hurried to get Rudi. He stood in bemused fascination while the harmonium wheezed and the Christian soldiers bellowed out the second verse – 'I am S-A-V-E-D, I am S-A-V-E-D. I know I am, I'm sure I am, I'm S-A-V-E-D.'

'Oh life, oh time, oh hell,' he groaned. 'Not this, anything but this!'

People strolling about waiting for the concert to begin stopped in mid-stride, uneasy and baffled. Rudi came as near to panic then as ever I saw him. Mozart and Haydn with a counterpoint of redeemed, tone-deaf bullfrogs? Grim enough to kill the festival stone dead on day one.

'Shall I get Father or Sonia or someone to speak to Aunt Hildegarde?'

'Can they persuade her to go away?'

'No, no-one can once she's made up her mind.'

'Then,' Rudi said, 'it must be underhand methods, dirty tricks. I suppose there's no way of putting that atrocious instrument out of action?'

'Well yes there is, but it's really rotten and mean.'

'Rottenness is the very thing, Amy, let meanness be our watchword. Can you do it? I'll make it up to her afterwards, I swear.'

'I'll need a very sharp knife, sharp enough to cut through leather quickly, and you'll have to keep them busy.'

'Go to the guests' buffet-tent, at the carving table. There's no-one in there so help yourself. I'll try diversionary tactics.'

The day was very hot. The pilgrims chewed on thick sandwiches that had already become dry. Rudi advanced, smiling his best curly smile, his face bland and calm. 'How are you, Aunt Hildegarde? Sweltering weather, isn't it? May I offer you and your friends refreshment? Iced ginger-beer is cooling to the vocal cords, I believe.'

'Thank you, dear, how kind.' I felt certain that she

was about to refuse but the young men were already saying, Ooh, yes please. 'Not for me, I think. Just a glass of water.'

'Or apple juice, perhaps? I have some pressed from Mr Bowell's own apples.'

I had played the traitor, and delivered Aunt Hildegarde into Rudi's hands. He never told me what he put into the ginger-beer. Whisky, I suspect, and lots of it. By the time my great-aunt had downed her third glass of Sammy's scrumpy the party had become very lively indeed.

'Let's praise the Lord with a hymn,' Aunt Hildegarde cried and took her place at the harmonium. It emitted through the slit I had cut in the bellows a squeal like a dying pig and then expired. She addressed it moodily. 'What's wrong with you, you silly cow?'

A couple of her young men wandered across. They opened the trap at the back and peered inside. ''Er's bust,' Avon said, ''er's witched.'

My great-aunt opened her mouth to say something that I feared might be snappish. But the concert was beginning. The orchestra struck up 'God Save the King'. The audience rose. We were unused in the country to launching events with the patriotic anthem. Rudi told me it was quite common in towns, sort of getting it over so that people could rush off at the end to catch their buses and trains. It was also providential.

'Dear me, is that the time?' Hildegarde said. 'I'd better get you all home before dark. Roll up the placards neatly and don't forget the harmonium.'

'If you leave it here, we can get it looked at and send it back when it's mended,' I offered.

I was feeling pretty sick with myself, thinking that she wasn't in much shape to drive the cart back to Sturminster Newton. Rudi had the same thought. 'Shall I find a groom to take you home, Aunt Hildegarde? You look a little tired.'

'Flapdoodle! I'm never tired. Thank you, dear, for a

most successful day of witness, and I trust we haven't disturbed you too much. Look after Amy.'

We saw her safely into the driving seat. Her petticoat seemed completely out of control. She hitched it up with a careless hand. Dear Aunt Hildegarde, she had mislaid her hat and her hair fuzzed out like a chimney-brush. Yet she sat steady as a rock. On her face she wore a smile of utter happiness. The Devil and his works were defied, the Lord was served.

'Damn,' Rudi said, 'I adore her, and now I've corrupted her converts and ruined her harmonium.'

'I'm the Judas. Oh, Rudi!'

'What can we do to please her? I know, I'll get that thing repaired – I suppose it'll need a new bellows – and you and I will take it back on a Sunday. Then we can escort her to her chapel, voluntarily and cheerfully. How's that?'

It had the right feeling of repentance about it. Not that I much wanted to endure Hildegarde's interjections. But in her church they might not be so embarrassingly noticeable. I nodded. 'Okey-dokey, Rudi, let's.'

Father gave Portia the chance of getting off school for the festival. She wrote to say that she agreed with her best friend (a duke's daughter, whose brother Portia eventually married) that stage people were impossibly vulgar. They belonged in theatres and not in one's home.

At fourteen she was a frightful snob though she became less of one as she got older. She never stopped being conventional to the point of absolute tedium, and she was hurt quite badly when the edifice of family respectability came crashing down around our ears.

Her brilliant suggestion for Claudia and me was that we should write out our impressions as an exercise and send them to her to be criticized. What a nerve! I wrote for myself and showed no-one. Only Rudi knew about my journals and about my dream of a white house. He understood about dreaming and he wasn't a tattle-tale.

With days and nights running into each other I just had time to pick out the best, most significant bits. Others stuck in my memory. There was the picnic on the Stour when Sonia lay back on cushions dreamily trailing a hand in the water, and watched Pan Mendel stare at her.

A lacy hat shaded her face. Her long legs, encased in white silk stockings, stretched out towards him, and once he stroked her ankle. She didn't move away. She seemed hypnotized by sunlight and shadow and the intentness of his dark eyes.

And stumbling over Marie Dearlove and Rudi kissing like anything under a hedge. Miss Dearlove's skirt was all rumpled. You could see her bottom and her lacy step-ins. Her legs weren't as good as Sonia's.

Then there was Mrs Moot who came to almost every event of the festival. Aunt Hildegarde's advice had no effect at all upon her ruling passion and the vicar got quite cross with her. 'I don't mind you having an enthusiasm, Rachel, but we are Christians, are we not? Do try to preach less of oosers and giants and more of Christ, I beg you.'

On the whole I felt glad that Portia didn't come. She missed seeing Grandmother and Claudia act, though I bet she would have been horrified and spoilt it. Oh, Rudi was clever. He performed the conjuring trick of mixing professionals with amateurs so smoothly and cunningly that the inevitable squabbles were contained.

Of Marie Dearlove my grandmother said, 'A vain, bullying, ill-natured trollop, with a fund of nasty tricks. She'll do well when I finish correcting her manners.'

Frankly, I worried. The trollop, Miss Dearlove, was

not noted for patience under criticism. If she chose to use those nasty tricks against Grandmother *Romeo and Juliet* might become a shambles. I shrank low in my seat, pretending I wasn't really there.

Only a child can experience fully the piercing shame and pity and guilt of watching a stately elder fail publicly, but it didn't happen. The small part of Lady Capulet fitted my grandmother. Her voice shook a little with true emotion at the speech:

'But one, poor one, one poor and loving child,
But one thing to rejoice and solace in,
And cruel death hath catch'd it from my sight!'

Tears came to my eyes. In acting out sorrow for a dead daughter Grandmother seemed to purge her own grief. And of course her old dream had come true. She was on the stage, an actress at last. At each of the two performances she got lots of bouquets, including huge ones from Grandpa.

'Will I be losing you to the boards now, my dear?' he asked after the first night, with a twinkle lurking at the back of his eyes.

She looked a bit bashful. It took years off her and I could see how Grandpa might have found her lovable. 'It's been an experience to enjoy. I'm glad to have proved that I can do it, but Papa was right. I should have been perfectly miserable among actors and actresses. No self-awareness, poor things, and no power of self-criticism either. All that wasted hope is pathetic.'

Her success was a great relief to me. 'You were jolly good, Grandmother,' I ventured.

'There you are,' Grandpa said. 'We all think so but I shall be relieved to have you back with me in the audience.'

The fascination of Sonia with Pan was not at first

obvious because it was so unlike the conventional ideas of falling in love. They never touched except to dance. They just looked. It had more the feeling of obsession, a kind of slow inevitability, as if events were fixed and moved onwards without haste. She had reacted oddly at the Ritz when Rudi first mentioned Pan's name, asking an unfinished question. Pan had no wife. I wondered why that was significant.

With him she was calm. With others her nervous state became exaggerated. As a result she and Rachel Moot had a public argument. It wasn't quite a row, because Rachel kept her temper and tried to be kind.

The young actresses were full of superstitions. When Rachel got on to her pet subject of local history and legend they egged her on. With a group of girls around her she told about the gabbygammies who came out of disturbed barrows, and of the Bronze Age horseman who haunted Bottlebush Down.

Naturally she couldn't miss out the Ooser or Cerne Abbas and the Giant on the hill. Claudia nudged me in the ribs. 'Oosers on the brain!' she said.

'Our prowler in the woods has an ancient motive – though nasty enough – and a fine sense of history,' Rachel said. 'Long before the Romans came the Celts were here, the dwellers by the water. Fertility of fields and flocks meant life. At the seed-time festival and the mating of the beasts, the chieftains were supposed to show the animals what they had to do. So they donned the bull-mask, and woe betide any unwary maiden.'

'Men don't seem to have changed much,' said one of the girls disparagingly.

Rachel Moot smiled at her. 'You might complain even more if they had, don't you think? Wearing the mask, the man became the Horned God, and no doubt the women he chose were flattered. It's no mean fate to be ravished by a god. Or to be made fertile by a giant.'

'Can we go and see this giant?' someone asked.

'You can hardly miss him from the village. The people of Cerne Abbas make sure that the grass doesn't grow over his outline and they give him a scrubbing now and again. It takes some doing. He's nearly two hundred feet tall and shown with erect phallus.'

With what? Could I ask her to explain? I left it too late. If Mrs Moot intended to tell us more it went unsaid. Sonia materialized out of nowhere. 'Stop it, stop it, d'you hear me, stop at once,' she said, the words falling over each other in her distress and rage. 'It's immoral and nasty. There are children present, my children, in my house.'

Claudia stood up. 'We aren't your children, and this isn't your house, it's my father's.'

Sonia burst into tears. Rachel put an arm around her. 'That's the remark of a cruel, silly child, Claudia, and not worthy of you,' she said without emphasis. 'My dear Lady Osmington, you are dreadfully distressed. I had no idea, none at all.'

At first Sonia tried to shake her off but she wouldn't have it. In the end Sonia clung to her and sobbed and sobbed on her shoulder. They were murmuring rather and I couldn't hear much. The actresses, used to backstage tears and tragedies, made twittering noises of sympathy. Claudia's rancour subsided. She sat down – on my hand – muttering that she didn't know what all the fuss was about.

'Shut up a minute, I'm trying to listen,' I said.

'I don't choose to be childless,' Sonia wailed. 'We try but nothing happens. Those rough village girls can behave as crudely as they like. And you make fun of me because I'm embarrassed by that horrible Giant and won't hang rags on oak-trees or drink witch-brews. It isn't how I was brought up – and I'm a Countess.'

'Make fun?' Rachel's voice got gentle and soft. 'No, not that, my dear, not that. I was thoughtless. I'm steeped in ancient nonsense but I truly want women to

121

be free. Don't let convention make you miserable; hold on to the magic of life.'

'I don't believe in magic.'

'Believe or not, it's there. Do what you want, follow your impulses now and then, rule your own fate.'

'You talk as though I were some kind of slave.' Sonia straightened up and mopped her eyes. She even cried beautifully, great clear drops that left no mark behind. 'I have responsibilities and I'm singing in two concerts tomorrow so I'm not going to cry any more or my voice will be ruined.'

'Rank and duty weigh too heavily on you. Morality can be flexible, tolerant, it doesn't have to be dull.'

'I'm quite able to do exactly what I choose, thank you, and it isn't to indulge in coarse country antics.'

Rachel said, 'I don't advocate them, Sonia, but I think you might see a doctor sometime. You're over-tired, highly strung.'

'No I'm not,' Sonia said unexpectedly. 'My health's perfect. But I bore Gervase, and his children hate me. I can't bear to think of the festival ending.'

As I said, sometimes she was clear-sighted, and so frank that I couldn't help admiring her. In a few words she made me understand the imperative nature of her wish to bear a child of her own. Dust and ashes. Locked into a marriage she had accidentally ruined, no art of friendship, no fire to warm her; unlucky Sonia.

Part of her tragedy was that she didn't have a reckless bone in her body. A few moments later I saw her go decorously down the drive at the wheel of her little two-seater. She enjoyed driving on her own. It can't have been speed that pleased her for she never went at more than about twenty miles an hour.

If she ever dreamed, the car might have been her dreaming place. Where did she go on her solitary ex-peditions? Was she not even a little bit tempted to visit the Giant and tell him her wish, or did she cut him dead?

*   *   *

122

That evening marked Claudia's debut. She appeared utterly calm. I was the nervous one. Unable to sit still, I chattered to Father and to uncles, aunts and cousins as they arrived.

Perhaps Father noticed that I felt jittery because he joked about Claudia's romance. 'I do hope she isn't planning to elope,' he said. 'Putting up the family is ruining me and I can't afford a wedding just yet. What a worry you girls are. Perhaps I should immure you both in a convent. What do you think?'

'Oh, Father, you wouldn't!' Belatedly I realized that he wasn't serious and I went rather pink. 'I don't think a convent would have us. Can you imagine Claudia as a nun?'

'Not easily. I'm told that I let you run wild, and that you are ignorant and quite unfit for society. And that you need the discipline of a governess.'

'You've had a letter from Portia.'

'I have, and Sonia supports her. Mr Longmire, on the other hand, speaks highly of your characters and takes a poor view of formal restraints.'

'Father, you do like Rudi, don't you? He's really kind, you know, even if he did ruin Sonia's cousin's maid, and he says he didn't actually. He's awfully good at protecting us, me especially.'

'Here's Sonia. Better not let her know what we're talking about.' Father smiled and patted my hand. 'I like him very much and I'm glad he gives you the security you miss.'

I knew he meant Gwennie, and I sensed in him the restraint that always seemed to prevent us from talking about her properly. I wandered off and prowled around the outdoor stage and the dressing-tents, peering through the gaps in the scenery where the actors entered and exited.

'Go away before you drive me mad,' Claudia commanded. 'And if you're sitting near the stage don't breathe through your mouth.'

'Sorry, I'm so excited.'

'It's only a poxy old play, stupid. What were you talking to Father about?'

'Nothing much. He said he hopes you aren't planning to elope with Emil, and perhaps we should go into a convent. He was joking.'

'I should jolly well hope so. How does he know about Emil, anyway? Has Soapy been spying on me?'

'She's too busy moping about things. Father doesn't miss much, if you ask me.'

'I don't. Get out of here and try to look as if you understand what's going on.'

Easy to say. Dimly I had begun to accept that I would always be a bit of a Philistine, rather preferring what intellectuals regarded as the second-rate. Modern plays, not old ones, weepy film romances, and music with tunes were my meat.

For Claudia's sake I had read *A Midsummer Night's Dream*. Most of it I understood. Sometimes Shakespeare meant to be funny. I didn't think I would be able to laugh much, any more than I laughed at Charlie Chaplin. My sense of humour was wrong and I was not too bright. With *Romeo and Juliet*, while I struggled to understand a sentence the play moved on and lost me.

I sat in the second row. In front of me was Sonia between Father and Pandel Metkin. Before that night I rarely saw Pan and Sonia touch each other unnecessarily, but in the darkness beyond the footlights his hand reached out and lay on hers. She didn't take it but she didn't move away either. I wondered whether Father noticed. He gave no sign. They stayed like that until the music began and the curtain rose, then I forgot to watch them any more.

The stage in our park emerged from the night like the moonlit forest clearing it purported to be. Since the orchestra could see the stage but were unseen to us, Mendelssohn's music flooded out of nowhere.

And there was Claudia. Awake, alive to her finger-ends, she bewitched. The green, shimmery costume that Cyril Fox had designed for her fitted close to her thin, undeveloped body. Under a little hat with a long curled feather even her hair looked green. She wasn't beautiful like Sonia, she was unearthly.

Rudi and the director drew from her brilliantly the sharp mischief, the busy help misplaced, the innocence and wickedness of the non-human presences that lurk beneath the safe surface world. Spellbound, I believed.

The audience gave a long sigh after Claudia stretched out her arms to them at the end and said:

> 'So, good night unto you all.
> Give me your hands, if we be friends,
> And Robin shall restore amends.'

They applauded for a long time, shouting as wildly as a genteel, mainly English audience can manage.

But I got anxious. The thin, placating arms trembled and under the silver-green make-up Claudia was chalk-white. She got through the principals' curtain-calls and her own. When they called the whole company she didn't appear. I followed a trail of dropped bouquets (she got loads of them) and found her crouched under a bush.

Putting my arms around her skinny shivering body I tried to hold her still. 'Bear up, Claudia,' I whispered, 'just one more, that's all. Then you can throw up if you want to.'

'I can't go back.'

She would miss her own triumph – unthinkable!

'What was all that bit about aunts and stools and bums?' I asked, throwing out a lure. 'You must have made it up. There aren't any bums in my book.'

Claudia sat up and gave a shadowy sneer. 'Of course not, yours is for children.'

'What a swiz, I'll kill that Rudi! Go on, they're all on stage and calling for you, and Emil, your leering lover, is there, and all the orchestra clapping. And Pan Metkin sent those roses you're sitting on.'

'Oh yes, my lover. Bugger, I'd forgotten him.'

She went then, to a roar of cheering. I sat on under the bush thinking how much I loved her and hoping that she would be happy. Just why I felt responsible for everybody's happiness was a mystery.

Yet I did. Claudia's and Portia's and Father's, even Sonia's. I wanted to help them. I expect that was why I watched them all. Or not. According to Rudi it was because I possessed the arts of interest and invisibility. 'You won't, thank God, grow to be a conventional beauty like your sisters,' he said. 'Better things await you. You'll be the comforter and have the greatest gift, which is charm.'

Well, he should know. He had lots, and lived by it. But oh, how I longed at times to be beautiful, and not comforting but comforted.

Chapter Nine

Darkness never quite fell on those fine midsummer nights. No-one hurried to go back to their hotels or rented houses or lodgings. Groups of champagne-drinkers gathered on the lawns. Impromptu parties broke out, and satyrs took the opportunity to chase nymphs through the shrubberies. Uncle Henry was completely outclassed.

I thought it all wildly sophisticated. Some of the nymphs were old enough to know better but they made strenuous and gallant efforts to appear young. Perhaps I envied their abandon. After the tension a queer kind of yearning made my heart ache. Among all those confident people I felt like a stranger from another planet.

Instinctively I made for my own quiet place. Ducking under the sweeping cedar-boughs I gave a long relieved sigh. A patch of white moved, the front of a dress-shirt. A man sat there in the darkness. I turned back.

'Don't run away, whoever you are.'

'It's only me, Mr Metkin, Amy. Sorry I disturbed you.'

'Lady Amity. I thought we had quite decided on Pan. Sit down, please, or I shall be uncomfortable.'

Still very shy of him, and feeling tearful, I sat gingerly on the extreme edge of the seat. 'Sorry, Mr Metkin – no, Pan, of course. It isn't usually done, you see. We're meant to be polite to our elders, and not behave badly to guests or bore them.'

'I shall be bored only if you treat me as a stranger. I

am a little bit of a snob, and to have titled friends enchants me.'

'Sorry,' I repeated.

'Why are you sad? Are you not enjoying the entertainments? I find them excellent.'

Sniffing back a stray tear, I said, 'Oh, I am, yes, but I got worried about my grandmother and Claudia in case the plays didn't go well. It's hard to work out whether people you know can do things properly, isn't it? And awkward for me to ask as I haven't any talents myself.'

'That isn't a thing I want to hear you say ever again, that you have no talents.' Pan sounded quite vehement. 'And please, never announce it is only me, Amy. In a year or two we shall know who you are going to become, and it certainly will not be "only me".'

'Won't it?'

'No. It's strange, is it not, that your father appoints no governess, no chaperone, no-one to bring you up? Among the best families in France such matters are handled more strictly, at least until the lady is safely married. Then, of course, she is free to take lovers, become divorced if she wishes, do what pleases her.'

France sounded a fearfully immoral sort of place. I felt awful. An earl's daughter and he was disappointed in me. 'Claudia and I bring each other up,' I said. 'Sonia is supposed to but she's rotten at it really. She doesn't much like us. It might have worked except for the accident, and then she made everyone tell me lies over Gwennie.' My voice wobbled humiliatingly. 'And she gave me beastly rabbits.'

I began to cry. 'Tell me,' Pan commanded, producing a large handkerchief too starchy to be of much use though it smelt deliciously of cologne.

And I found myself pouring out the whole story of my mother's death, and how I felt abandoned by Gwennie and looked for her everywhere, and how Father came to be injured. I even told about my white

128

house and my longing to be anyone but Lady Amity Savernake. 'Portia says middle-class ambitions are degrading, but I can't help it, that's what I want to be. I hate living at Gunville. It's lovely now but it'll go back to being awful just as it was before.'

He let me talk without interruption. My voice came out muffled because he held me firmly against his shoulder. 'Sorry,' I said at length, trying to sit up, 'I didn't mean to be such a baby.'

'Stay there,' he ordered, and seemed to go off into a dream. Then instead of just making comforting noises he asked, 'Who is with you in your white house?'

'Just me, I suppose.' But I became aware of another faint shadow in the sunny imagined rooms, scarcely even a figure and certainly not a 'who'. 'It's only a sort of make-believe, you know, so I haven't thought that far. You won't tell anyone, will you? They'd laugh or be angry with me.'

'Amy, I have an extraordinary feeling, just as I do when I pursue some rare and highly covetable object. Well, we shall know in time. Of course I will say nothing, we are friends. Tomorrow you and Claudia must come to tea with me.'

'Alone? We'd like that very much.'

'One day you must try to forgive Sonia if you can, if only because she is so extraordinarily lovely. But she is not invited and no-one will call except possibly Rudi. I shall show you some of the treasures I prefer not to live without. Come at four. Jimmy will collect you in the car. He is my great treasure for whom I would gladly give up the rest.' He paused as if he waited for a question. I had none so he asked, 'Is that all right for you?'

'Oh yes, Pan, lovely.'

We stood up. I got a little shiver down my spine, standing there so close to him in the darkness. Moonlight filtering through the branches striped his hair with pewter and picked out little gleams from his shirt-studs.

I wondered whether I was falling in love with him. But I decided quickly that I wasn't. Like Rudi he had an air of belonging in the Arabian Nights, the wealthy young merchant who turns out to be the lost prince and marries the princess.

Unburdened of some of its aches my heart felt empty and free. Somewhere there must be a magic that might, just might, make all our dreams come true.

I wanted to tell Claudia at once about going out to tea but after the last curtain-call she had disappeared. Thinking she might really be sick, with nobody to hold her head, I looked in her room. She wasn't there. I found her sitting alone at the back of the stand seats, staring down on the stage with her chin cupped in her hands. I crept along the row and sat down beside her.

After a while she said, 'Was I truly all right? I don't seem to remember much of it.'

'You never looked tired once. It was really creepy. Pan Metkin told Sonia you had an alluring elfin quality that convinced him Puck was a creature of upper air. She wasn't half irritated.'

'I bet.'

'She put on her soapy voice and said that she'd always thought there was something of the bad fairy about you. Father gave her a very straight look so she shut up.'

A cloud crossed Claudia's face. 'He came and found me, and sort of apologized for not spending more time with us. Sonia kept trying to send him to bed. I think she'd hide him away for ever if she could because she can't stand being reminded of her crime.'

'It wasn't exactly a crime, was it? More of an accident. She didn't mean it.'

Unrelenting, Claudia said, 'It's a crime to me when she pretends it wasn't her fault, and acts like a suffering martyr, and goes on to strangers about being a second mother to us. Her! She hates us, me especially. And Valentine too, because if Father dies he'll inherit and push her out.'

Unless Sonia had a child of her own, who would have a perfect right to grow up at Gunville Place. An odious plot, compounded out of Ivy's sensational magazines and Grimm's fairy tales, flashed through my mind: wicked stepmothers and poisoned apples and murdered children. Even as I thought I knew it was nonsense. If we had been properly docile and biddable and not shown how we disliked her, Sonia would have done the conscientious things.

'It's no use going on about it, Claudia,' I said as firmly as I could. 'When you think of us, we're not all that nice, especially to her.'

She got up and capered gleefully along the seats. 'You're a nice, kind rat; I'm a horrible, nasty girl with elfin allure!'

'Sit down, you'll get sick again. Rudi's ever so pleased with you.'

Subsiding, she said, 'I told him I don't want to be an actress. He thinks the talent probably won't last anyway when I become a woman, and I'm glad.'

'Because of feeling upset afterwards?'

'No, you bloody fool. It's terribly hard work and I've decided to make a good marriage and have lots of pleasures.'

'What about Emil?'

'Oh, bugger him. I did think he might want to ruin me, but he's quite barmy and hateful in some ways. He only wants me to join a thing called the People's Revolutionary Theatre and do plays about turnip-planting and blowing up Parliament and killing off the landowners and bosses. Can you imagine more dreari-ness?'

I was indignant. 'The awful nit, what poisonous ideas.'

'And he's dreadfully nosy, especially about what

everyone owns – and other things.' She frowned, puzzled and angry. 'I told him Father's going back to the House next session and he'd better stop scoffing our food if he wants to hang us all from lampposts. He got in a miff and said all property is theft and a lot of other stuff I can't remember.'

No wonder Emil was stateless. I couldn't see why we had to put up with him either and I was glad Claudia had miffed him. Also I felt relieved. It had been a game to her and it was over.

'Pandel Metkin has asked us to tea tomorrow. I said we'd go.'

'Someone as rich as him will do. Is Soapy-bitch coming with us?'

'No, but Pan says we should try to forgive her.'

'I don't trust her.' She put an arm around my shoulders. 'Thanks, Amy, you were the top. I'm dog-tired.'

'Me too. Shall we go up to your room and talk about everybody? I'll get Ivy to bring us some chocolate milk and biscuits.'

'Will you read to me out of that book of hers? The one about where they feel pagan passion, naked and unashamed, and the girl swoons and wakes up to find the imprint of a man's head on her pillow; I'm dying to know what he did to her.'

We still didn't find out. 'It's only a row of dots again,' I said.

'Go on, it might say later.'

By the time I got to the bit where the girl was deep in trouble and cast out into the world to starve, Claudia was asleep.

Pan's car pulled up at the front door. Ivy chased us down the steps. 'Wait, both of you. Ow, my foot!'

She had cut a big hole in her right shoe and she seemed to be in pain. 'What's the matter, Ivy?'

'Me corn's gone septic. I'm under the doctor for it.

Here's your hats. Her ladyship says not to let you outside the gates without – it's common.'

Claudia looked at what had been her school panama with a purple and black striped ribbon round it. She had left it out in the rain and it had gone into a kind of pimple at the top. 'You might have brought a decent one,' she groused.

'You haven't got anything better. I don't know what you do with them.'

I squashed mine down over my ears and fixed the elastic under my chin. 'Hurry up, the car's here,' I said. 'We can take them off once we're out of sight.'

Jimmy let us squeeze in beside him in the front seat and coaxed us into singing the duet from *Floradora*. '"Tell me pretty maiden are there any more at home like you?"' he sang.

'"There are a few, kind sir, all simple girls and proper too."'

We forgot the words and the song petered out into la la la. 'Why did you give up acting, Jimmy?' Claudia asked.

'Because Pan found me and took me in. I wasn't awfully successful.'

'He's such a kind man,' I said. 'I like him tremendously.'

Jimmy glanced down at me and gave a funny little smile. 'Good. I owe him everything and I shall always love him.'

Ignorant of the world, and conditioned to extravagance by Ivy's novelettes, we found nothing excessive in his statement. Claudia said, 'He's handsome, and so are you, Jimmy. I do wish one of you would elope with old Soapy.'

'Shut up, Claudia,' I muttered.

'What for?'

'It isn't proper etiquette to suggest things like that to guests, and she's married to Father. And you ought to call her Sonia.'

133

I sensed a rude word trembling on Claudia's lips but fortunately Jimmy laughed then. 'I suggest that poor Lady Osmington might be equally glad, Claudia, if you eloped with the musician who's taken your fancy.'

'Oh, Emil. Does she hope he's trying to ruin me?'

Jimmy said, 'Take it from me as a world-weary ham and reformed rake, Claudia, it's better not to be ruined too soon. Savour experience, don't bolt it down like a rich pudding.'

'I don't want any more experience just yet; I expect I'll wait until I'm about sixteen. Amy thinks Emil's a beetle. He asks barmy questions about people and what their secrets are.'

'If you ask me, you're the barmy one,' I said.

She screwed an elbow into my ribs, doubling me over with a stitch in my side. 'I didn't ask you, rat.'

'The china and those jewel-ornaments are heavenly, but I like the pictures best – well, some of them,' I said to Pan when he had finished showing us round his house.

'Which are your favourites?'

Claudia was decking herself out with lots of gold things, helped by Jimmy. 'Try the earrings; they're supposed to have belonged to Cleopatra.'

'These,' I said, leading the way back into a small lobby off the hall. 'Especially those pinky-blue trees by the river. It is a river, isn't it?'

'The River Epte, yes.'

'And I love the girl sweeping, and the little country road, and the orchard, and the lady combing her hair.'

'So,' Pan said, 'Monet, Pissarro, Van Gogh and Degas, not yet completely arrived, but when they do, ah, then we shall see the dealers fight each other. Amy, you disclose to me that you have a talent and one of importance, for you recognize genius.'

It pleased me to be told, but I knew myself to be a

fraud. 'I hadn't realized about genius, Pan. I was only thinking about how I'll furnish my house.'

'Modesty is a charming virtue in the very young but you must try as you grow older to be less *douce*, less kind, less undemanding. People take advantage and they will put upon you the value you put upon yourself.'

'Does everybody pretend?'

'Of course. The world would be intolerable if we showed always our naked souls.'

The tea was heavenly. No wholesome bread and butter in sight nor bright-coloured jellies dithering coldly on their plates. Pan's chef gave us tiny pastries filled with cheese, or caviare, or mashed-up ham, or mushrooms, and followed them with a huge chocolate cake. There were almond macaroons and brandy-snaps piped with cream to fill up the corners.

'Gorgeous,' I said, leaning back in the padded chair with a groan. 'Sorry to be such a greedy pig but we only get nursery tea at home unless we're invited to join the adults.'

'My chef would have been hurt if you hadn't eaten well. One day you must come to stay with me in Paris and find out the full extent of his talent.'

That was the kind of polite meaningless thing that people say to new acquaintances. As soon as we were out of sight Pan would have forgotten. I smiled and nodded and thanked him. Then it slipped from my mind. Twelve years later I went to Paris and I did visit him. But by that time I badly needed help that only he could give.

Sonia, so inept at dealing with people, became transformed by music as though, mermaid-like, she stepped off the land that pained her and swam back into her proper element. Once she sat at a piano all her tension vanished. It remained to be seen whether she could sustain a long singing role on stage.

The Marriage of Figaro came in the second week, the last big event of the festival. 'Our friend Rudi will be busy,' Pan said to me. 'I should be honoured if you will sit with us. And your sister too.'

Of course, Sonia would be busy too, and not available, but I felt very flattered. Claudia was even more the Mottesfont favourite. Now that they had a knowledge (slight) of drama to share, Grandmother hunted her down all the time. She and Grandpa joined us.

Compared with Rudi, so exuberant and outgoing, Pan gave an impression of remote cosmopolitan elegance that I adored. Meanness of spirit flourished in some other of the guests. Here, they reasoned, was a trader in rare articles privileged to enjoy the company of gentlefolk. Why not try to acquire some of his goods at a discount?

Pan smiled the frank, sweet smile that had often wooed from reluctant sellers the treasure he desired. 'Thank you for your interest but I cannot transact business at a social gathering. May I suggest a visit to my Paris showroom? There I shall be overjoyed to welcome you.'

I heard one lord of recent elevation say to Uncle Henry, 'The fellow's a capitalized nobody from the stews of Cairo. He ought to be grateful to be noticed.'

For all his little foibles Henry had a sense of fair play and an uncompromising tongue. 'Made your pile during the war, didn't you? Nails or somesuch. I like Metkin. He's neither a social climber nor a bounder. It doesn't do, the pot calling the kettle black.'

I applauded silently. I liked Pan too, an awful lot, for we had interesting conversations and he never talked down to me. Some of the men who hung around Sonia showed impatience in my company. Pan never did. If sometimes he reminded me of a sleek cat watching patiently at a mouse-hole I pushed the image out of my head.

Not all the family was present for not all were musical. The minstrel group (lutes and counter-tenor) had not gone down too well with them. 'Don't tell me that voice is natural,' Uncle Henry said. 'Fellow sounds like a blasted eunuch.'

Aunt Phyllida reined him in. 'It's mediaeval music, and much admired in its day.'

'They must have been mental. Last thing I want to do is hear eunuchs squawking. I need a drink – my throat feels sore as hell just listening to the brute.'

He wandered away, still grumbling under his breath. With the *Arabian Nights* at the front of my mind I was interested to know why he so much despised eunuchs. I had assumed they were a race of people like Cossacks.

'Doesn't Uncle Henry like eunuchs then, Aunt Phyllida?' I asked. 'In my books they look after people, especially ladies, just like our upper servants and everyone respects them.'

Aunt Phyllida laughed. 'Better not call your father's butler one. He wouldn't like aspersions cast on his manhood.'

Another puzzle to be unravelled.

I got Grandmother on my left. She certainly wasn't musical, not the least bit, or literary except for plays. She positively detested Tennyson and Wagner and had been known to walk out of concert-halls and poetry recitals if there were danger of exposure to either. So her knowledge and mine were on a par. She had the extra handicap of loathing Sonia and she probably hoped for a fiasco.

There wasn't one. Having no standard by which to judge I couldn't measure the degree of success. Sonia's newly acquired high notes sounded all right though I preferred the warm, creamy sound of the low ones.

The three professional sopranos were fat – not plump, really fat. Among the bolster fronts (Marcellina and Susanna), and the big bottoms (Marcellina and the

137

Countess), Sonia in knee-britches made a neat and pertly charming boy.

Pandel Metkin thought so too. At the second interval Grandmother got on to the subject of governesses and began fussing about Sonia not bringing us up properly.

Claudia woke from a half-sleep. 'We can bring ourselves up without any old governess,' she said indignantly.

I faded, not wanting to be embroiled in a typical family argument. These consisted of all the protagonists talking at once, and loudly, without listening to a word the others said.

Under cover of the noise Pan said softly, 'My God, Jimmy darling, doesn't she stir your blood? Those melting curves of flesh and muscle round out the britches and tempt the hand.'

'Even a dedicated "so" like me isn't immune from straight desire, as you know. After all, I was married for eight years. My blood, yes, that's stirred.' He smiled at Pan. 'But somehow she has no power to stir the emotions. Can she possibly be as cold as Rudi maintains?'

'Unpossessed as yet, except in the most basic sense; chaste and at the peak of tender ripeness. If only such moments in human lives were collectible!'

Jimmy said, 'Memory is the greatest collection of all. It can't be sold or stolen and it attracts no death-duties. Does it occur to you that we may be given a destiny here?'

Pan laughed. 'It occurs to me that we might do our best to find out. They are so likeable, this family, so without false pride except for the poor Sonia, that I wish for the power to make them happy, to give each one the perfect gift.'

'What you are really saying is that their lives are untidy and you itch to tidy them up as you did mine.'

'True, I detest a muddle, but you, my dear, are quite different.'

My light burned dim while Claudia fought our battle with Grandmother. Pan and Jimmy could not know the sharpness of my ears and my incurable habit of listening, so they were unguarded with me. It ought to have been mortifying. Somehow Claudia never got overlooked. She would have burst in with the questions I hesitated to ask, like what did Jimmy mean when he called himself a so? and did Pan love Sonia? and did he want to clasp her in his arms with a frenzy of mad, passionate joy like Paul did the lady?

Jimmy was to play Paul in *Three Weeks*, an interesting prospect if his blood got tremendously stirred when Sonia set about purring like a tiger and covering him with kisses.

He was definitely a man one might like to kiss and he looked like Paul. But then Pan mesmerized. Every gesture he made had elegance of a wholly masculine, muscular kind. His beauty and his fabled wealth excited women. You could tell it from the little smile they gave at the sight of him. If I were Sonia which would I choose?

'Thrilling but difficult,' I said aloud.

'Do stop chattering, Amy, the music's starting,' Grandmother said.

'I've only spoken three rotten words in hours,' I muttered, stung by the unfairness of it. 'I could die sitting here and no-one would even notice.'

'Be quiet or go out.'

Pan took my hand and gave it a squeeze. I saw Claudia's nose edging around Grandmother's massive bosom and I pulled a face at her. She looked quite jealous.

'Opera uses up an enormous amount of energy,' Rudi said. 'The singers get ravenous.'

He had arranged for a substantial hot meal to be served after *The Marriage of Figaro* and strolled around making sure that everyone had plenty. An astonishing amount of drink stood on the tables. Marcellina spurned the wine and drank stout. ('You should try it, Sonia duckie. Nothing like it for giving power to the lungs, except perhaps Irish porter.')

Rudi took a glass and dropped in a cube of sugar. He added something out of a dull, black bottle, poured on champagne and stirred.

'What's that you're mixing, Rudi?'

'A little cocktail for Sonia. She looks quite weary and low-spirited, and I do wish she would make an effort to talk to the other singers.'

Without a doubt she regarded them as common to an impossible degree. I noticed how she recoiled and froze with resentment when fat, vulgar Marcellina called her, the Countess of Osmington, duckie, and recommended stout.

'Will she drink it?' I asked.

'It's mostly champagne and she quite likes that.'

Sonia enjoyed the drink and had several more. The effect startled me. Her spirits roared up to the roof and pretty soon she had a large laughing group around her and men flirting like anything. Intrigued, I drained a few drops left in a glass.

'Gosh, Rudi, it's strong.'

'Adults only. Delicious when you grow up a little more.'

'What did you say it's called?'

'Champagne cocktail. Infallible for all ailments of the heart and mind. Remember when the time comes that two is sufficient unless you intend an indiscretion.'

'Sonia's had about four already.'

'So she has, but don't they make her a lot more interesting?'

Others, hearing the laughter, filtered into the room. The singers still wore full make-up and their stage costumes. Sonia's eyes glowed green and huge. She took off her wig and shook her hair free. The slight

140

dishevelment enhanced her beauty, making her less of a perfect shell and more of a woman who might be loved and touched. Her permanent air of faint desperation vanished. I began to feel nervous.

But she saw Father and went to him. And she was gentler and sweeter to him than I had ever seen her. She bent and kissed him then sat down beside him, holding his hand as if she could never bear to let it go.

'Just look at her. Wouldn't you think she'd prefer to avoid the limelight after what she did? She half-killed that poor man.'

The speaker was a raddled fast-looking woman who sometimes called on Sonia. She was munching a mouthful of stuffed olives and spilling bits as she talked. Her front was bony and freckled.

'I know for a fact that she took a horsewhip to the youngest girl. One of the undergrooms told somebody who told my chauffeur. It was while Gervase wrestled to get the whip away from her that the horse panicked and the accident happened.'

'That's not true,' I said.

Flinty eyes stared down at me without recognition. 'Go away.'

'Who is that girl?' her companion asked.

'I've no idea. Anyway, as I was saying, she inflicts awful cruelties on those step-children.'

I realized that Claudia stood behind me, probably thinking me a traitor and a rat. I didn't care. I tapped bony-front on the arm and said loudly, 'She does no such thing. It's a lie and you've no right to say so.'

'How do you know? Who do you think you are?'

'I'm Amity Savernake, the youngest child. I was there, and you're a liar. Lady Osmington has never hit me in her life, or any of us.'

There was an awful silence while I waited for Claudia to blurt out that Sonia had once slapped her face. I did my sister less than justice. '"These are the forgeries of jealousy,"' she said. 'Both our parents are

141

present. Why not ask them instead of listening to servants' gossip. Would you care for some more olives?'

No answer. 'More gin, perhaps? No? Then do excuse us. Come, Amy.'

'Beastly women,' I said.

Claudia looked desperately hangdog because she had actually referred to Sonia as a parent. 'Is it going to be like this when we grow up, Amy? Having to mix with our own class however stupid and boring, and not mind when they talk behind our backs? What a grisly prospect.'

'We might get just like them. That's even worse.'

'Oh no we won't. You're much too stupid and nice,' Claudia said kindly. 'And I intend to live abroad as much as possible when I'm married. Everyone will be busy doing sex and won't care about Society one bit. Where are you going?'

'To talk to Sonia and Father and show that skinny woman that we can stick together. You come too.'

She scowled. 'Oh, all right. It won't work.'

I did the talking. 'Sonia, we've come to say good night. The opera was jolly good. Did you enjoy singing?'

The way she was astonished us. A dreamy expression softened her face and gave a sweetness to the curves of her mouth. She smiled at us or past us, I couldn't tell which. The brilliance illuminated her beauty to an almost hurtful degree. 'Oh yes, yes I did. The teacher Rudi sent me stretched my range by an octave though I prefer my natural voice.'

But she seemed *distrait* as though her mind was on something quite other than singing. Claudia looked at her open-mouthed and said nothing.

I bent and kissed my father and on impulse planted a kiss on Sonia's cheek. 'Good night then. We're going to bed now.'

She looked at us, then at him, and smiled. 'Perhaps

142

we should do the same, Gervase, unless you wish to stay longer.'

'An excellent idea. Good night, Claudia, good night, Amity.'

'Cor,' Claudia panted as we raced up the stairs, 'what's got into Soapy?'

'Champagne cocktails,' I said.

Chapter Ten

Without a singing voice Sonia might have lived out
her life on a cold peak of propriety and never
discovered the warmth of the valleys. Her new tran-
quillity made her vulnerable. A melting, accessible
quality increased her loveliness. Half the men then
present at Gunville Place would have given a great
deal to change places with my father. I could see by
the way their eyes followed her. The older, the sillier!

Uncle Henry said to Grandpa, 'Is Sonia changing,
or is it me? I rather pitied Gervase with nothing
warmer to cuddle under the blankets. Now I seem
to imagine doing the most extraordinary things to
her and it's sending my blood pressure through the
roof.'

'Small harm in imagining, Henry. Better not let
Phyllida find out though, or she'll dose you with
something lethal – brimstone and treacle probably.'
Grandpa nodded at me. 'Are you listening in to our
conversation, Amy? I hope you aren't a tale-bearer.'

'I never am! How will I learn anything if I don't
listen?' I said indignantly.

'Doesn't she have a nurse to go to?' Uncle Henry
asked vaguely, just as if I were too young to speak for
myself. 'Not like her sisters at all, is she? They'll be
beauties in a year or two.'

'I'll have you know, Henry, that Amy favours me.
She has some very good points.'

'Can't say you're much to look at, or the rest of the
Mottesfonts, so it's no recommendation for the girl.
Quite nice eyes, though.'

144

'Very kind of you to say so, Uncle Henry.' I spoke with some bitterness. 'Has Aunt Phyllida thought of trying castor-oil for your blood pressure? My maid swears by it, especially for the elderly.'

A look of absolute horror crossed his face. 'Gad, what a vile idea,' he said, fishing in his pocket. 'Here's half-a-crown. Not a word to your aunt, I beg you.'

I took it with an innocent smile which seemed to alarm him. He added another. Five shillings for absolutely nothing. Blackmail paid well.

I don't agree that time flies when you are enjoying yourself. In fact, I don't agree with most sayings of that kind. Honesty isn't necessarily the best policy, and cheats do prosper, and virtue isn't its own reward, it's pretty unrewarding in every way.

Time neither flew nor dragged, it simply disappeared altogether. The twenty-second of June, the last day of the festival, took me by surprise. A few people went off in the morning but most stayed for the final concert of English music.

'I'm rather sorry the paying guests won't see *Three Weeks*, and Jimmy kissing Sonia,' I said to Rudi. 'They're having such fun, and falling in love like anything. We all are – having fun, I mean. Even Sonia isn't miserable any more, and just look at Gunville! Flowers and waving palm-trees and fascinating Arabs dressed like Rudolph Valentino. They smell of Christmas, have you noticed? As if they bathe in rare spices. It's Sinbad and Aladdin and Scheherazade in the *Thousand and One Nights* all wrapped up into one.'

He laughed at me. 'That's the longest speech I ever heard from you, Amy.'

'It's only with you and Claudia and Pan and Jimmy I can talk.'

'But you listen? Being unnoticeable can have great advantages up to a point.'

'Yes,' I said grudgingly, 'though now and then it

would be nice to be as beautiful as Sonia and flocked around.'

'Awful, though, to become frozen into virtue. Do I imagine it, or is she thawing just a little?'

'Rudi Longmire, I think you knew what those champagne cocktails would do. You *are* wicked!'

'But isn't she happier – and lovelier? After all, your father wanted her to have an interest and being courted by every man over sixteen is surely that?'

Was it the kind of interest Father meant? He didn't seem the least bit disapproving, but after his accident he had sort of faded out of our view so that I understood him less than ever.

'I suppose she is,' I said doubtfully. 'Pan and Jimmy said they were tempted when she was dressed as Cherubino. Jimmy said he's a dedicated "so". I wonder what he meant? And some of the women who pretend to be her friends were saying awful things about her.'

Instead of explaining about Jimmy as I'd hoped, Rudi taught me a bit of what he called philosophy. 'A lovely woman is bound to attract jealousy and spite. Never try to silence the gossips, Amy dear, for it simply makes matters worse. Ignore them as I have had to do more than once. "They say? What say they? Let them say."'

He had surmounted the scandal over his engagement to Sonia's cousin, and possibly other indiscretions as well. I overheard some waspish remarks the cousin made about him and the trollop, Marie Dearlove, and not being able to resist carrying on with women of loose morals, but I never repeated them. Rudi was a man who would always have some kind of woman trouble yet always be liked.

'By tomorrow it will be over. Why oh why can't magic things last for ever?'

'Then they wouldn't be magic, just everyday. And it won't quite be over. Don't forget our party when we

146

can all throw off responsibility and be as frivolous as we like. Come and choose a costume for the evening.'

'Who are you going to be?'

'I wanted to be Charlie Chaplin, but Pan and Jimmy insist that we shall be the Three Musketeers. Those two love dressing up. Sonia's to be the Queen of France so that Pan can deck her out in some of his gorgeous jewels.'

'Real ones? Gosh. Can I be a boy for a change?'

'Don't you want to be glamorous? An eastern princess in filmy harem-trousers, or a Spanish Infanta?'

'I haven't got enough shape yet, and I'm plain.'

We rummaged in the huge wicker costume-baskets and I came up with a dear little embroidered red and gold waistcoat. 'Look, this is eastern, isn't it?'

'Persian page to Cleopatra, the nineteen-twenty tour. There are gold trousers and a shirt and turban somewhere.'

The costume charmed me. The turban had a huge glass jewel in front and a plume, and the toes of the matching slippers curled up. 'Perfect, Rudi, that's just perfect. What about Claudia?'

'The Witch of Endor?'

'Seriously.'

'I hope she'll agree to wear her Puck outfit. Cyril designed it for her and it suits her, don't you think?'

'Yes, and it makes her different, more comfortable to be with.'

'Acting gives licence to display emotions rather than push them out of sight. Many people in the profession are only truly themselves when they are on stage pretending to be someone else.'

'I think that's awfully sad.'

He turned to see my face. 'Claudia's growing up, and she'll be all right, I promise you. In a few years' time when she comes to make decisions about her life you won't recognize her for the same girl.'

'Won't I?'

'Take that anxious look off your face at once. I promise she'll be all right.'

It was almost time for the final concert to begin. In the twilight hands grasped my arms from behind. 'Aha, you are my prisoner, Amy.'

I jumped and tried to pull free. The voice was heavily accented and full of a false joviality that gave me shivers. It could only be Claudia's beastly Emil. 'Let go of me, please.'

'We have liddle talks about these peoples and you tell me secrets, yes?' He swung me round to face him, tightening his grip painfully. 'I am journalist and mekkin propagandas is good thing for me.'

'I don't want to talk to you. Leave me alone.'

'But no. You are spawns of decadent capitalists without morals. The Countess mekks many fockinks, I think, and Clowdia perhaps also mekks fockinks with boys.'

Having no idea what he was talking about didn't spare me a feeling of helpless disgust. I opened my mouth to scream, but a sudden force detached Emil from me. Rudi shook him as a terrier shakes a rat. He said in a harsh voice that betrayed his London origins, 'Come near Lady Amity again and I'll tear the head off your body, you filthy little wretch.'

Emil sneered. 'Not so filthy as you, I thinks, who mekks f—'

Rudi hit him hard in the mouth and he fell over. 'Some words we don't use in front of ladies and children,' he said, stirring the prostrate form with his foot, 'and that's one of them. Make sure you leave here immediately after the concert. It will save the embarrassment of having you thrown out.'

He put a warm arm around my shoulders. I was shivering a little. 'Come along, Amy, he won't hurt you. I shall have something to say to Claudia when I can find her.'

148

'Don't blame her, Rudi, please. She's not nearly as smart as she imagines but she does know what a beetle he is. They had an awful quarrel.'

'I wish she'd told me. He sounds a pretty vicious type.'

I hugged him. 'You were wonderful. I didn't know you could fight.'

'All London street-kids can, but it's been a long time. Will you be all right?'

'Yes, fine.' I grinned at him. 'He looked just like a fat cockroach, lying on his back with his little legs kicking in the air. Is fockinks an awfully rude word?'

'In good English it is – and an ugly one. You'll hear it again but I hope you'll never, never use it until you are forty and grown-up, unless you're so angry that nothing else will do. Now we shall talk of other things – shoes and ships and sealing-wax, and cabbages and kings.'

'And why the sea is boiling hot, and whether pigs have wings. Rudi, you are positively the dearest person.'

'No, you are. Let's start an argument of our very own and never resolve it.'

'Let's.'

'Are you quite sure you're only eight? If you were fourteen I might wait and marry you.'

I giggled. 'Am I your goddess and Queen, like in *Three Weeks*?'

'Oh, absolutely.'

'Don't bother to wait for me, Rudi. I can't marry such a liar. Try the trollop, Marie Dearlove. I expect you suit each other.'

'Amy!'

He was genuinely shocked. It occurred to me that trollop was probably also a bad word. Grandmother's tongue could blister varnish when she got in a mood.

'Do you like her a lot? Sorry, Rudi dear, it's what Grandmother called her,' I said.

'She should be ashamed, and so should you.'

'I am, Rudi, I am.'

Not wishing to see Emil again, even from a distance, I sat on the terrace while the concert was on. Light spilled out over the palm-trees. In the warm night the scent of roses and myrtle wafted over me, and as the rich, measured beauty of Elgar's cello concerto sounded across the park the nightingales began to sing.

However ugly my home, the county of my birth enraptured me with its tranquil grace. The music was its voice, the voice of an English summer. I looked up at the moon, waning but still bright, and understood why Claudia wanted so badly to grow up and fall in love.

We were housed and fed and clothed yet we had no place. If we vanished we would not be missed for long. To come first with someone, to be necessary to someone's happiness, that must be real magic.

Some of the string players asked if they could stay on for the cast party, though most members of the orchestra packed up immediately. They were to be taken by car to Southampton to catch a night train for the north.

Emil left. We discovered afterwards that he had gone round the house from room to room helping himself to what money he cou'd find. A practical step towards redistribution of the national wealth, but not at all appreciated by the losers. My house fund (six pounds eleven and fourpence) was fortunately well hidden and intact.

'For once, Amy my dear rat, you were right,' Claudia said. 'He's a cockroach. I feel vindictive and I shall stop his nasty little games.'

She did too, by means of a cousin whose friend's father was a diplomat. We heard some time later that Emil had been deported. The country from which he came declined to have him back. For all I knew he sailed on around the world for ever, looking for peasants and turnip-fields, and aristocrats to overthrow.

The cast set to on the last of the wine. I noticed Rudi keeping Sonia well supplied with champagne cocktails though I think she scarcely needed them. Her looks possessed an extra stunning quality that put all the other women in the shade, even the trollop, Marie Dearlove, who could by no means be described as a hag.

Rudi had barred everyone except the players from the rehearsals of *Three Weeks*, and he scarcely mentioned the play. When I asked questions he said, 'Wait and see.'

'Is it like the book?'

'Better, I hope, or I'm in the wrong business.'

The audience, all in their fancy dress except for my father, showed a willingness to be entertained but no particular excitement. Claudia and I sat near the front, and as the curtain rose on a hotel dining-room in Switzerland, Rudi slipped into the seat beside me.

'You've got an awfully wicked look in your eyes,' I said.

'Shsh. My nerves are twitching. Here we go.'

Paul sat at a table, frowning and glancing at a newspaper. A woman dressed in black entered, a servant poured red wine into a glass, and suddenly the atmosphere on stage became tense.

I would never have believed Sonia could be as she was, never in the world. Rudi told me afterwards that Jimmy had tutored her, going over each scene time and again until he got the response he wanted.

Needless to say, she looked magnificent. Her exquisite costumes stayed close to Elinor Glyn's descriptions and the jewels – her own and Pan's – and the furs were real. What stunned was the emotion. Passion overflowed from her as if her body could not contain it. She undulated and enticed and clung.

In 'a garment of pale green gauze', clinging 'in misty folds around her exquisite shape', she wore pearls and a diadem of emeralds and diamonds, just as in the book. Her bust peeped through the thin cloth and then hid in a fascinating way. Paul and the lady were in Venice, and it was the Feast of the Full Moon.

'"My darling one,"' Sonia said, lying in Jimmy's arms, '"this is our souls' wedding. In life and in death they can never part more."'

And then Jimmy started kissing her. His kisses were long and deep and terrifically thrilling and Sonia kissed him back as hard as she could go. I went all hot, and Claudia gave me a great nudge. We had no doubt that this was exactly how SEX should be done.

Behind me a man gasped like someone dying of thirst, and said 'Chirst Almighty' under his breath. I stole a look at Father. He had an admiring expression on his face but his mouth curled and twitched as if he wanted rather to burst out laughing.

I whispered to Rudi, 'Jimmy kisses her as if he could easily eat her up.'

'Who couldn't?'

'But she seems to like it.'

'It's acting. Hush.'

Then morning came and Sonia got up and kissed Jimmy a lot more and gazed at him in anguish. She wasn't as good at the anguish as at the passion. It made her look a touch constipated. I thought she seemed quite inclined to jump back into bed if only Jimmy had woken up. Then she wrote a note, told God to keep him safe, and left.

After this scene a lot had been cut and the action departed somewhat from the book. It was an improvement. Paul arrived in time to take the dying lady into his arms and have a really touching parting, while faithful Vasili killed the brutal, murdering husband. Everyone on stage cried and some of the audience. Final curtain.

'Whew,' Claudia said, 'did you see Jimmy stroking her bosoms when he was lying on top of her? I feel all tingly, don't you?'

'And he rubbed her legs too, high up near the top, and she kissed his chest.'

'We'd better remember those bits for when we have lovers.'

'My face is all red. Let's get some lemonade and listen to what people are saying.'

A crowd of men collected around Sonia. Jimmy had an arm about her waist. Pan lifted her hand and kissed it for a long time. The musketeer outfits weren't a bit what I expected – no fancy coats or plumed hats. Pan wore tight-fitting black trousers and a frilled shirt open to the waist.

He didn't have hair on his chest. At that time I was dreadfully squeamish about hairy men, realizing dimly that there were sex overtones that intimidated me. His skin had a honey colour – mouth-watering. And he looked totally beautiful, like a picture of the death of Chatterton only vibrantly and excitingly alive.

Men, even Rudi, changed in the worst kind of way when their minds dwelt on sex. They brushed aside good manners and could hardly be bothered to talk to people other than the object of their desire. Their eyes went all glazed and blind-looking too.

Rudi forgot to get our lemonade. He pushed through the little crush and handed Sonia a champagne cocktail. I never saw any woman so elated. She still wore the white dress in which, as a queen, she had died. Against it her flesh looked warm and soft as cream. She couldn't keep still but swung around, smiling into eyes glazed with lust, and not attempting to remove her hand from Pan's.

Claudia lost patience. 'Oh God, this is getting boring,' she muttered. 'There's dancing in the barn, let's go.'

'In a minute. I'm watching.'

She drifted off alone. By exerting gentle pressure Rudi gradually drove the admirers away, back to their wives or girlfriends. 'Sonia dearest, I've rarely been so moved,' he said. 'Not a man in the audience, and I include myself, but would cheerfully have killed Jimmy for a chance of taking his place.'

I waited in vain for her to tell him that he was common and not a nice man. Her full red mouth curved in an odd smile. 'As the lady says, "I feel myself ennobled, exalted." I should like more champagne please.'

'First some food, if I may borrow her from you, Pan my dear, just for half an hour.'

The Bowells family ran the buffet. Most people had eaten before the play so it was quiet and the conversation had reverted to local matters. Rudi sat Sonia at a table.

'Fill a plate for Lady Osmington, please, dear,' he said to Gladys Bowells.

'She took a lovely part, Mr Longmire. Surprised us all, it did. Mrs Moot were just saying.'

Bearing dishes they all advanced on Sonia like a string of eastern slaves, twittering praises. Rudi gave her another champagne cocktail. Rachel Moot said, 'An experience to remember, Sonia. No doubt my husband would think the morality dubious, but if we are to understand that the husband is made impotent by disease the urgent need for a child can be accepted. The queen had to die, of course, to reassure the prudes.'

I thought Sonia might get miserable again at the mention of a child, but she blinked at Rachel and half-smiled. Her eyes were distant and empty of feeling. They shone like the emerald diadem she still wore around her reddy-black curls. 'You once told me, Rachel, that morality can be flexible and doesn't have to be dull.'

154

'Be happy then,' Mrs Moot said quietly.

Conversation roared around us. The Bowells family had prospered greatly during the festival and they now relaxed. Sonia picked dreamily at her food and sipped her cocktail.

'That Ooser's getting beyond 'isself,' Gladys Bowells complained. 'A'showing off up along by the strawberry-fields 'e were day before yesterday, in broad daylight. Us'll need to be doing something drastic afore long.'

'Carstration,' said her married daughter, 'that's what 'im wants.'

Rudi backed away with a distressed air. Rachel smiled. 'It may well cure itself quite quickly.' She glanced through the open window at the groups wandering in the moonlight. 'Midsummer's Eve, the magic heart of the year and the night of the Giant. Also a lesser Sabbat. Bonfires will be lit on the grave-mounds tonight.'

I saw Sonia lift her head and stare. Colour drained out of her face, leaving her skin white and pure. There was something frightening about the way she looked, the kind of elevated, holy madness that is said to afflict some of the saints.

Behind the broad backs she got up and slid silently from the room. Pan and Jimmy stood talking to Aunt Phyllida. I plucked at Rudi's coat-tails. Sammy Bowells had him pinned down and was booming at him. They didn't notice me. Everything felt strange and threatening, and a growing anxiety for Sonia made my heart thump in my ears. She ought not to be alone.

I hurried after her, hoping to find my father, but he had gone and Sonia was nowhere to be seen. Dodging through the groups of people chattering and laughing in the rose-scented dark, I reached the great beech-trees where the nightingales sang. The birds were silent, waiting for us to go away and leave them in peace.

My turban had fallen over my eyes. I discarded it and strained my ears. From the stable yard came the sound of a car starting up, and I heard it rattle away down the drive. I raced round through the archway under the little clock-tower. The yard was crowded with motors, from Father's new Rolls-Royce Silver Ghost down to a baby Austin with a ragged cloth top. I checked and checked again. Sonia's car was missing.

It would have been wise to tell Father or Rudi, I suppose, but my hatred of telling tales stopped me. Wheeling out my bicycle I exchanged the Persian slippers for a pair of old plimsolls I kept in the basket and set off in pursuit. At the gates I hesitated. Distantly an engine died for a moment, then complained as it took a hill. I guessed that Sonia had paused at the Piddle-trenthide crossroads and climbed up into the downs beyond.

At the crossroads I saw the signpost for Cerne Abbas and I shivered. The shadows under the trees were pitchy-black though the moon freckled the road with blue light. A bonfire blazed on the top of Bulbarrow. The witches were out and the forces of the past pressed upon me. I wished that I had Claudia for company.

Ahead loomed Giant's Hill. But Sonia despised pagan traditions and her little drives never lasted for long. I expected at every moment to see her returning. Behind me I heard the noise of a powerful engine and headlights lit up the trees. I pulled to the side of the road. Pan's motor swept past and disappeared around the next bend.

Half-blinded I pedalled on and found Sonia's car by almost running into the back of it. She had parked it badly. The nose and the front wheels dug into the verge. It was empty.

For a moment I felt totally at a loss. Where was she? The white outline of the Giant loomed huge and distinct. Staring upwards, I saw him fully for the first time. He *was* naked. What in my foolishness I had taken for a belt proved to be the very essence of his nakedness.

'He's nearly two hundred feet tall and shown with erect phallus,' Rachel Moot had said. The behaviour of rabbits and the disgraced boy showing off his crumpled little winkle in Sunday School came into my mind. Was this what men were like and what made them look at Sonia the way they did? A hazy understanding percolated through my ignorance.

Sonia. On the path up the hill a white-clad figure moved quickly in spite of the steepness of the ascent. Was it her? I didn't dare to call but I was certain. Her desire for a child had become too desperate to be borne. Through champagne and the play and Rachel Moot's legends, the dwellers under the land called out to her. Sonia had gone to lie down on that fearsome nakedness and sleep in the lap of the Giant.

Chapter Eleven

Well-bred, virtuous Sonia, Countess of Osmington, high as a kite on champagne and acting, had gone clean out of her mind. So what was it to do with me? Anyone with a grain of sense would leave her to her madness. My bicycle lay on the verge. I picked it up and wheeled it back to a spinney on the far side of the village, leaning it against a tree.

The moonlight seemed unnaturally brilliant. Every church clock for miles around chimed midnight, more or less together. I decided not to intrude but to wait just a little while. It was then that I heard sounds. Someone struck a match and the smell of cigarette smoke drifted on the air. A voice, Jimmy's, said, 'Go if you want to, my dear. I'll wait for you here.'

My slave-trousers and embroidered waistcoat hardly blended with the landscape. Keeping low on my stomach I wriggled through the dewy grass and peered. The big motor car was parked only yards away. The lights were out. Two burning cigarette-ends moved like slow fireflies.

'She responded to you. Come with me.'

'I suspect that each of us closed our eyes and imagined it was you. You're the prince of gifts. I'm not much dedicated to giving others their heart's desire.'

'Can I manage, do you think? I suppose it depends on whether Titania or Bottom is in the ascendant,' Pan said, and they both laughed.

'You've wanted this from the beginning, and so has she, though she may not know it. Go after her quickly. I'm not immune to envy.'

Those two muddled up my ideas dreadfully. I couldn't sort out in my head what they intended but I realized that they wouldn't let Sonia be harmed. She didn't need me. Pan got out of the car and turned on to the path up the hill. Jimmy threw away his cigarette, sighing heavily, and leaned his head against the leather seat.

Walking back along the road I thought I heard movements in the trees on the far side of the road, keeping pace with me. A poacher? A fox prowling? It was Midsummer's Eve, and other people beside Sonia might want help from the Giant.

I stopped to listen. All was still. Feeling uneasy, I found my bike and bumped it down the low bank. One of the costume slippers bounced out of the basket. Awkwardly I bent to pick it up. Something white blurred across my vision and was gone. I straightened and peered across the road, nerves tautening with an instinct both to hurry and to do so silently.

I saw the head first, hanging in the air and glaring with dead malevolence. My heart gave a thud and began to race at suffocating speed. The bushes swept apart. A creature stood there, not ten feet away, watching me.

Polished curving horns crowned the hideous beast's head. A broad animal snout flared red at the nostrils. Teeth snarled out of the long slack jaws and shaggy hair hung over the forehead and from under the chin. The unhuman power of the thing weakened me with horror and disgust.

The head swung forward. Some kind of rough animal skin cloaked the upper part of the chest. It got caught on a twig and a muffled voice said, 'Fuck un then. Come off up.' I moved. ''Old still, you, or I'll brain you.'

The command was for me, and the voice human. So was the rest of the body – human and naked, aggressively, loathsomely naked like the Giant on the hill made flesh.

159

For the first time in my life I knew true fear, so huge that it destroyed all other senses. I tried to cry out but I was dumb. Run, my mind said, but my paralysed body refused to respond. The beast that was a man had me trapped.

Above all things I wanted not to look at that threatening excrescence, growing stubbily out of a mat of hair, and the sack-like lumps below it. Yet I couldn't look away. The Ooser stepped on to the road. He wore a pair of filthy broken boots without socks. A stench of uncured hides and dung and, curiously, burnt lavender wafted across to me.

He swung a heavy billet of wood. The bull's muzzle nodded in amiable travesty with the gesture, and the awful object bobbed in rhythm. The lower jaw of the mask dropped and disclosed an open scarlet mouth. 'I be King and bigger nor the Giant,' it – he – declared.

A local accent, a Dorset man, and somehow my terror altered. I heard uncertainty and a touch of madness. On such a night and in such a guise a virgin might be raped and pillaged or a disappointed maniac might kill.

My teeth chattered and I shook uncontrollably. 'Keep away from me,' I hissed, and hurled the slipper at him.

He can't have seen it through the slits in the bulging painted eyes. Certainly it was too light to hurt him, but it struck him on the chest and he stopped for a moment.

Whimpering, I threw my shaking body on to the saddle. Panic almost defeated me. The bicycle wobbled and I half fell. Behind me came the Ooser, slip-slapping in his broken boots, calling in a mad, hoarse voice, calling what? The threat of that gross nakedness lent strength to my legs. I picked up speed and left him behind.

Past Piddletrenthide my breath began to labour

painfully and I badly needed a lavatory. Oosers hid behind every hedge. But my clothes were borrowed and I dared not wet them. I found a bush. Rage and disgust and shame overwhelmed me and I crouched there and sobbed.

After a while I pedalled wearily home. The party still went on. Keeping my head down I ran past groups of revellers and didn't stop until I reached my room. It spelt safety, yet I thought that I would never, never feel properly safe or clean again.

I locked the door. The Ooser haunted darkness and I put on all the lights, fearing to lie down in case he came for me. Still dressed I got under the covers and sat there, bolt upright and shivering, hugging my Bonzo dog, waiting for morning.

People came and knocked, and getting no answer went away. After a while Rudi called out, 'Amy, are you in there?'

The handle of the door turned. 'Locked,' said Aunt Phyllida. 'Perhaps she's asleep.'

'She seemed very distressed. I'm worried.'

Eventually I heard Claudia's voice, sleepy and rather cross. 'She never locks her door usually, and the lights are on. You'd better all go away.' Some shuffling movement. She said, 'Let me in, Amy. If you don't they'll send for Father.'

That would truly be the last straw. How could I speak of the unspeakable to anyone? And him I could never tell because of Sonia. 'Who's with you?' I whispered.

'What? I can't hear you.'

'Are you alone?'

She spoke to someone else. 'Please, Mrs Moot, go downstairs.' All of Gunne Magna seemed to be making a night of it in the upper hallway. 'There, that's everybody. Now can I come in?'

I slid off the bed and opened the door wide enough for her to squeeze through, then locked it again. She stared at me and said in a tender, exasperated tone, 'Oh God, you look awful. Now tell.'

I began to cry, bawling as I had done on the day I last talked to my mother. Claudia locked her skinny arms around me. She must have extracted some sense from my babble about the Giant and the Ooser and erect phalluses for she showed deep interest.

When my howling subsided to a mere snivel she said, 'Did it really jiggle about? How unnerving. Naturally you stared. Where else could one possibly look? Never mind, it's over, but what were you doing out there?'

'If I say, you must swear your holiest oath not to tell anyone else.'

She put a finger in her mouth and crossed her heart. 'See that wet, see that dry, cross my heart and hope to die in screeching agony and go straight to hell. Will that do? It's my biggest swear.'

It didn't seem necessary to mention Pan and Jimmy so I left them out. But I told her about all the champagne cocktails and Rachel Moot talking about Midsummer's Eve and how odd Sonia seemed. Then her going to the Giant after all. 'I know you hate her, Claudia, and I expect you despise me for bothering, but she's pathetic in a way.'

'Idiot rat! We'll have to say something,' Claudia said. 'Rudi's out of his mind with worry. Shall I make a sort of statement for you and tell about the Ooser but not the rest? You're feeling better now, aren't you?'

'Yes, but don't leave me and don't let anyone else in yet.'

She went out into the passage and called. 'Listen please. Amy went for a ride on her bicycle and got frightened by the Ooser. She wasn't hurt but she can't talk about it now.'

'Why did she go out on her own so late?'

Claudia learned early in life when to answer a

162

question with a question. 'Why shouldn't she if she wants to?' She put her head round the door and said, 'Can Rudi come in?'

I nodded. He looked at me with gentle concern, then picked me up and held me against his chest. 'Bath – hair too,' he said. 'Come on, Claudia, lead the way and start running the water. You can soap, I'll dry.'

Probably half the family was scandalized, but they didn't understand Rudi's protective streak like I did. As he wrapped me in a towel and rubbed vigorously he said, 'I used to do this for my little sister.'

'I didn't know you had a sister.'

'She died of diptheria when she was seven.'

'That's terribly sad.'

'Yes. Are you warm enough for your nightie now?'

The uncontrollable shivering had gone. The slave costume lay on the floor. Streaks of green marred the gold trousers and one of the shirt-sleeves had a great rip in it. 'I've ruined your costume, Rudi, and I've lost one of the slippers. I threw it at the Ooser. I'm sorry. Do I have to go to bed alone? I don't feel safe undressed just yet.'

Without another word he sent Claudia off to bring clean day-clothes for me. She came back in a state of high excitement. 'Sammy Bowells is getting up a party to track the Ooser. He wants you, Rudi, and he wants to know exactly where Amy saw it so that he can take his hounds along.'

'I'm not staying here on my own,' I said, knowing that Claudia wouldn't miss such a treat for worlds.

'Shall I ask your grandmother to sit with you – or Sonia?' Rudi asked. 'I think they're both in bed but I can wake one of them.'

He hadn't even noticed Sonia's absence. 'They'll ask questions. I can't tell them, Rudi, I can't. I want to be where you go.'

'We'll find out exactly what's happening. You won't

mind talking to Gladys Bowells, will you? She's seen the creature and it made her furious.'

Feeling clingy, I made him carry me. 'Can we go to the stables first, please, to make sure my bike's all right?'

My true purpose was to find out before half of Gunne Magna gathered near Giant's Hill whether Sonia had come home. Her car stood in its place. All was well.

The sun would soon be up and the sky was already light. 'There then,' Gladys said, 'us can get off upalong at once. A nasty old article and we'm going to nab 'im. You just show us where.'

'I can't look again, I can't,' I said. 'He might follow me. He said he'd brain me.'

She recognized shock and panic. 'Him'll be gone but the dogs'll find un. We'll not lose hold of you one minute. Can you find the place, d'you reckon?'

Rudi said, 'It's close to Cerne Abbas. She threw a slipper at him and it may still be there.' He put Bonzo into my arms. 'There, hang on to him, Amy. Do you feel up to helping us at all? We really can't let this go on and once he's caught you'll be safe, won't you?'

'I suppose so. You swear not to leave me for a second?'

'I swear.'

'All right then.'

'Brave girl.'

Soon after six in the morning we set off. Sammy Bowells and Rachel Moot were in great spirits so it felt more like a picnic than an ooser-hunt. We went in a farm-cart with Sammy's dogs sitting up in front. He loved those dogs. 'Best trackers in Dorset,' he said several times.

'Carstration's the thing,' his daughter maintained grimly, loading on several stone jars of scrumpy. 'I 'ope you brought a sharp knife.'

Rachel Moot, who had been going on again about the Giant and fertility, grinned. 'A basic cure, but we do it to other animals so why not our own kind?'

Sammy said sternly, 'Hush up now, women. Not in front of Miss Amy, if you please. 'Er's 'ad a nasty fright.'

Gladys brought an enormous basket of food. She opened it the minute we began to move. 'Try a strawberry tart, my dear, all on the 'ouse,' she said to me. 'You'll be empty with no breakfast. You too, Miss Claudia.'

I was – empty and ravenous. 'Thanks, Mrs Bowells.' There was no point in asking what carstration involved since delicacy clearly forbade the mention to creatures of gentle nurture like Claudia and me. 'You make lovely pastry. Won't you feel dull now the festival's over?'

'Nothing after till 'arvest. I 'ope us gets a good apple crop or us'll be going dry. Sammy's near sold out on beer and scrumpy. This little lot's the last.'

I gave Rudi a bite of my strawberry tart. 'Leave me some, don't eat it all,' I said, watching it anxiously. 'Mrs Moot does go on so and she's only got one weedy son. I don't call that fertile, do you?'

'You know, Amy, I begin to understand why Sonia gets the teeniest bit irritated with her.'

'I hate the country,' Claudia said. 'It's a mad kind of place. As soon as I'm out I shall live in cities.'

The shoe lay where I had left it. 'There, he was there,' I said, pointing at the bushes. 'The skin over his shoulders got caught up in the branches and made him cross.'

Mrs Moot jumped down, followed by Sammy and Claudia. 'Look at this. A clump of hair, ox-hair I think, red with some white in.'

'The skins smelt awful,' I said, 'not properly cured, and he had dung or mud on his boots.'

'A farmer, maybe?'

'I'm not sure. There was another smell as if he'd been burning lavender on a bonfire.'

'Did you say 'e spoke? What sort of voice then, posh was un? What did 'e say?' asked Gladys.

I remembered reluctantly. 'Local definitely. He said, "Fuck un, come off up then."'

Mrs Bowells went pink in the face and the back of Sammy's neck seemed to swell. Claudia didn't hear me. She stood on the bank, craning her neck to see the Giant. A revision course on phalluses?

Mrs Moot swung round and looked a bit shocked. 'Hush, Amy, there's no need to shout.'

I felt really indignant. 'I'm not shouting. You asked me what he said and that's it.' Rudi tried not to laugh. 'Is that word dirty, like mekkin fockinks?' I asked him in a whisper.

'Very like. Take no notice of them. They've all heard it before.'

'I'm not saying any more so they needn't ask me. But he seemed puzzled, the Ooser.'

Rudi ruffled my cropped hair. It curls a little but not in soft fruity bunches like Sonia's or crisp and nutty like Pan's. 'The last thing he can have expected to see was a child in baggy gold trousers. Girl or boy? A baffling mystery for an Ooser.'

I hadn't thought of that. Gladys gave me another tart, perhaps to keep my indiscreet mouth shut, and uncorked a jar of cider. Sammy Bowells and the dogs both sniffed about and found a clod from the Ooser's boot. The dogs got tremendously excited. They dashed in and out of the trees, returned to the road and set off at a steady trot towards Minterne Magna.

Claudia wore a thrilled look. 'Will the dogs mangle him into bloody shreds, Sammy?'

'Now then, Miss, there's no call for bloodshed. We do only want to find un, not kill un.'

She subsided, wearing a 'you speak for yourself' expression, and dropped into a doze against his massive shoulder. He refreshed himself with a long swallow from the stone jar.

If we had tried to use cars instead of a horse we would have come to grief. The trail led over fields and along the narrowest of lanes. At Fifehead Neville the hounds showed intense interest in a shack-like house set in the middle of ploughed land.

'Is this un?' Sammy asked the air. 'A poorly sort of place.'

It looked haunted. My heart began to thunder and I gripped Rudi's hand. 'All right, Amy; look, the dogs are moving on.'

The trail must have been fresh. We rumbled into Sturminster Newton and stopped when the hounds dashed through the gate of a small manor house. Neatly trimmed lavender bushes edged the drive. A bonfire burned fiercely at the bottom of the garden, tended by an old lady wearing a holland overall and a straw garden hat. Behind her stood a shed. The hounds made straight for it. The door was closed.

'Call off the dogs, please, Mr Bowells,' Great-aunt Hildegarde said. 'I realize that he must be punished but you are not to hurt him, do you understand? The police in Dorchester have been called. They'll be here quite soon.'

'We want 'im bad. Miss Amy here were frightened 'alf to death. 'Er won't never do, speaking up in court.'

'Certainly not. He'll plead guilty to the other charges. I'm so sorry, Amy. I did try to warn you.'

Rudi said quietly, 'You've known all along who it was, haven't you?'

'Of course, dear, Avon Werlock usually, though sometimes the older brother in makeshift costume. You met Avon once at our little demonstration. He came to my Sunday School class a time or two and then joined the young men's Christian Endeavour.

167

When my gardener retired I hired him to do odd jobs, to keep him under my eye.' A worried frown creased the soft skin of her forehead. 'One can't watch all the time. The poor boy tried so hard but it's in the family, you see. The Werlocks are all a little wanting, and that wretched mask has been an object of worship for goodness knows how many generations.'

The self-congratulatory look on Rachel Moot's face hardened into anger. 'You knew about that too? How dared you hide such a treasure from me, Hildegarde? It belongs to the county, our heritage.'

'On the contrary, it belongs to that wicked old man, Werlock. He tutored his sons in evil and he it is who should be locked up.'

Mrs Moot dodged round Great-aunt Hildegarde and wrenched open the shed door. A youth crouched in the farthest corner with his eyes closed and his hands clasped protectively over his head. He neither moved nor looked up as the light fell on him. 'Come out here,' she said.

I recognized the cracked and filthy boots. From them my mind created instantly a complete picture of the horror of the night. 'No,' I said on a loud hysterical note.

Aunt Hildegarde pulled Mrs Moot away none too gently, shut the door and padlocked it. 'Come into the house, please.'

'He doesn't have the mask. Where is it? I must see it, Hildegarde, before the police impound it,' Mrs Moot said.

'Oh, it's out there, dear, what's left of it.'

Aunt Hildegarde pointed vaguely through the window at the bonfire. Rachel seemed puzzled for a second. Then she caught on. Purple in the face with rage she gripped Aunt Hildegarde by the shoulders and shook her until her head wagged like a rag doll. 'You can't have burnt it, you can't! You wicked, wicked old woman.'

'Steady on,' Rudi said, and pushing between the two he gradually prised Mrs Moot away.

My great-aunt smoothed her dress. With great dignity she said, 'Poor Rachel, can you really not see that you are the wicked one, wilfully infected? Your husband is the servant of God. You so forget and betray him that you are halfway to worshipping the Devil in the guise of that pagan atrocity.'

Mrs Moot burst into tears. She cried loudly like a child, wah-ah-ah. 'Years I've tracked it down and now it's gone. All that research wasted.'

'Don't cry so, dear. If only you'd thought a bit you could have found out long ago. I haven't half your brains but the names are unmistakable. Werlock surely is obvious, and then Avon, and his brother is Aedo — from the Celtic words for water and fire, two important elements in the old religions. They are a very ancient priesthood.'

'I only know the mother, and her name's Ruby,' Rachel sobbed.

'Not at all witchlike I agree. Women priests were drawn exclusively from the royal families and were few. Poor Ruby is a nothing, a vessel to breed sons. Only the men count.'

'How do you know all this? You've never been a scholar.'

'But I'm a Christian,' Aunt Hildegarde said stoutly, 'and it's necessary to understand evil in order to defeat it. Now do stop blubbing, Rachel dear, and be sensible. I believe the police have arrived.'

Mrs Moot looked out of the window. 'They've brought a Black Maria. You've destroyed evidence, Hildegarde, and it wouldn't surprise me if they arrest you as well.'

She smiled benignly. 'They might, of course, but the sergeant from Dorchester was in my Bible class and I stood sponsor for him when he entered the police force.'

                          *   *   *

'Can you believe old Hildegarde?' Claudia asked me. 'Aren't you going to watch them take the Ooser away?'

That huddled, dirty youth with dirty habits? He had taught me to be afraid and I didn't want to see him or think about him ever again. 'You go if you want to.'

Rudi was mopping up Mrs Moot who began to apologize profusely as my great-aunt came back into the room. 'Forgive me if you can, Hildegarde, though my behaviour was inexcusable. I can't think what got into me. Have I done great harm, have these incidents been caused by me?'

'Of course not, Rachel. Let us stop dramatizing ourselves and be sensible. Both the boys are sub-normal to say the least. Werlock told them all the old tales about fertility rites and how the Ooser had a duty to the land. He also has a still on that disgrace he calls a farm. Sometimes the boys get at the liquor – pure rot-gut. The result we know.'

'How can I face my husband? He asked me to stop and I ignored him.'

Hildegarde patted her hand. 'Don't tell him, dear. Men are usually far happier in their ignorance. I do feel that the role of vicar's wife is rather dull and narrow for you. Have you ever thought of taking pupils? You give your own little boy lessons, don't you?'

'Well, yes, but that doesn't make me a teacher.'

A determined expression crossed my great-aunt's face. She glanced at me and then at Claudia outside in the garden, raking the bonfire for traces of the ooser mask. 'Amy and her sister are growing up with no discernible education. Neither would be comfortable at a conventional school but they might enjoy learning from you. I'll speak to my nephew.'

I stood in the crook of Rudi's arm with a thumb in my mouth, something I hadn't done for years. Reaction from the ooser-hunt had set in and I trembled violently. Aunt Hildegarde raised her eyebrows at him.

'Amy saw, but she doesn't understand,' he said helplessly. 'Sonia's told her nothing and she's still innocent, you see.'

'Ah, and ignorant too. I would like you all to go now please. Amy will stay here for a while and we shall have a talk.'

So in the end it was Great-aunt Hildegarde of all people who told me about sex. And she did it simply and clearly and without embarrassment so that I didn't feel a bit uncomfortable. She answered my questions and told me the proper words. ('Unfortunately all rather ugly, dear, and the colloquialisms hardly less so.')

Also she explained why the Ooser looked the way he did. 'Erection occurs in men, poor creatures, at the thought of sex, and some have precious little control,' she said. 'We women are luckier, more secret.'

'Is that the only way to get a baby, then? It can't happen by sleeping on the Giant?'

'Only if a man goes with you,' she said dryly. 'Why do you ask?'

I thought of Sonia and Pan and Jimmy. 'I just wondered. Have you ever been in love, Aunt Hildegarde?'

'Well, dear, I haven't always been seventy-five years old, or a good Christian for that matter. Will you have lunch with me? Then I'll show you some ways of defending yourself against unwelcome advances before I take you home.'

Jogging along on the box beside Aunt Hildegarde I passed the spot where the Ooser had caught me without a second glance. Imagine her knowing about knee-jerks and gouging at the eyes with thumbs, and bending fingers backwards. ('The Girls' Reformatory, dear, where I taught plain sewing. They gave me such useful advice.')

The festival was over. It had been wonderful, but I wasn't altogether sorry. Feeling light as air and carefree with my new knowledge, I said, 'Thank you, Aunt Hildegarde, thank you very much.'

Chapter Twelve

'The mouldy police wouldn't let me go in the Black
Maria with the Ooser,' Claudia complained. 'I asked if
he'd get the birch or be thrown in a dungeon and they
said "Go and play, Miss," as if I was about four or
something.'

'Precocious, bloodthirsty girl,' Rudi said. 'Do keep
still.'

We were sitting at a table under the palm-trees. She
kept scraping her chair on the paving-stones in a way
that set the teeth on edge.

'You stop yawning then. I was up most of the night
and I'm exhausted. Did Aunt Hildegarde go on about
Jesus, Amy? You were absolutely ages.'

I evaded her gimlet eyes. 'Not exactly. She just
explained some things. She's with Father arranging for
us to have lessons with Mrs Moot. Will you mind?'

'Not much. If it isn't her we're bound to get landed
with a governess soon. One can see Portia's point. It
doesn't do to be ignorant if one's to mix with people.'

Rudi looked amazed. 'Good Lord!'

'It's all right,' I said, 'she's not ill. Grandmother's
been nagging her about going to school again.'

Already men were removing the boxes of flowers
that had given Gunville Place a temporary beauty. The
big banner was half down. Cyril Fox clung to a rope
like an acrobat and shouted, 'Lower it, for Christ's
sake, lower it! Don't drop it,' terrified that his work of
art would get damaged.

Sonia wandered along the terrace. In a floaty
handful of flowered silk organza she looked the acme

173

of romance. I watched her eagerly. Heroines who have Lived bear faint but indelible marks; shadowed eyes, perhaps, hollowed temples, a single strand of white in the hair. Ivy's novelettes were definite on the point.

Sonia disappointed. No emotion disturbed her coolly exquisite face. In the sunlight her hair had the dark smoulder of a dying fire, but every curl was in place. She oozed primness.

Claudia wore an expression of demon interest. 'Hallo, Sonia, did you sleep well?' she asked. I kicked her shin and she gave a strangled yelp. 'Ow, a mosquito. After the play, I mean. You must have felt jolly tired with all that acting. Do you think Jimmy's amazingly handsome? I do, though usually I like dark men best.'

'He and Mr Metkin are coming to lunch tomorrow so you can tell him,' Sonia said, blankly uninterested. 'Should you be sitting in the sun without a hat?'

Not a word to me. Oughtn't I who had nearly been raped and pillaged by the Ooser be the heroine? She never so much as mentioned it. Bitterly I concluded that I could sit in the sun stark naked and frizzle to death without Sonia raising an eyebrow. She passed on.

'What did you kick me for?' Claudia asked.

'You swore not to tell.'

'I didn't tell.'

'Questions like that are the same as telling.'

'No they're not. She never notices, she's *boring*,' Claudia moaned. 'How can she have slept in the lap of the Giant and be so *boring*?'

'Well she did – at least she went there. The grass was damp. Perhaps she didn't actually sleep.'

'Ivy says damp grass gives you piles and chronic rheumatics. I must ask Soapy about those next time.'

'Has Sonia got piles?' Aunt Phyllida asked, advancing unexpectedly. 'Nasty, painful things. They bleed, you know. Henry and I are off in a moment, dropping a

174

gaggle of cousins at the station first. Come and say goodbye.'

As I stood up Claudia fell suddenly asleep, her head nodding towards the iron table. Rudi fielded her neatly and propped her against his shoulder. 'She only slept for six hours,' he explained. 'My regards to Henry.'

'Rudi, will you tell me something, please? It may be secret or I may be wrong.'

'Ask and we shall see.'

'I'm not innocent any more, I promise. Aunt Hildegarde told me all about sex.'

'What you mean is that you're no longer ignorant. Innocence is something different.'

'Is it? Well, I can't bother now. She explained about forbidden things, avoiding unnatural acts if possible as they put you in prison unless you're a lady. It's cruel and very bad manners to pry into people's private lives, she says. Rudi, I wouldn't do it, I swear, but I have a reason.'

'Offhand I can't recall committing a single unnatural act. All too natural I'm afraid.'

'It's not you, silly. I know what you did to Sonia's cousin's maid, and I expect you do it to the tr— to Miss Dearlove too. That's quite all right.'

'Thank you, dear,' he said.

'I'm a tiny bit worried about Pan and Jimmy, I can't tell you why. Do they love each other with a forbidden love? Is that what being "so" means?'

He went silent for quite a long time as if he were mulling things over in his mind. 'Suppose I say yes, will you stop liking them?'

'Of course I won't. I love them both like anything, almost as much as I love you.'

'Pan is mainly Jewish but he has a strong dash of Cretan Greek in his blood. To the Greeks the greatest love was, and possibly still is for all I know to the contrary, that of man for man. The devotion between

175

him and Jimmy is unshakeable. It's like a marriage.' I began to feel greatly relieved until he added, 'That doesn't mean that neither is capable of enjoying a relationship with a woman, but as your great-aunt so wisely said, one doesn't pry.'

'Oh.'

Did he guess what troubled me? I expect so. Rudi seldom missed much. He said, 'Stop worrying about us all, Amy. If you frown and the wind turns east you'll stay like that and spoil your face.'

'You don't say "beautiful face" like you do to Sonia, I notice.'

'Beauty becomes tedious. I shall never get tired of looking at you.'

'What a smooth old fibber you are. I shall kill you if you say I have rather nice eyes.'

'Ridiculous! They're small and piggy, not nice at all.'

'Like yours? Exactly how old are you, Rudi?'

'I'm twenty-five. Why?'

'I thought I might marry you in ten years' time but you're far too ancient.'

'Touché,' he said, with what was supposed to be anguish. 'That's a thoroughly bitchy remark.'

'Is this a quarrel or part of our argument that never ends?'

'Argument of course. It's a great bond.'

'Thank you for taking care of me last night.'

'When I'm old and wrinkled, with piles and chronic rheumatics, you can take care of me.'

'Okey-dokey, Rudi.'

At lunch on the following day I could detect no sign of the fever that had infected Sonia and Pan and Jimmy. We were informal and amiable and relaxed. Father and Pan held an inquest on the festival, exchanging views on high points and weaknesses and discussing the merits of modern plays. Rudi and Jimmy gossiped about the theatre.

Sonia listened politely and said the proper things like, 'Do have some more salmon,' and, 'How dull we shall be without guests,' and, 'I hope the weather will stay calm for your flight home.'

As he and Jimmy rose from the table, Pan said, 'Dear Countess, we leave this afternoon. I cannot express adequately my gratitude for your hospitality. The organization, the artists and artistes, all have combined to make a memorable occasion.'

His dark, longlashed eyes smiled gently into Sonia's. He bent over her hand but did not kiss it. With that curly head and handsome face so close surely now she would react, show emotion, sadness at the imminent parting?

A polite smile lifted the corners of her mouth. 'Very kind of you to say so, Pandel. We can't pretend to compete with the culture of Europe but I'm glad that you haven't been too disappointed.'

There might have been irony in the last remark but I doubt it. She wasn't really attending. When the aeroplane was turned to face into the wind and Pan and Jimmy flew away, she let them go without troubling to come down and wave them off. The mounting tide of passion existed only in my over-heated imagination. After all it had been just acting and champagne.

The next morning at breakfast the butler brought parcels for Sonia and Claudia and me – presents from Pan. In mine I found the Pissarro painting of a girl sweeping a floor. There was a note. It read, 'Hang this in the drawing-room and invite me to tea.'

He sent Claudia the Cleopatra earrings, and to Sonia a little silver monkey reaching up to steal golden fruit from a tree. 'What an ugly thing,' she said and left it standing on the table.

Soon afterwards Father went away. He wanted to build up his strength in time for the next Parliamentary session. Rudi stayed until Gunville Place returned to its grey, tidy self.

The palm-trees in their terracotta pots also stayed. They wouldn't all fit into the conservatory and I knew that the first icy winds of winter would kill them. The stage revolved once more. All the scented glamour of Baghdad and Africa disappeared, leaving us where we began. And we had used up all our wishes.

Were we much changed? Had we been given our hearts' desires? I didn't think so then. When Rudi went away it felt as though a dreary frost settled on me. He hugged me. 'So long, Amy dear. Trust me to write and telephone whenever I can.'

I knew I could trust him. But letters are never the same as just talking. 'I feel miserable. You're dearer to me than almost anyone.'

'Only almost? I bet I'm fonder of you.'

'No you're not, you like the tr— sorry – Marie Dearlove much better. Are we still arguing?'

'Naturally, so no goodbyes if you please, not until I manage to have the last word. And do shut up about Marie Dearlove.'

'I'm sorry Grandmother called her a trollop.'

'Mrs Mottesfont's a thoroughly bad example to you. I'm to visit her in London. I'll take it up with her then.'

'You wouldn't dare, she'll eat you alive. Write soon.'

Lessons with Mrs Moot began almost at once. She had overcome her obsession with pagan worship but she did teach us history and taught it well. We gained a smattering of French, some arithmetic and geography, and enough of English literature eventually to wean us off sixpenny novelettes.

Towards the end of September my letter to Rudi contained an aftermath in the following vein:

The Ooser's been sent to the lunatic asylum. The Assize Judge said something about persistent delusions and thinking he was God. Great-aunt Hildegarde is upset and knitting away like mad. She visits the Ooser sometimes and takes him warm gloves and tracts.

Then the Judge called Mr Werlock a thoroughly wicked man and sent him to prison for five years for a lot of things, mostly for having a still. The other son only got a year – I forget what for.

Mrs Moot says that Ruby Werlock has taken on a new lease of life and goes down to Bournemouth on the train to dances. Gladys Bowells laughed (sarky, not amused). 'Ha, ha,' she said, 'a funny kind of dancing if you asks I. 'Er does it lying down and charges ten bob for un.'

Do explain what she meant, dearest Rudi. Sammy got all pious and told Gladys to shut her trap in front of the little un (me).

Rudi didn't explain. He simply wrote, 'How could I ever have thought the country dull!'

But without him and all the glamorous people it was dull. In late October, a few days after her eleventh birthday, Claudia fidgeted around in front of my bedroom mirror hopefully examining herself for signs of breasts. 'I'm going to stick like this for ever,' she said fretfully, 'I'm never going to get a bust.'

'What's the hurry? You're not in love or anything, are you?'

'Who's there to fall in love with in this hole? I wish we lived in London.'

'You're Grandmother's pet. Ask if you can go and stay.'

'Oh, shut up. That bloody house is full of loony old women drinking tea with their hats on. I think I'll have an Eton crop. It might make me look more sophisticated.'

'It'll make you look a freak.'

She opened my manicure case, took out the little

polishing pad and began to buff her already highly polished nails. Regarding them critically she slipped the pad into her pocket. I held out my hand without speaking.

'Oh, bugger.' She dropped her trophy into my palm. 'I can't think why Grandmother gave you such a pretty set when you've got paws like a monkey. You ought to let me have it.'

'Well, I won't. It's almost the only thing I have of our mother's. You and Portia bagged the rest. Go away please, Claudia, I've simply lots and lots to do.'

'Crazy rat, you only ever come up here to read or scribble. You're retarded in sex.'

Knowing that I knew more of the subject than she did I said a smug nothing. Ivy bumped open the door with her bottom and came in backwards carrying a pile of linen. 'I'll want this room, it's clean beds,' she said. 'Heard the news, have you? She's expecting at last.'

'Who's expecting what?' Claudia asked.

'Yer stepma, of course – in the fam'ly way. She's having a little brother or sister for yer. Lovely, in't it?'

Claudia looked like a small thundercloud. 'It's foul,' she said, 'we're all right as we are. Parents are rotten and useless and don't care what happens to us. A bloody baby'll only make it worse.'

All my excitement over the Giant bubbled up. I began to imagine the old nursery occupied again. And Gwennie? No, Sonia would never bring her back. I said, 'It might be quite nice. If Sonia's happy perhaps Father will stay at home more. When's it getting born, Ivy?'

'Let's see, she's about four months gone, March then. Get up off there, both of you.' She lugged the blankets off my bed. 'You going to give us a hand, Miss Amy?'

'Cheek, it's your job,' Claudia said, and left before she got drawn into unwelcome activity.

I helped smooth sheets and tuck in blankets,

positively seething with speculation. Too soon had I discounted marvels. The Giant had given Sonia her heart's desire. I silenced the echo of Aunt Hildegarde's dry voice declaring that magic alone had no power. 'Only if a man goes with you.'

Before I had time to write the news to Rudi, he telephoned. I heard the voice of the post-mistress chatting away to him while he waited for me to get to the phone. 'Might be an Easter child, you never know. Here's Miss Amy now, Mr Longmire. You're through-hoo.'

'Blast,' I said. 'Hallo, Rudi dear. She's got in first about Sonia, hasn't she?'

''Fraid so. It's good news. I told her a festival might do the trick, but I was lying a little.'

'Naturally. The magic sort of took off though, and perhaps it's still at work. I'm ever so excited.'

'Amy, I can't bear to write my own news in a letter and I hope you won't be upset. Marie Dearlove has been offered a Hollywood contract. Talking pictures are all the go over there and a lot of their silent stars are useless because they sound appalling. Marie has a pleasant voice, you'll agree.'

'Yes.'

I thought I knew what was coming. Rudi was going to marry the trollop, Marie Dearlove, and that would be the end of our friendship.

'She wants me to become her business manager. It means I shall have to go with her.'

At least not marriage, not yet. 'Is it going to be for ever?'

'I hope not, I do very much hope not. In my own way I'm unshakeably English. It's just such a wonderful opportunity for me, but telephoning will be difficult.'

'You'll write still?'

'Of course. Aren't we friends?'

The operator butted in with her special telephone

181

voice. 'So sorree. I heard what you said about Hollywood, Mr Longmire, the switch sticks sometimes. I must say congrats. You're bound to meet all they film stars. If you come across Mary Pickford, do let us know if she's really so pretty as at the pictures.'

'Rudi, I'm going to hang up now.'

'Don't go yet, Amy, wait.'

Sadness came over me and I wanted to cry, but not while the operator could hear me. There had always been comfort in the knowledge that a train ride would get me to Rudi. America was too far away. I replaced the receiver.

Claudia and I were sent away to Bournemouth in the care of Ivy while Sonia had the baby. 'So's you don't get frightened by the screaming,' Ivy said with relish. 'It's agony giving birth.'

We pumped her for details but she refused to be drawn. Of all deadly dullness, the seaside out of season takes first prize. Everything was shut and our hotel empty except for an old man who was pushed out once a day in a wicker bath chair. He was papery yellow. His legs bundled into a tartan rug looked like a narrow parcel of wood.

Ivy longed to know what ailed him. She tried to get into conversation with the man-servant but he was morose and unfriendly. She loved Bournemouth as much as we hated it. 'I wish I could find a little place for Mum here,' she said.

When the motor came to take us home, Claudia and I rejoiced.

'You got yourselves a little brother then,' the chauffeur, formerly the head groom, said. 'Mother and child doing well I hear. You'll be pleased.'

'I'd rather have a puppy,' Claudia muttered, and was shushed by Ivy.

Yet like everyone else she adored David at first sight. He was such a confiding baby, liking to be cuddled and talked to, and absolutely charming with his huge round eyes and crest of darkish hair.

Father must have been proud when Valentine was born but by the time it came to me I imagine any thrill had worn off. He can't have expected another child after a nine-year gap. Yet with Davy he was wonderful. While Parliament was sitting he customarily lived at his London club. Suddenly he took to coming to Gunville Place for long weekends and spending most of the time making friends with his baby son.

Grandmother Mottesfont said sourly, 'From the time of the accident Gervase abdicated as a parent. We can only hope this child may remind him of his duty to his neglected daughters.'

In the trio of Father, Sonia and David I sensed a faintly discordant note. They were like points of a triangle, joined but never meeting. The compassionate affection he bestowed on Davy seemed somehow to make Sonia uneasy, and her own attitude to the son she had so much desired was curiously detached.

She had soppy ways with Davy at first – lots of huggies and kissies. And she didn't exactly follow the convention of handing him at once to someone else and arranging to pack him off to boarding-school the minute he was old enough. Yet she rarely saw him for more than an hour a day.

Davy didn't live in the nursery or have a proper nanny. He had his own bedroom close to Sonia's. Several nurses took care of him but they changed frequently. 'I won't have him grow up spoiled by women,' Sonia declared. 'He's to have a tutor as soon as he begins to walk, and learn to be a man.'

Most of his waking hours he spent with me. Either Sonia decided it wasn't worth fighting me or she didn't regard me as a woman. She made no objection even when the first tutor came.

Claudia always said that I was slow-witted and

backward. She may have been right. But I noticed more about others than she did. Before Davy's third birthday she had grown two inches taller and achieved womanhood at last. Ragtime gave way to spoony songs like 'What'll I Do?' and 'Can't Help Lovin' That Man', and selections from *Bittersweet*.

Being Claudia she crowed about her budding front and moaned over the other signs that heralded the moment. 'Amy, it's ghastly, I'm covered all over with hair.' She showed me a couple of sparse blonde tufts. 'Can you believe the shame of it? I've tried cutting it off and it just grows again.'

'I expect it's meant so why bother? You'll have to get a bust-bodice. Flatteners will soon be out, it says in Ivy's fashion-mags.'

'We're staying at Grandmother's before Christmas, aren't we? She's bound to give us five pounds and I'm going to do lots of shopping.'

'Well, I'm not, I'm saving up for things I shall want when I'm older.' (House fund, fifteen pounds seventeen and twopence ha'penny, and one treasured painting!)

'Whatever for?'

'I told you, things.'

'Why are you saving, I mean? We're all going to be rich when we're twenty-one – you, me and Portia. Grandmother told me. Mother left us lots of money in a truss or something and it gets more each year. We're heiresses.'

All those years of hoarding sixpences for nothing. 'You might have told me I was an heiress before,' I grumbled, feeling cheated, 'I could have afforded sweets and stop-me-and-buy-ones when we go to Dorchester.'

'I thought you didn't like buying ice-cream off a cart, that's what you *said*. And twenty-one is ages away; seven years.'

And nine-and-a-half for me, but at the end the

fulfilment of a dream. I wrote at once to Rudi, telling him of my expectations and asking him to describe the trollop, Marie Dearlove's house in America. I didn't call her that, naturally.

For Christmas of 1930 Grandmother took Claudia to Marshall and Snelgrove and bought her a coat. It had a big blue fox collar and a matching fur hat. I think that Claudia must have had a natural *chic* that showed off her beauty to advantage and made her seem older than her fourteen years. I tried it on and it made me look like a caterpillar.

The effects of the gift delighted Claudia. Grandmother was dismayed. Traps lurked everywhere – in Selfridges and William Whiteleys and Gunthers, even in the streets. She got busy. On the day before we were to return home she said, 'Now, Claudia, you enjoy idleness but soon you will crave a social life. Portia is at ladies' college; she's bound to marry well and be useful to you. I have the name of an excellent finishing-school in Switzerland.' Claudia pulled a long face. 'None of your looks, please. You won't be called upon to be academic, and we shall visit the place together first.'

'What's the point of it then if it's not just lessons?'

'You learn good social manners to begin with, and not before time. Also you will be trained in the difficult art of coping with young men and their appetites.'

Claudia gave me a nudge. 'What appetites, Grandmother?'

'You may well discompose Sonia, it's far from difficult, but you cannot pull the wool over my eyes, child.' She leered in a well-bred kind of way. 'Sex will come under discussion I don't doubt. Practical experience is not part of the curriculum and activities are supervised. Not repressively, I understand, but sensibly. If you detest the place on sight I will say no more about it.'

'What about Amy? Who's going to look after her?'

'Those whose responsibility it is. I've a few words to say to your stepmother though the wretched creature persistently avoids me.'

Who could blame her? Grandmother's face in repose began so closely to resemble Queen Mary's that the King might have confused them, and the Queen was not a smiling sort of lady.

'Sonia does salons now,' I said. 'The house is full of poets and musicians and secretaries and tutors and hags. There's to be another festival in two years' time; it's going to be a regular thing.'

'Please don't refer to ladies as hags, Amy, even if they are, and don't chatter so.'

'Okey-dokey, Grandmother.'

'Americanisms! Speaking of America, how is young Mr Longmire getting on, d'you know?'

'Homesick, about to be rich, worn to rags with temperaments, he says.'

'I imagine the trollop, Marie Dearlove, gives him a rough time,' Grandmother said.

I wanted to ask why 'trollop' was all right but not 'hags'. A glance at the Queen Mary expression deterred me.

Nothing happened about me, of course, other than getting forgotten again. Claudia went to Switzerland. Except for the servants below at the back of the house I lived quite alone in a wasteland of high, echoing rooms and holland-shrouded furniture.

We had the holidays but inevitably Claudia changed and grew away from me. Only the growing intensity of affection between David and me kept me from utter loneliness.

One day I went up to the nursery where I had been protected and happy. It felt drearier than a tomb. Mattresses from my bed and Gwennie's leaned against the wall, drawers and cupboards were bare. My rocking-horse lay on its side in a corner. The hob had rusted with disuse.

186

No memories awoke to comfort me. I closed the door quietly and turned the key in the lock. At first I thought of running away. Then I realized I had nowhere to go and no-one to run to.

Ivy took care of me when my periods began. My nature changed in the most awful way. I was miserable and sometimes bad-tempered and, unlike Claudia, I found breasts a nuisance, though mine were humiliatingly small. Also I got secretive. 'Don't tell Lady Osmington, Ivy, don't dare tell anyone.'

As if Sonia was interested anyway. I could have grown an extra head and she wouldn't have cared.

'It's us women that pays,' Ivy said, lugubriously cheerful. 'You can have kiddies now, so watch yerself. You oughter be pleased.'

'Well I'm not, I hate it.'

'Nowt you can do about it,' she said.

When Father stayed in London Sonia sometimes asked me to have tea with her and to bring David. She accepted me, I think, as a reliable nursemaid. Usually the tutor joined us. He had little to do other than give a few simple lessons. Not much of a job for a young man but he wasn't terribly bright.

On these occasions Sonia made a great fuss of her son. 'Darling little man, Mummy loves you more than anything in the whole world.'

Probably she knew how touching the scene was, with her cheek resting against Davy's dark curls, a bit like an Italian madonna. Sometimes he would spoil the effect by saying, 'Where's Daddy gone? I want Daddy,' and his tutor would say, 'Won't I do? Ha-ha-ha.'

He was one of those men who seem to be bursting with blood: red-faced, stocky and strong, with straw-coloured hair and very bright blue eyes. I believe that at games he excelled.

For quite a while Sonia had been wearing again her softly rumpled look. She undulated nicely as she walked and her enticing bosom moved without restraint. I thought little of it after her cool dismissal of Pandel Metkin. Since the original festival she had thrown herself wholeheartedly into preparation for the next. Parties became frequent and I supposed she must be at the champagne cocktails again.

One afternoon on returning from a walk I put Davy down for a rest and sat with him until he fell asleep. Creeping away I heard noises in Sonia's room next door. It was not talking, but the huffing, scuffling, panting sounds the trollop Marie Dearlove had made when Rudi kissed her under a hedge.

The door stood ajar allowing me to see through the crack. I didn't dare to move. The top of Sonia's dress was around her waist. The tutor eased down the narrow shoulder-strap of her silk chemise and one of her roly-poly white breasts dropped out into his hand. He stroked it and groaned a lot then bent down and began to kiss it. One arm pressed her right up against him. Their hips sort of ground together and he pushed her backwards on to the bed.

How did I know that it wasn't the first time, possibly not the first man? I felt a bit sick and terribly hot and bothered and miserably upset all at the same time.

Was my father aware of what went on? He showed no sign. On the rare occasions that we were alone together I felt that there was no longer a proper meeting-place between us. We talked in commonplaces. The tutor left soon afterwards and was replaced by another, older man. Sonia sulked for a while. But the flood of casual visitors continued and she cheered up.

In 1932 the second Gunville Festival of Arts took place and was judged a success, though not on the scale of the first. I saw nothing of it and it meant nothing to me without Rudi and Pan, Jimmy and Claudia. Sonia arranged to take a house in Cornwall for David and, of course, me. She sent staff with us. We stayed for a month and returned when the festival was over.

Another revelation occurred in a sandy cove near to St Austell. Davy then was four. One day I left him with Ivy while I went to buy us all ice-cream cornets. As I picked my way back over the beach I thought how sweet he looked in his white cotton hat and shirt and brief blue knickers.

He looked up and smiled. From babyhood his likeness to his mother was marked, and commented on by everyone, including me. His eyes had darkened a little to golden-brown. They beamed up at me, and the smile and the long lashes were oh so familiar. I had seen an older version of the very face, bent towards Sonia five years before. There was no doubt in my mind at all. David was Pandel Metkin's son.

Chapter Thirteen

Cloaked in her reputation for virtue and culture, Sonia got away with it for a long time. Her passion for the arts naturally brought her into the company of men, good-looking and plain. The late flowering of her other desires went unnoticed. Only the hags gossiped, but they always did and they were ignored.

Yet she hardly bothered to be discreet, and the men became younger and younger. Rarely at home, she was spotted flying to Biarritz or Deauville, playing chemmy in the casino at Monte Carlo, dancing at the Ritz and the Kitkat Club.

Rumours began and spread. In a time of slump when bitter poverty was rife, Sonia lost large sums at the gaming-tables and showered expensive gifts on her lovers. Insinuating paragraphs, naming no names, appeared in the gossip columns. Other married women in her circle lived the same frenetic kind of life but Sonia the unlucky had been rather ostentatiously chaste. Those frailer vessels she had snubbed began to gloat in anticipation of her fall.

A lonely little boy and virtually motherless, David clung to me and to Father. He loved to ride in the wheelchair. 'Are we comfortable? Now what shall we talk about today, Daddy?' (Sonia had got her way and Father was Daddy at last!)

The wider family, including my siblings and grandparents, insensitive as they were to innuendo and undercurrents, noticed no scandal. They had made up their minds about Sonia and saw no reason to waste more thought on her.

In 1934 Claudia left finishing school. Our old closeness had weakened and she had become self-absorbed to the point of denseness. Yet beneath the poised young woman lurked still the odd, permanently weary, impatient, hateful, lovable child.

Her numerous boyfriends dashed to and fro. They got a wonderfully gracious welcome if Sonia happened to be home. I considered warning Claudia. But she treated the boys with casual indifference and her interest in Sonia extended no further than the arrangements for her official 'coming-out'.

She noticed the hangers-on. 'Any eligible ones among them do you suppose or are they all climbers?' she asked.

'A mixture; art, craft, bored heirs waiting to inherit, younger sons. Why?'

'A rich husband is essential to me,' she said, 'and I mean bottomless, filthy riches, not noble wealth encumbered by entails and huge estates like Portia's fiancé. And it must be someone amusing and kind as I don't seem to be the type to fall in love.'

Something about Switzerland bothered her and gave an extra urgency to her desire to be 'out'. 'We were a hotchpotch,' she told me, 'all nationalities and all colours – Indians and Chinese and Italians and Jews from about every country you can think of. Nice, most of them.'

'But not all?'

'Well, there was this truly weird German girl who tried to make passionate love to some of us. The principal was jolly good on sex, though she made sure none of us got the chance to do it. She explained afterwards, a lot of guff about a poetess called Sappho who lived in Lebanon or somewhere.'

'It wasn't Lebanon, it was Lesbos; Aunt Hildegarde told me about it. Did the girl make up to you?'

Claudia raised her eyebrows into her hair. 'Oh yes, it's just the kind of thing Aunt Hildegarde always talks about, I don't think. How can I tell this if you keep interrupting and telling lies?'

'Sorry, Claudia, go on.'

'You wouldn't have guessed what she was really like because she was rather beautiful, and noble and heroic to look at. I had to kick and pinch her a bit when she tried to kiss me. But she never touched or even spoke to the black or yellow girls or the Jews, especially not the Jews, and that was the most awful part. She said they were all filthy animals and that in Germany they were spat on and Adolf Hitler was going to turn them out. They heard her. Some of them cried.'

The name of Hitler rang the faintest of bells. I rarely looked at a newspaper though I had seen the uniformed, shouting figure in the Pathé Gazette news at the cinema. Home and its little wars absorbed all my attention. I had no political awareness.

That conversation gave me my first inkling of the deep unrest in Europe and the perils of the Jews. I said, 'She sounds a complete wart.'

'We were awfully close to Germany, just across the Bodensee and we heard a lot of rumours. It scared me, Amy. Can you imagine what it must be like to own a little shop and have gangs come at night and beat you up and smash in the windows and doors? And be called a pig-Jew.'

I thought of the fat jolly Jewish lady who kept a secondhand clothes shop in Dorchester and joked and teased me. 'You get hard-up, my Lady, you bring me good clobber and we split the profit, eh? Now here I got stout working boots – your size.'

And then I thought of Pan saying that he wouldn't be let into Father's clubs, and the Metkin Fine Arts showroom in London, all plate glass and one lovely object displayed against silk or velvet. 'It won't happen in this country, Claudia, will it? Some people here don't much like Jews.'

She cheered up. 'Of course not. We may be awful

snobs but not cruel. I've been invited to Ascot, the Royal Box. Come and see my dress, it's a dream – full-length – and a gorgeous cartwheel hat. Aunt Phyllida and Uncle Henry are going so I must watch my rear. Do you want an invite too?'

I shook my head. 'I don't have anything posh enough and Uncle Henry makes me feel hideous and deformed.'

'If only you could grow a bit and bleach your hair you might have more It.'

'I don't want to bleach my hair; I'm only fifteen.'

'So what? Henry began pinching me to bits years ago. He's a kind of sexual barometer.'

'Then my pressure must be low,' I said. 'But I've got nice eyes.'

David grew tall and graceful. At eight years old he was relaxed and charming and kind, and considering the way Father and Sonia carried on his tolerance was phenomenal. We spent much of our time cycling together or playing draughts or bezique in his room. At cards he possessed a fiend's cunning. I always lost.

One early evening I heard loud and angry voices. David was rummaging in the box where he kept his treasures. 'Here, Amy,' he said, emerging with a model biplane, 'I made this for you. If you hang it from the ceiling on a string and squint up your eyes it looks real.'

'It's beautiful,' I said. 'What's going on in Father's room?'

'Oh that. They shout at each other sometimes. Take no notice, they'll shut up in a minute.'

Humming to himself, he knelt by the box and began to tidy the contents. His unconcern was genuine. He had a knack of concentration that enabled him to shut out everything but the immediate interest. I felt grateful. The quarrel unnerved me because it concerned David and I could hear almost every word.

With cold distaste Father said, 'I accept that I'm a cuckold but your gigolos and the presents you lavish on them make us both look ridiculous. Don't force me to withdraw your allowance and publicly refuse payment of your debts.'

If Sonia felt no shame I did. Those revealing announcements in *The Times* and the *Daily Telegraph* always made me shiver with embarrassment. I missed the next bit. Davy said, 'Can we go down to the village tomorrow, Amy? I've run out of paint for the wing-markings and they promised to get some in for me.'

'It'll have to be after your lessons.'

'That's fine. Oh dear, I forgot to put my bike away. I'd better do it now. It sounds as if Mamma's in a wax and she'll confiscate it if she sees it.'

He dashed out of the room as Sonia said, 'How pious you sound, Gervase, and yet you're every bit as bad. Do you think I don't know where you go and who it is you see? Am I supposed to spend my life dancing attendance on a cripple who cares nothing for me, all because of an accident I couldn't help?'

'I've never blamed you, either for the accident or for minor indiscretions, but I won't have the boy exposed to shame. Change your ways or leave my house.'

There was a silence. Sonia said, 'When I go David goes with me. You can't force me to give him up if I choose to fight.'

'Teaching ethics to a bitch on heat is a complete waste of time.' The bitter rage in Father's voice made me shiver, as did the thought of losing David, my friend and ally in the growing desolation of Gunville Place. 'The boy's my son until you prove otherwise. Hurt him and I'll destroy you.'

Sonia laughed. 'Give up, Gervase. There's really nothing you can do. Take it or leave it.'

I heard Davy returning so I thundered around on the floor and the voices stopped.

*   *   *

194

King George the Fifth died in 1936. Claudia's coming-out had to be postponed. Her language had improved a lot since the finishing-school. 'Damn them all to the hottest pits of Hell,' she said savagely. 'Does Edward stop having fun because his father's dead? No he does not.'

'The King couldn't help dying. I don't suppose he wanted to. D'you think they're true, all the stories about passionate goings-on at the Palace? Grandpa said if that damned American woman's intent on marriage it must be rank she's after as it's rumoured that Edward's private parts are practically invisible to the naked eye.'

Claudia gaped. 'Grandpa said that to *you*?'

'Of course not to me. He was talking to Father who shut him up jolly fast.'

'Wouldn't you think a King would be the last word in rampant unbridled lust? Poor Edward, no winkle.'

'The proper word's pee-nis – I told you ages ago. Winkle sounds prettier though. I suppose it matters dreadfully and makes it awkward if you have to have heirs.'

'She's seen off two husbands already so perhaps she can't have children,' Claudia said. 'Or perhaps she doesn't want to ruin her figure. A friend in France told me she's tremendously *chic* and beautiful.'

'Then he'd better keep her as his secret lover and stop upsetting Grandmother who thinks he's a sense-less nincompoop and steadily killing Queen Mary in her prime.'

We both considered that lady and her prime, and decided that nothing less than a well-directed cannon-ball could destroy her.

Claudia yawned and stretched. 'I missed our talks in Switzerland. Let's go to the pics – my treat. It's Ginger Rogers and Fred Astaire – *Top Hat*. I saw it in London last year but I don't mind seeing it again.'

A curious thing happened. The newsreel came on. It

consisted of a lot of political stuff from places we'd
never heard of and we began to chatter in low voices.
A face on the screen arrested my attention. 'Look,
Claudia, behind that man who's making a speech,
surely it's Emil, your childhood lover.'

'Well, strike me pink, so it is, our cockroach puffing
out his chest. Doesn't he look important? I wonder if
he's killed off all the capitalists and stolen their money
to spend on turnip-fields.'

'Mekkin fockinks, more likely.'

Fortunately the programme had almost got to where
we came in because we began to giggle in the stupidest
way and irritated our neighbours. I enjoyed the treat.
But seeing Emil reminded me of the thrill I felt when
we saw *The Merry Widow* with Rudi and Claudia
danced all the way down the street. We had grown out
of magic.

She went off to Town again soon after. Valentine had
a batchelor flat in Mayfair where livelier company
than mine could be found. Now engaged, Portia spent
much of her time in Leicestershire with the Duchess,
her future mother-in-law.

Sonia's indiscretions were eclipsed by rumours about
the King. Pictures of Wallis Simpson began to appear
in the newspapers, outraging Claudia. 'A hag,' she said
on the telephone, 'and you wouldn't believe the
vulgarity of her jewels. Queen Mary's livid. So shall I
be if I can't be presented next year. They say that
pathetic ass, Edward, might abdicate.'

For the remainder of the year I feared no public
family disclosures. In December the King abdicated
and married Mrs Simpson. It was mad and sad and
turned out to be deeply disappointing to them and to
some people in Britain. We got George the Sixth
instead.

As preparations for the third festival began my unease

196

returned. Undercurrents of emotion eddied about the house like smoke. Where Sonia and her army of young men were the atmosphere vibrated with furtive excitement. A political element added nervousness. Among the men were some who belonged to Sir Oswald Moseley's British Union of Fascists and they didn't like Jews. They tried to persuade Sonia not to engage an orchestra with Jewish refugees among the players.

Whatever she had become, she cared nothing for foreign or home politics or for race. 'Don't talk nonsense, please. If the orchestra is the best available, hire it. There are enough of you to organize these things, surely. Rudi Longmire managed single-handed. I only wish he were in England.'

I wished it too. Each time a letter came I expected to read that Rudi had married the trollop, Marie Dearlove. My mind gnawed away at so many things that I couldn't write down. I needed advice more than ever in my life.

Occasionally I cycled over to Sturminster Newton to talk to Great-aunt Hildegarde and get cheered up. She was then well into her eighties. Her wire-brush of hair had softened and become silky white and there was a change in her relationship with Jesus. She thought He had made a false move in permitting the appointment of the new minister at her chapel. 'His sermons remind me of the barber's cat,' she said.

'What do you mean, Aunt Hildegarde?'

'All wind and piss, dear, and before you become shocked those are two good old English words and found in the Bible.' She smiled benevolently. 'And they explain him rather well. How is that beautiful boy of Sonia's?'

'He's a lamb.'

Naturally Hildegarde had wanted to know how I came to be near Cerne Abbas at midnight in time to meet the Ooser. I didn't tell but I think she probably worked it out for herself. She said, 'Bring him with you some time, I'm curious. And, Amy, don't take too much responsibility on your shoulders. The world is a wonderful maze, a place to enjoy – "Heaven in ordinary", "the land of spices". Those aren't original thoughts but they do express my opinions. We all pick our way through as best we can.'

She so often surprised me. 'My land of spices vanished a long time ago, Aunt Hildegarde. I shall never find it again.'

'You will, dear, oh yes. The young seldom pray nowadays though it's a useful method of clearing the mind. I shall pray for you. It's a pity about our minister but I dare say there's a reason somewhere.'

In spite of her advice I began to worry myself thin over Davy and Father and Sonia. Yet on the surface all was calm. It seemed that Sonia would have her cake and eat it and be lucky after all.

The suddenness of the explosion took me by surprise. It was early June of 1937. Portia came home. Valentine and some of his friends had promised to visit and Claudia was to travel down with them.

A pre-festival hush fell on the house. Everything was ready. The invitations had been sent and accepted or rejected. Rooms were prepared for the family and distinguished guests. They, the guests, were less distinguished than formerly. Several lords and their ladies had made their excuses, and pretty trivial they were. We had become dubious.

And then, of course, right at the last minute, Sonia chose to prove that she truly was unlucky. Heat lay over Dorset, muggily, languorously, dewing the skin with sweat and conjuring up voluptuous images of oases cool among desert sands. Life seemed to slow to an erotic amble. The gardens and the house had the stillness of an enchanted forest.

Davy and I played a desultory game in the ground-floor corridor. From the hall came the sound of muted voices and the rubber-tyred wheels of Father's chair whispering over the parquet. A knot of men moved towards the ballroom. Like a moth caught in a draught I drifted along in their wake with Davy lagging behind and touching alternate patterns on the wallpaper in some complicated ritual of his own.

Sunlight poured in through the ballroom windows. And there on a velvet-padded bench, overcome one imagines by sun and silence and searing passion, lay Sonia, frantically making love in broad day. The room itself seemed to move with the spectacle of heaving buttocks and writhing limbs endlessly reflected in the dozens of long mirrors that lined the walls.

Her partner was the youngest son of a Methodist peer. And the stricken peer stood there in the doorway with Father and a group of interested caterer's assistants from London, a horrified, helpless observer.

Suddenly the peer moved. He hauled his oblivious offspring to his feet and clouted his head savagely. The boy's white summer flannels fell to his feet and he scrabbled to pull them up. Sonia too wrestled with her tumbled clothes, lying sprawled and ungainly and obscenely, erotically lovely.

I judged instantly. Surely my adulterous stepmother ought to have reacted with penitence, with utter humiliation, yet I sensed a measure of defiance – a 'do your damnedest' air.

My unwilling voyeurism had, I felt, destroyed sex for me for ever. I would never marry. My virginity would be carried intact to the grave. Coupling like this, semi-clothed, semi-public, was just sordid and ugly and horrible and ridiculous. I could have died with shame and howled my anger aloud.

Sonia sat up. 'We love each other,' she said in a small, flat voice.

And that was the kind of thing that made her touching. It was such a brave statement. She wore no make-up. Fine lines around her eyes and a slight heaviness under the chin betrayed her age. She was forty-one, the boy seventeen. Poor Sonia, she was about to be torn to pieces.

My father swung his chair round abruptly, his face gaunt with defeat and determination. He saw me. 'What the devil are you doing here, Amity? How dare you stand there and gape? Get out, get out at once.' My face must have betrayed me. I was never much good at concealing my deep feelings. In a softer voice he asked, 'David?'

'Outside. He hasn't seen.'

'Thank God for something. Look after him. Now go.'

I went, not wishing to hear or witness what came next. One of the caterer's men said, 'Cor, she's a goer, ain't she, on the job in daylight? Wish she'd give my missus a lesson or two.'

'Shut up, damn you,' I said, 'mind your own business,' and grabbing the hand of a surprised David I dragged him away to the farthest end of the house.

Being unused to the company of children he was what Ivy called an old-fashioned boy. He shrugged his slim shoulders. 'They're fighting again, are they?' he said. 'Don't be upset, please, Amy, you take it too much to heart. We'll manage, you'll see. I promise I'll always take care of you.'

He wound his arms round my waist. His handsome, betraying face was almost on a level with mine when he leaned forward and kissed me. It dawned on me fully then that Davy was not my brother, no relation at all. I wanted to keep him with me for ever and I had no rights – we had no rights.

Curse Rachel Moot and her blather about fertility and giants and oosers. And God curse, I prayed with vehement spite, Pan Metkin who was 'so' and had Jimmy as a wife, and still crept up after Sonia on Giant's Hill and casually seduced her. He had started all this. I hoped he would drop dead among all the lovely objects he cherished – now, at once.

*   *   *

The very next day Sonia left in the big Wolsey, driving herself. Beside her in the front, resigned and patient, David craned his neck towards me as I raced down the drive after them. He waved. One palm remained pressed like a starfish on the window. We hadn't even been allowed to say goodbye to each other. Tears choked me. The car turned into the lane, gathered speed and disappeared.

I walked back. Davy's bicycle lay on its side on the terrace. I picked it up and rested it tidily against the balustrade. Father leaned on his crutches behind the glass door, staring blindly over the park. He saw me and turned away.

So there we were two days later with a roomful of indignant relatives and no festival. Somebody – one of the secretaries, no doubt – had cancelled most of the performing artists and sent off to members of the family telegrams that might or might not have arrived in time. ('Telegram? I received no telegram. I shall certainly speak to the postmaster.')

Portia coped with the practical things like lunch and orders to the staff and timetables to get everyone home. 'I'm disgusted with that woman and with Father,' she said coldly. 'I can't imagine what the Duchess will think.'

She made me snappish. 'Does it matter what the damned Duchess thinks? It's her son you're marrying, not her.'

'When I've got rid of this rabble I swear I shall never set foot in this house again.'

I could hardly say that she would be sadly missed since she only set her foot about twice a year. But I didn't want to upset her while she was being useful. I said, 'Give them lunch, Portia, and I'll try to explain to Grandmother. You know what she's like, she'll clear them out in a trice and take Claudia to London with her. Val and his friends have already gone.'

Underneath Portia's fuss and snobbery lay true concern. 'What about you, Amy? You oughtn't to stay here, you know. If this becomes public the scandal will smear us all.' She offered the supreme sacrifice. 'I could ask the Duchess to invite you down to Leicestershire I suppose.'

'Not just now, thanks, Portia. I shall wait awhile. Father has already lost David, now you and Claudia. I won't leave him here alone.'

'If you're sure. Call on me if you change your mind, won't you?'

Her face brightened with relief. I smiled a brave, sweet martyr's smile which was the kind of thing she understood. 'I'm absolutely sure.'

A revealing babble of voices emanated from the small drawing-room. 'Amity, it really isn't necessary to tell everyone in there remember, just Grandmother.'

'We can plead a nervous breakdown for Sonia, perhaps. Hurry up with lunch if you can.'

Everyone left at last. A strained expectant silence fell on the house. I watched and waited for Gwennie Hughes to arrive but she didn't come and as far as I could judge she wasn't expected. Father kept to his room and I kept to mine or wandered in the garden.

I thought what a strange old bird Grandmother was. She seemed quite glad to know that Sonia had lapsed from gentility and I could see that she was dying to laugh when she heard about the scene in the ballroom. 'That starched-up old Methodist, I wish I'd seen his face – like a French po, I dare say.' (Suppressed grin. Why a French po and not an English one?)

'Don't tell the family, will you, Grandmother?'

'They'll find out sooner or later but I'll concoct a yarn and see them off.'

Grandpa whispered in my ear, 'One look should do it.'

I snorted. 'Blow your nose, girl,' Grandmother commanded, 'there's nothing to blub about. Your father was a fool to marry the woman.' She made a joke. 'Slipped off the pedestal on her own soap, I dare say, and into a heap of dirty washing.'

Grandpa and I pleased her by laughing immoderately.

A week later Father sent for me. Rain was lashing down and the weather had turned cold for June. He said, 'You realize that I shall have to divorce Sonia? My lawyers will be here in a day or two.'

My low spirits fell another notch. Lots of people got divorced but when they were well known or titled the newspapers reported every detail. 'I suppose so. What about Davy, can't you make her give him back?'

'I have a choice – heartbreaking whichever course I choose. I won't explain, you must take my word that if I fight for him I risk humbling him in the eyes of the world. I love him too much for that, so no, Amity, I can't get him back.'

'It's not fair. Sonia didn't bother with him. I'm the one who looked after him. He's a lonely boy and I love him too. People shouldn't have children if they won't look after them.'

He tapped a paper-knife on the edge of his desk and frowned down at it. I thought he might lose his temper. He said quietly, 'Go away now, Amity. I can bear no more reminders of failure.'

At first Sonia intended to contest the divorce and cross-petition on the grounds of Father's adultery. It became nasty. Detectives dragged up a story about Sonia going to a private nursing-home in Paris, hinting that there had been an abortion. This in turn began to involve fashionable French doctors. The pressures on her became too much. She truly adored her boy-lover and his father threatened suits against her. Eventually she was persuaded to take the least damaging course.

Newspaper reporters hung around Gunville, accosting anyone they could catch. I stayed immured and alone in the house until it was all over. In due course my father's petition was heard and granted. He asked for his own adultery with an unnamed woman to be taken into consideration which came as a shock as I hadn't believed what Sonia said.

Portia was utterly furious. 'The Duchess is shocked beyond measure,' she said tightly – on the telephone since nothing would persuade her to visit Father or speak to him. 'I shall be lucky if she doesn't forbid the wedding. It's foul.'

'I wouldn't want a man who let his mother rule his life. Can't you be a bit more tolerant?'

'Tolerant, how can I be tolerant?' Her voice rose to a well-bred screech. 'The first thing we all see at breakfast is my family name on the front page of the papers and pictures of Father and that frightful woman. I wish they were dead, both of them.'

'It hasn't stopped Claudia's presentation. You'll come to her ball, I hope. Father won't be there.'

'We'll be hounded by scandalmongers from the Press.'

'Really, Portia,' I said impatiently, 'you talk like a complete drip at times, and you know you love having your picture in *Tatler*. I'm going, come hell or high water, and if you let Claudia down I'll set Grandmother on the Duchess and you know who'll win.'

To give her her due she wasn't completely lost. She stifled a laugh. 'All right, Amy, if I must. Is there any word of David?'

'No,' I said, miserable again. 'I had one card from Italy then nothing. Sonia would stop him from writing or telephoning. She never liked us.'

'The feeling's mutual.'

I wore a slinky simple dress to the ball. It cost a fortune and I was proud of my sophistication. 'Lovely dress,' Claudia said. 'It makes you look about twelve. I've found a filthy rich man and we're getting engaged. He's Scottish and rather gorgeous.'

Why did I bother about being a lady and struggling to look the part? More fervently than ever in my life I wished that I could give up trying and become anyone except who I was.

I returned to my ugly prison. My nineteenth birthday came and went without much notice. I began to count the months until I was twenty-one and possessed of my inheritance.

In February of 1938 my father said, 'I'm going away next week. I want you to come with me. Will you do that?'

The weather was cold and wet. I didn't want to go anywhere. In my heart I still hoped that Davy might come home and I must be there when he did. 'I'm not at all keen. Where are you going?'

My voice sounded chilly in my own ears. He hadn't said one word to me about the divorce or the settlement made for David. The long depression in the country had begun to take its toll on the traditional wealth of the landed gentry and he must, though still rich, have been less so then. I knew that Sonia had sole custody of her son.

Father raised his eyebrows. 'You'll see. Pack enough for a week or so.'

Overcome by the complications of fate and fear I froze into indifference. 'Very well.'

The Rolls-Royce purred silently towards the mountains. We had crossed from England into Wales and below us ran the River Wye. The chauffeur obviously knew the way for he asked for no directions and didn't consult a map. I assumed when I saw the sign for Builth Wells that we would stop at a spa but we went through the little town and steadily climbed uphill. It was still raining.

Outside a small farmhouse the car stopped. 'Go on in,' Father said, 'you'll find the door open. I'll follow in a few minutes.'

I had a sudden moment of foreknowledge as I stepped into the room. A dark-haired, pretty woman stood looking at me, smiling and holding out her hands. Over and over again I had dreamed that vision. All through the years of loneliness I assumed that I loved Gwennie Hughes still with the tenacious love of childhood. And, of course, that she loved me. I had grown, but never away from the nursery time that was all I had ever known of mothering.

A wave of pure rage shook me. I had no need to ask questions; I knew that once again they had betrayed me, Gwenefer Hughes and my father, and that the betrayal had gone on for years. They were lovers. I ignored the outstretched hands and blundered blindly to the door.

My father stood in the doorway leaning on the chauffeur's arm. Gwennie hurried over and helped him to a chair – 'his' chair, I was sure. 'Sit down with you, Amy,' she said.

I stayed where I was and glared at them both. 'What on earth's the matter with you?' Father asked. 'Aren't you pleased to see Gwennie again?'

'Twelve years ago I would have been pleased.' My voice was so hard and choked I scarcely recognized it as mine. 'All that time and not a word, not a line, though you knew I was breaking my heart. How could you, how could anyone be so cruel?'

Father said, 'We met again by chance after the accident, in a nursing-home. There was Sonia. I'm sorry, Amity, the secrecy was my fault – I tried to tell you once, then I thought it best to say nothing to anyone. You seemed settled. Gwennie and I are to be married. We can all be together at last.'

He understood nothing. Not the nights of tears, the painful growing-up alone, nothing. Callous, uncaring, stupid, heartless; neither of them was worth a minute of my agonizing, frustrated love.

'Go to hell,' I said. 'I won't live with you. I hate you both. I never, never want to see either of you again.'

At that moment I meant every word. And I truly didn't want to live with them, not after this. Gwennie burst into tears. 'Amy, please. There's a room ready for you upstairs, see.'

Why did they always try to comfort me with rooms or rabbits or something equally stupid? 'May I have some money, Father? I suppose there's a hotel somewhere?'

'In Builth,' Gwennie said. 'Don't go off like this. We can talk.'

'It's too late for talking. Until I have my own money I shall need a regular allowance, and I should like you to arrange it please, Father.'

He was dreadfully angry. I didn't care. I had lost everyone, David, Claudia, Rudi, Gwennie, worst of all I had lost a large chunk of dreams and memories. He commanded roughly, 'Sit down, stay where you are. I won't tolerate this rudeness.'

'Let her go, Gervase,' Gwennie said softly. 'She's right, isn't she? We should have told. Cruel we were, and selfish, and I am sorry for it. But no use crying now.'

Chapter Fourteen

As I walked into the hall at Gunville Place a few days later the telephone started to ring. I picked up the receiver, expecting it to be Father or Gwennie. A strange voice said, 'May I speak to the Earl of Osmington please?'

'I'm sorry, my father's away. This is Amity Savernake, can I help?'

'Oh, Lady Amity, you may remember me, I'm the maid for the Countess's suite at the Ritz. I'm a bit worried about her, she's gone off and left the Honourable David here on his own. He's been trying to reach you for several days.'

'Do you know where she went?'

'It was supposed to be just a weekend but it's over a week now.' A discreet note crept into the voice. 'We can get the sack for gossiping so please excuse me, but I did hear that the young man, the one in the papers, had talked her into going on a boat trip – a cruise or some such.'

Mumbling went on at the other end of the line. I heard the click that meant our operator was listening in. Damn. Then David said, 'Amy, at last. I've missed you dreadfully. Mamma's not there, I suppose?'

'No, darling, only me. It's lovely to hear from you.'

'She made me promise on my honour not to write or anything until the divorce became final. I don't know whether it is yet or not but I truly don't care. Our life's an awful mess. I'm bored to my toes and she hasn't done a thing about money or anything so I can't even go out much. Should I come back to Gunville, d'you think?'

'Stay where you are, Davy. I'll explain why when I see you. Ask the maid to make sure there's a bed ready for me tonight, will you?'

'Yes.' He had sounded firm and confident, older than his age, but a slight relieved shakiness reminded me that he was still a deserted ten-year-old. 'Are you really coming, Amy?'

'Of course I am. We'll have supper together so don't go to bed until I get there. You don't know how I've missed you.'

'Me too. I hated leaving, and everyone makes jokes about Mamma. She doesn't really want me, only her friend, and yet she throws a tantrum if I ask to come home.'

Conscious of listening ears I said, 'It'll be fine, you'll see. We'll talk it all over together. OK, Davy?'

'Super-duper, Amy. Hurry up.'

I added Sonia to the list of those I could cheerfully kill. Claudia was right, parents are useless and go on sickeningly about loving their children until it comes to a question of putting aside their own desires.

At the Ritz Davy and I had supper in the suite. I told him the bare bones of my quarrel with Father. 'I won't go back there to live,' I said, 'so we're both orphans of the storm.'

'What will we do, then? I can't think of anything so is it all right if I leave it to you? You're good at standing up to my mother.'

'Am I? I get sorry for her sometimes.'

But I felt as baffled as Davy. The suite could be charged to Father but I hadn't a great deal of money, only about twenty pounds of my own and fifty I had borrowed hurriedly from Great-aunt Hildegarde. I didn't want to ask Grandmother for help, and I couldn't and wouldn't take David back to Gunville. High time that some of these people who behaved so casually got their come-uppance.

After a sleepless night I made a long-distance telephone call. 'Hallo, that's Jimmy, isn't it? This is Amity Savernake. Is Pan there? No? When he comes in will you say that I shall be in Paris with a friend the day after tomorrow and I need to see him urgently. Thanks.'

I packed suitcases for us both. Davy hopped up and down with excitement. 'Why are we going to Paris?'

'Tell me first, do you terribly want to live with Sonia always?'

'No. I'm in the way though she pretends not. I miss you, Amy, more even than I miss Father.'

'Then we'll visit an old friend of mine. You'll like him, I think, and he's about the only one who can advise us properly.'

'I want you to meet Sonia's son, my half-brother, the Honourable David Savernake,' I said to Pandel Metkin. 'We have a problem.'

Davy bowed nicely and smiled at Pandel with his own smile. The emotional temperature of the lovely, lovely room whizzed up to boiling point. Jimmy gave a long low whistle. Tears dampened Pan's eyes and his pale olive skin went even paler. 'How do you do, David?'

He held out his hands to me, palms upwards, in a very foreign sort of gesture, looking as though he was about to burble something embarrassing. 'Davy, I need to speak privately to Mr Metkin,' I said before he could utter. 'Will you go with Jimmy? I'm sure he'll find you some tea.'

Pan stared at me without seeing me. He said, 'I didn't know, on my truth I didn't.'

I covered the awkwardness by admiring the evidences of wealth that surrounded us. The room seemed to do homage to one flaring, flamboyant painting that hung alone above the magnificent fireplace. It was of a woman, her arms raised, breasts half-revealed. She looked as bloomy and voluptuously full-blown as the roses she was tucking into her hair.

'You notice the likeness of course,' Pan said, coming to life. 'Renoir. A sensualist, overwarm at times. The proper ambience and careful hanging are essential.'

'Sonia, yes, it's very like, but she's flesh and blood not just a pretty decoration.' I was deliberately hostile, blaming him for awakening Sonia from her frigid slumbers on a whim. 'You'll have read about the divorce and the young man she's mad on. When you followed her on to Giant's Hill you certainly gave her what you thought she wished for. But it was a Savernake son she truly wanted, not a Metkin. I suppose dreams have to come true in the right kind of way to be any good, and you've caused a lot of harm.'

'But how did you find out about the Giant?'

'The way she acted at the party worried me so much that I followed her. I saw and heard you in the car, that's how I got caught by the Ooser. I didn't understand some of what you said then but later I did. Was it really such a good joke?'

That hurt his feelings. He drew in his cheeks as if he were sucking a lemon. 'The unnoticed watcher, and how you judge us all! You think me cynical and cold but I swear it isn't so. I saw Sonia, a woman of potent loveliness, strangling in her strait-jacket of British respectability. She ravished the senses, and if I couldn't love her I couldn't resist her either.' He glanced up at the painting. 'The Renoir would not hang in this room had I felt no affection, no passion for her. Tell me, does David know?'

'Of course not. One day he may realize. He looks just like you, but then Sonia looks a little bit like you too. She's gone utterly man-crazy these days. Davy's neglected.'

'Is it truly all my fault? Can one self-indulgent act have so deep an effect?'

More than ten years had passed. Pan, ageing a little,

remained the romantic, handsome Caliph, trailing the glamour of Baghdad, and the waft of warm, spice-scented breezes.

'Our lives had been ordinary, dull, you can't imagine. Then Rudi conjured up magic for us, and you came flying out of the sky, so wonderful, so beautiful, bringing all the riches of the Orient. That's how we saw you; I did anyway, silly and ignorant as I was.'

'Amy, oh Amy,' he said softly, and my heart gave a jump as I suppose Sonia's must have done. 'You shame me, and yet my son – *my* son – is so beautiful how can I regret? What of the Earl? Is he angry, is that why he didn't ask for custody?'

'He adores David but Sonia threatened to say publicly that you're his father. Illegitimate children have a bad time in England.' I sighed and steeled myself. 'If Rudi were closer I would ask him what to do but he's too far away. I want you to keep David here for a while. If anyone can influence Sonia, if anyone has the right, it's you.'

Pan got to his feet, walked across the expanse of carpet (the rarest in the world, I expect) and stared out of the window. 'Here is not safe, not for him, not for me,' he said sombrely. 'I'm a Jew and David is the son of a Jew. What is happening in Germany will, I believe, bring us to another war, and soon. I'm forty-three, Amy, too old to fight for France and too foreign to be trusted in England. The Germans will know what to do with me and with the millions like me.'

Is it the heart or the soul that gets sick at hearing a dreadful truth? I remembered what Claudia had told me about the German girl in her school and I felt as though I had begun to bleed somewhere deep inside me. 'Where will you go?'

'I'm rich. First I shall go to America. Already I am moving my rarest goods there. Many of my race are trapped in Germany, that unspeakable charnel-house of a country, for want of bribe-money. Each day a few risk the frontiers. Some are shot by the guards, others succeed only to die later of privation.' He moved an ornament on the window-sill then moved it back again. 'My childhood was a battle against dirt and hunger and exploitation. I shall find a role somehow, help the children if I can.'

'But you can't help Davy and me?'

'Oh yes, that I can do. Who most wants the boy?'

'I do. I've loved him since the day he was born and he trusts me. He's my dearest friend. But I have no home and no money until I'm twenty-one.'

I told him about Father and Gwennie and why I wouldn't go back to Gunville Place. He said, 'Yes, I understand that. What of the white house? Does the dream remain?'

'Oh yes, always, but I'm the only one who can make it come true.'

He nodded. 'Hands off then, and no more interference. Leave me to arrange matters. I will deal with Sonia, with them all.'

And it was through Pan that I found myself with a neat house in rural Sussex, not square, not white, not mine but rented, with David officially in my charge and servants, including Ivy, to look after us. Pan bought me a little Ford motor car.

'A temporary arrangement,' he said. 'When war comes I shall make sure of David's safety, I promise. Will you trust me with him if I take him to America?'

'Only if you're willing to make the effort to know and love him.'

'How often is a middle-aged queer suddenly blessed with a son?'

'I thought the word was "so".'

'Fashions in words change. Is there anything, Amy, that you didn't notice? No, I think not.'

'Everyone overlooked me. I expect I seemed stupid.

213

While I hung about waiting to be noticed I could hardly help noticing other people, could I? Then after the Ooser tried to rape and pillage me my Great-aunt Hildegarde told me all about sex and let me ask questions, so I did. She's the darling of darlings.'

'Rape *and* pillage?'

'A joke. I know pillage only means to plunder, but Claudia and I used to think everything was sex, and perhaps at that time it was.'

Davy went as a day-boy to a local school. I swear to the world and to myself that I encouraged him to make friends of his own age and bring them to the house. But we were happiest together. Grown tall and slim and marvellously, gravely debonair, he drew the eyes of women like a magnet. It was easy to forget that he was still a young boy.

'You orter have people in more, or get wedded and have kiddies of your own,' Ivy said glumly. 'It'll end in tears.'

In the September of 1938, the Prime Minister, Neville Chamberlain, came back from Germany and said he thought we would have peace in our time. No-one really believed it. The digging of air-raid shelters in the London parks didn't inspire confidence.

Father telephoned from Gunville Place, polite but cold. He imagined for a time that I would 'come round' and behave like a loving daughter. My appropriation of David through the mediation of Pandel Metkin threw him into a terrible state of rage. 'You are killing your father,' Gwennie wrote. 'We love you and want you home by us. Forgive and make up, there's my old lady.'

Her old lady didn't answer. I had already forgiven as much as I could manage but I wasn't going to say so until I felt ready.

Anyway, Father rang about Chamberlain. 'It will be

214

war, definitely, in a few months. Sussex is far from safe. You had better bring David here.'

'Sorry,' I said, 'he's sailing for New York on the *Queen Mary* next month with Pandel Metkin and Jimmy.'

From the other end of the line came a brief explosive sound. 'I will not have my son corrupted by a pair of homosexuals, do you understand me, Amy?' Instead of making the obvious reply I kept quiet. He said, 'All right, that shouldn't have been said. I gather that David doesn't know and he mustn't imagine that I don't love him. Ask him to write without fail, will you?'

'He won't live with them,' I said gently. 'They do very much respect his youth. He's to stay with friends of Pan, a big family of boys and girls and mother and father, the kind of life he needs. They'll make sure he's happy.'

'What about you, Amy? You'll be alone.'

'As ever,' I said. 'If it comes to war I shall join one of the services, supposing they'll have me with next to no education. My regards to Gwennie.'

An awful thing had happened. David, self-possessed in most things, overwhelmed me with a warm, shy devotion that drew the heart out of me. I was twenty years old and I had fallen deeply in love with him, a boy of eleven, my half-brother. The secret absence of a blood relationship made no difference. The thought of parting from him cut me to the heart. Yet I would be relieved when the ship sailed and put an ocean between us before I could betray an emotion that could only do him harm. Ivy's gloomy prognostications were justified. It was going to end in tears.

War came with a forgiveness of sins. What had been shocking and scandalous got lost in the greater turmoil. I tried to find Sonia. She and the peer's son seemed to be missing. Pandel Metkin wrote to say that he had seen her last at the Hotel George Cinq in Paris and advised her to return to England. 'She feared, I think, that her lover might enlist and be killed, for she refused to listen. I hear that they went south to the Riveria but I have not been able to trace them.' Although it was none of my business I fretted about her.

Half of Gunville Place became a boys' school. The other half, the rooms where Claudia and I had grown up and discussed doing sex, and read *Three Weeks* and other steamy works, were given over to evacuees from the dangerous ports – Plymouth and Portland, Southampton and Portsmouth.

A flying visit from Claudia, looking stunning and every inch an English rose in the uniform and rings of a WRNS Second Officer, cheered me up. 'It's all the greatest fun – I can recommend it,' she said. 'Sex abounds and it's one's duty to try to stamp it out before it turns into pregnancy. I've broken my engagement.'

'The tricorn's heaven, do let me try. I thought you meant to marry next year.'

'In England he was perfectly fine and generous and quite fun. But you wouldn't believe Scotland – all scenery and haggis and Rabbie Burrrns and hacking about over moorland in tweeds. Hell, sheerest hell! His father died and he became the M'Gurk of M'Gurks or something equally strange. He and everyone else disapproved of me like anything.'

'Poor you. Of course I see how dismal it might be. Not bagpipes, though, do swear there were no bag-pipes.'

'On the battlements at dawn, I promise you. Imagine! And an ancient retainer who wore the shortest kilt and showed his bare bottom and etceteras when he bent over to make up the fires. They smoked.'

'The etceteras?'

'No, idiot, the fires. Then the dancing! So dangerous – people prancing up and down on swords. When I merely ventured to ask why they bothered, and couldn't the butler wear woolly combs or something, everyone looked at me as if I were the great whore – you know, out of Revelation.'

'The Mother of Harlots and full of abominations?' I asked interestedly.

'The very same, and they mumbled in Scottish. It was sheerest luck that I happened to fall in love just when I thought it impossible. He's only a commander and hasn't a bean except his pay and he thinks I'm the bee's knees but an entire waste of the love of a good man. I think that last bit's a joke.'

I hoped it was. I could see that Claudia felt deeply at last. Even with an income of her own she would need a lot of love to cope with being the wife of a poor man.

She must have mentioned somewhere my habit of keeping a journal for I was asked officially to write a diary record for a year concerning my life in wartime. Lots of other people did the same thing. I wondered how they fared. From mine evolved a weird kind of employment. Officially I was a Wren but not all the time, and I could not then and still cannot write about it as it was secret.

On the records I was quartered at Southampton. In practice I continued to live in Sussex, missing Davy and writing to Rudi. Letters were delayed and censored. For ages nothing much would happen except for dodging bombs if I went to London, or watching aeroplanes fight and fall out of the sky. Then a plain-clothes courier would come and put an end to boredom.

Odd things happened. I guessed rather than knew that Pan had organized an escape line for fugitives from occupied Europe. It chanced that my duties took me to ports to keep an eye on arrivals from abroad. Thus on a bleak November day in 1940, months after the Dunkirk evacuation, I got to Sheerness in Kent in time to meet a tiny coaster coming in with a load of refugees.

I recognized a face. From beneath a layer of coal-dust Sonia's lover peered out at England. He didn't recognize me.

I said, 'I'm Amity Savernake, Sonia's step-daughter. Where is she? Is she on board?'

An old blanket draped his shoulders. Beneath he wore only a pair of flannels and a torn cotton shirt. He shivered and shrugged, totally indifferent. 'Still in Le Lavandou, I imagine. We quarrelled. There was only enough money for one passage.'

I wanted to slap the young, hungry face and knock some concern into it. 'So you took it and left her there to chance the Germans?'

His eyes had a cowed look and I saw that he had lived with fear too long to be ashamed. 'She made me. She'll be all right,' he said. 'She'll be all right, I know she will.'

Another year passed before Pan managed to trace her and bring her home. What Sonia suffered for love cannot be known for she never spoke of it, but at forty-five she looked an old woman and, despite everything, a beautiful old woman. Her black-cherry hair had turned almost white. The opulent curves were quite gone. She had an emaciated, spiritual look.

I took her to live with me in Sussex. Ivy had left to work in a munitions-factory and accumulate the money to buy her mother a house in Bournemouth. Sonia vaguely took charge. She was a dreadfully expensive guest for she drank like a fish and was rarely quite sober.

Happily she proved to be a silent drunk. Just beyond my garden lay a huge private estate. Sonia often wandered there and although sometimes she listed alarmingly when she walked she never quite fell over. The staff, few and mostly elderly, grew quite fond of her. Often a bailiff, carrying a brace of pheasants or a rabbit to help eke out our meat ration, would see her safely home.

*   *   *

Portia married in 1942. She telephoned me. 'I shall need absolutely all your clothing-coupons for material for the dresses, Amy,' she said briskly. 'Put them in the post right away, will you?'

'But, Portia, I simply must have a new dress myself, always supposing that I'm to be invited.'

'It's perfectly appropriate to wear uniform in war-time. After all, I'm not asking you or Claudia to be bridesmaids, and naturally I will in no circumstances receive Sonia.'

Savernakes clearly were not to be over-represented. Portia expected much for little. The hope of buying something civilian and feminine departed – for months. 'You can have most,' I said, 'but I shall have to keep some back for stockings. Not even for your wedding am I prepared to wear regulation black woollen ones.'

'Rather selfish, isn't it?' The tone was her haughtiest and I met it with a long silence. After all, she was paying for the call. Getting no response, she went on, 'I suppose I must invite Father and his present wife, and hope that they have the decency to refuse.'

'You can be fairly sure of it. They keep very much to themselves. Who will give you away?'

'Valentine. One can be proud of him.'

He was doing something important and clever at the War Office and wore comforting red tabs. The occasion bored me. Claudia yawned and fidgeted through it and left at the earliest appropriate moment. On the death of her father-in-law soon afterwards Portia became a duchess, demoting the old one to dowager and keeping her firmly in her place.

Living in the country had its drawbacks. Grandmother Mottesfont, having thrown her considerable energies into a war effort of her own, lacked eggs. I was commanded to find some on the rural black market and take them to London. ('And do keep them out of sight. So inconvenient if you're arrested and they are confiscated.')

Hurrying across Waterloo Bridge on my way back to Sussex I got the feeling as I entered the railway station that someone was following me. At the door of an empty first-class compartment I glanced over my shoulder. An American voice said, 'Do you mind if I join you, Ma'am?'

I considered the speaker. He was tall, fair, and madly good-looking. 'I can't prevent you,' I said, 'but if you're intending to make a nuisance of yourself I had better warn you that this is a stopping-train and I have a particularly piercing scream.'

He laughed and bowed from the waist like a nice little boy at a party. 'Nothing of the kind, I assure you, though you have the loveliest legs I ever saw. Major Naughton, US Medical Corps, a bored and terribly well-behaved doctor and token soldier.'

I became fond of Naughton and enjoyed having a handsome escort. After our first few meetings he kissed me and mentioned love. His kisses weren't a bit like those that Jimmy bestowed on Sonia in the play or like those Rudi and the trollop, Marie Dearlove, exchanged under the hedge. They were gentle but without fire.

The speeded-up relationships of wartime left me bemused. Opportunities abounded. I was simply no good at them. ('Have a drink; have another; your bunk or mine?') When maidenheads were being lost in their hundreds because of these urgencies my virginity remained intact. It had, I suppose, a certain rarity value in the marriage market. Yet I felt a touch of pique that Naughton never tried to relieve me of it nor even made token advances in that direction.

I discovered why eventually. 'I've asked for a posting to North Africa,' he said one evening. 'I love you deeply, Amy, but I can't ask you to marry me. It's wrong of me to take up your time.'

'To be truthful I hadn't thought of marriage at all. I like you immensely, Naughton, but love is a different matter. Why can't you ask?'

'English soldiers complain that the Yanks are overpaid, oversexed, and over here,' he said. 'My dear, I'm not sexed at all, and that's the most difficult confession a so-called man can make.'

Could it be possible that I had managed to find the only American in Europe unable to dispossess me of my virginity? Apparently it could. Who said Sonia was unlucky? The awful thing was that I liked him so much and I had a cruel desire to laugh.

'You don't need to explain to me, Naughton, honestly you don't. In fact I'd much rather you didn't.'

'I ought never to have – oh, damn it, Amy, I adore you.'

There were tears in his eyes. I looked away and thought how glad I was that I hadn't managed to fall in love with him. 'It makes not a bit of difference to being friends,' I said. 'Sex isn't everything and my sister says I'm retarded in that line. We make a good pair.'

That was our last meeting. 'If you don't mind I won't write,' Naughton said on parting. 'I'm man enough to feel intense jealousy at the thought of you marrying someone else.'

So much for my one essay into wartime romance. I never saw him again. It depressed me and I didn't dare tell Claudia. She would probably have blamed my lack of sex appeal and burst her uniform buttons laughing.

One marvellous day later that year the phone rang and Rudi said just as though we had never been parted, 'I have precisely two hours before I go to Southampton. Come and lunch with me, the Dolphin in half an hour.'

He looked sun-tanned and familiar and friendly and so very, very nice. I hugged him vigorously. 'Is the tr— is Marie with you?' I asked.

The laughter still lurked behind his blue eyes. 'No,

dearest Amy, the trollop, Marie Dearlove, isn't with me. We're alone. You look tremendously fetching in that hat; and black silk stockings – wow!'

'It's uniform. I had to wear it because of using official petrol. They put a dye in so that the police can tell if we're up to no good with rations. The regulation stockings are wool and itchy; practically no-one wears them.'

'You have lovely legs, did you know?'

'Thank you, yes. An American major told me so. How do you come to be here? I know that Marie's a screen goddess and a pin-up for the troops, and I've seen her at the pictures. I imagined you lying back on silk cushions and eating grapes from the hands of houris.'

'Slippery things, silk cushions. I'm off to mysterious foreign places talent-spotting for ENSA, that being my business. It's good to be home. The Americans go in for flag-wagging in a big way. I began to find them embarrassingly sentimental and they thought me impossibly stolid and English.'

'Surely Marie will miss you?'

'Not a bit. She's quite above herself and surrounded by admirers.'

Because of shortages the food was fairly dull but I had no idea what I was eating anyway. The ease of friendship that allowed us to pick up where we left off fifteen years before warmed and relaxed me. 'I expect you'll get around to marrying her one day. Will you have to go back to America after the war?'

'No way, as they say over there. I've made some money and I dare say I can beg a crust.'

'Lovely! Will you ask me out sometimes? My treat. I've come into my inheritance though it's worth less because of the war and Sonia drinks quite a lot of it.'

'We can always go Dutch – that's American for paying for ourselves. How old are you now, Amy?'

'Ancient, I'm twenty-three. What about you?'

'Going on for forty. I expect my hair's white with age and my eyes rheumy. What is rheumy, d'you suppose?'

'Something nasty. Your hair's still tidy and brown. I used to think you had terribly wicked eyes but they're not now. Did you do your look at lots of women and lure them into bed?'

Rudi gave me a pained scowl. 'Unfair question. Do I enquire about your virginity? No, I do not. Please change the subject.'

'Gladly,' I said, thinking of Naughton and my lack of success in the love stakes. 'Grandmother's having a lovely war. They've been bombed out several times and lost most of their servants. She's organized a canteen for the ARP in her basement and serves them tea and buns herself. Do go and see her if you get the chance. You're one of her favourite men.'

'I did toss up as to whether I'd rather see her or you. You won by a whisker.'

'Well thanks, Rudi. It's nice to know that I can compete with someone.'

We smiled contentedly at each other. 'You're an absolute dear, Amy Savernake,' he said. 'How's Great-aunt Hildegarde?'

'Ninety, can you believe, and getting quite peeved about it. She says that she's waited for Heaven so long that it begins to look as though Jesus doesn't want her. I hope He lets her stay with us a while yet.'

Our two hours were almost up. We parted with the usual wartime urgings: come back safely, don't forget to write, take care, do please take care of yourself, et cetera. Rudi kissed me on both cheeks. 'Next time – oh hell – I wish I could stay.'

'Off you go or you'll miss your train.'

'Who's this American who says you have lovely legs?'

'You mind your own business.'

'Okey-doke, Amy,' he said. 'Oh, by the way, the

trollop, Marie Dearlove, married her producer last year. Goodbye for now.'

Drizzle began to fall. I smiled up at the clouds. Some idiot had parked right in front of me and I couldn't move the car. Leaning against it I waited. Under my breath I began to sing 'The White Cliffs of Dover'. Not my favourite wartime song but just then it seemed to have a meaning.

Chapter Fifteen

The meeting with Rudi stiffened my rather limp backbone enough to move me towards making a proper peace with my father. Also I needed to talk to him about Sonia. I applied for and was granted a long-overdue week's leave. Gunville Place being conveniently full of schoolboys and evacuees, and having no idea of what my reception would be, I preferred neutral territory. I drove to Dorchester and took a room at the Wessex.

Although we had spoken on the telephone, I had seen neither my father nor Gwennie since my abrupt departure from the house in Builth Wells. The initial awkwardness was on their part rather than mine.

'Uniform, there's smart,' Gwennie said, not quite daring to kiss me. 'Brought your ration-book, have you?'

This was the polite wartime way of asking, Oh God, are you staying? The laundry hasn't come back yet and we're down to our last egg.

I saw that we could spar for ages so I stated my case at once. 'Only a passing visit, Gwennie. I'm not coming back to live, or even to stay. But with people we know getting killed every day it seems idiotic for me to go on sulking about things that lost their importance years ago. Do you think Father will agree?'

'I'm sure he will, oh yes. I'm glad. Selfish we were and not thinking straight, being in love.'

'Why on earth didn't you take him before he married Sonia? He wanted you, I'm sure.'

'He did and he didn't.' Gwennie blinked and

swished imaginary dust from the table. 'I was only a servant, see. An unsuitable match and we both knew it. Pride then, nose up in the air, not wanting to be talked about and pointed at. "On the make, that girl, marrying above her station." Foolish. I'll tell him you're here and get some coffee sent up.'

The interview was difficult. Father sat at his desk, writing or pretending to. Neither he nor I intended to apologize if we could help it though the words kept trying to force themselves out of my mouth. Did all daughters go in awe of their fathers? I know that I did though I hadn't understood it before that moment and I didn't know why.

We exchanged trivial remarks then he took up his pen and said, 'Well, I expect you're busy.'

'Oh dear, this is getting nowhere, is it? Do help me a bit, Father, please. Family quarrels hurt badly and I want us to make up and be friends if that's possible. I'm glad about Gwennie, truly I am.'

'You girls, I never managed to understand you. Or women in general for that matter. So many causes for bitterness, beginning with your mother's death.'

'But you *are* happy now, aren't you? Gwennie is. She radiates contentment.'

He smiled. 'Yes, Amity, I am. We're a comfortable, ordinary couple. Much of the money is draining away in taxes. As soon as Valentine marries I shall hand this house over to him, and when the war's over Gwennie and I will look for a small place somewhere by the sea.'

I grinned back, feeling very much easier. 'You'll let us visit?'

'If you must,' he said, and laughed. 'Stay to lunch, won't you?'

'I'd better not. It's unkind to eat other people's rations.'

'Bowells killed a black-market pig and sent us up a leg and some offal. You're welcome to share.'

226

'Just coffee, thanks. Gwennie's sent for some, but before we go in I need advice. Don't be angry with me please, Father, but it's Sonia. You know she's living with me?'

He swung his wheelchair round so that I couldn't see his face. I expected an outburst. All he said was, 'I've suffered enough damage at her hands. How does she concern me?'

'She lost everything she had in France,' I said, soldiering on, 'jewels, money, pride, health, all her possessions. She's old and sad and silent yet not a word of complaint. It's pathetic to watch her struggle. Could you, would you help her a little, give her a small income, perhaps – a kind of token forgiveness?'

'And what of my pride? Why doesn't that idiot boy help her?'

'You know perfectly well that he deserted her, and I'm sure you expected it to happen.'

His temper began to sizzle. 'Humiliating, the whole wretched business. Why should I care what happens to her? Throw her out and let her fend for herself if that's what you want. It's not your burden, you owe her nothing.'

The peace between us was fragile but it had to be risked. 'I don't mind about that but I do mind the sense of guilt. Sonia had the rottenest luck with us. We're all to blame in part. You because you married her when you were in love with Gwennie, then Claudia and me. We hated her taking Mother's place, and showed it. What chance did we give her either to like us or be liked?'

I watched the back of his head, trying to guess what went on in it. For all his detachment he was a man who could be kind and generous, and he had suffered the loss of his health and youth without complaint.

'A trust fund to bring in a couple of hundred a year, with you as trustee, will that do?' he said without turning. 'Tell her she's forgiven, tell her what you like,

227

but I can't see her or write to her or have any direct communication with her at all.'

'Thank you, Father, thanks awfully.'

'You're being pretty decent taking her in, Amy, so she's not entirely unlucky with us. Shall we get our coffee now? It's muck, I'm afraid, liquid mud, and we've had to settle for a half-baked girl from the village as a cook. David seems happy in America, don't you think?'

The hidden love I trailed like a second shadow gave a painful twinge. Yet at Gunville Place, more hideous than ever in its wartime neglect, strong emotion seemed to wither. Goodbye desire and folly. Putting aside my immature and hopeless longings I said, 'It's a saner life than he had with Sonia or with me. His adopted family are keen to keep him and he wants to go on to Harvard when he leaves school. I rather suspect he'll become an American citizen eventually.'

In the afternoon I visited Great-aunt Hildegarde. On that fine autumn afternoon she sat in the sun on a garden seat with a Bible in her lap and a bronze chrysanthemum pushed somewhat drunkenly into her bushy white hair.

'Oh, there you are, Amy dear,' she said comfortably. 'It seems a pity to cut back the roses while they're still flowering, don't you think?'

I kissed her softly wrinkled cheek and sat down beside her. Directly in my line of vision stood the shed where Avon Werlock, the Ooser, had hidden. 'How are you, Aunt Hildegarde?'

'I haven't left you this house, dear, because of the fright you had here, but I haven't forgotten you, not at all. You are to have the contents.'

'Please don't,' I said, 'don't talk about it. I've always relied on you and loved you.'

She turned serene shortsighted eyes to me. 'You'll stay the night, dear?'

'I hadn't meant to. I've a room at the Wessex.'

'Time's short, I think, and everyone's so busy with this war. You'll stay?'

'Yes, darling, I'll stay.'

'Supertax is iniquitous, nineteen-and-sixpence in the pound, and then estate duty on the little that's left. But with so much destroyed in the bombing furniture and silver will be worth having.'

She seemed to be wandering a bit. 'I'll tell you all my gossip and then you can tell yours,' I said.

After dinner we went back into the garden. Not a light showed anywhere because of the blackout, but the stars burned and shimmered brilliantly against the dark of the sky.

Aunt Hildegarde looked up. 'Do you know the poems of George Herbert, dear? A favourite of mine,' she said, and then quoted in a soft voice:

'The Milky Way, the bird of Paradise,
Church-bells beyond the stars heard, the soul's
    blood,
The land of spices, something understood.

'So modern in its way and yet he died in sixteen-thirty-three. I wish I'd known him, though I dare say I should have been disappointed.'

'It's odd about the land of spices. You mentioned it before and I thought it was a real place where everyone glamorous lived – princesses and wazirs and eunuchs and caliphs.'

'Perhaps it's real and here, among the myths and fables, for each of us a different reality. Life as it passes seems a muddle, all unconnected bits and pieces, but they come together when we get things right. Then we begin to understand.' She took my hand. 'Think of me on your happiest days.'

I felt that she had separated herself from me. The atmosphere, though peaceful, was strange and made me desperately sad. The next morning at breakfast she put down the square of toast she was conveying to her mouth and smiled. 'How very interesting, Amy dear,' she said.

Great-aunt Hildegarde died at once, without fuss or pain, leaning against the high back of her chair. Perhaps her land of spices was Heaven, or perhaps it was no place at all, only an idea in our minds.

Her elderly maid helped me to move her to the chesterfield and fold her hands neatly on her breast. We sat with her until the doctor came. I thought of her oddities and the happy air she always carried with her. I couldn't stop crying.

After the funeral I went back to the graveside and found Claudia there, weeping like a water-spout and drenching her best uniform. 'Imagine her leaving me the house,' she said, sniffing vigorously. 'I wish I'd been nicer.'

'Aunt Hildegarde understood people. She knew more about us than we knew about ourselves,' I said. 'More about everything, come to think of it. After the Ooser she told me all about sex.'

My sister gave me a characteristic scornful glare. 'You really are a fearful liar at times, Amy. That isn't true, is it?'

'Where do you think I learnt all the proper words?'

'Pee-nis, see-men, amazing! I should have known you were holding out on me. What a rat!'

'But you so loved being superior and simply wouldn't listen. You hate the country. Will you ever live here, do you think?'

'Anywhere with the right person.'

'Even Scotland?'

Claudia smiled. 'It's perfectly lovely really. I just couldn't take being trapped there with the M'Gurk. Being in love makes the difference.' She put her arm through mine. 'I bet all the little angels in Heaven will soon have pairs of nice warm gloves, don't you? Shall we go?'

It wouldn't be true to say that Sonia perked up at all on hearing about the trust fund. Somewhere inside she still mourned. I couldn't question her so I never knew whether her sorrow was for the young lover who behaved much as one might have expected or for her son or for her lost respectability.

She showed neither gratitude to me nor resentment. 'Gervase would much prefer that I had died, I expect. He needn't worry, I shan't trouble him, but you had better get your lawyer to say so and thank him,' she said with flat lack of interest.

But with a bit of urging she bought some clothes and shoes instead of leaving her clothing-coupons to go out of date. She still drank rather too much when I was away on duty and she was alone in the house at night. I worried about her on those occasions.

After one absence of six weeks in the late summer of 1944 I returned to find Sonia missing. Shortly afterwards her bailiff friend knocked at the door. He said, 'I saw your car come up, Lady Amity. May I have a word? It's about the Countess.'

'Have you seen her? She isn't here.'

'That's right. I've got her down at my place. There were doodlebugs coming across last night and a lot of gunfire. I came to see if she was all right. She gets restless after France, see, and turns to the bottle, so I took her on down to stay with me.'

'Thank you, that's kind. I do get anxious when she's on her own. Shall I walk back with you and bring her home?'

'There's something else that I'm going to ask. If you think I'm out of line you can say – I shan't take offence.'

I began to get an inkling of what was coming though I didn't quite believe it. 'You'd better tell me quickly before I start making wild guesses.'

'We've got pretty close, Sonia and me. She's a lovely

woman and we go along well together.' He cleared his throat and twirled his cap so nervously between his fingers that he dropped it. Red-faced he retrieved it and said quickly, 'I want to marry her if she'll have me and if it won't upset you. Not much of a match for her, I know, but she needs company and someone to look after her.'

I smiled to reassure him which only seemed to unnerve him more. 'Have you asked her yet?'

'Why no. She's upper class, titled. I thought there might be a law or something and I ought to ask you first.'

What a joke, asking me for permission to marry my stepmother. Claudia was going to laugh her head off. But this was a good man and loyal and not to be hurt. And Sonia's self-esteem was as low as it could be. If she accepted him she would never know the pain of rejection again.

'There's not a thing to stop you from marrying tomorrow, only if Sonia herself refuses. And I shall think her beyond hope if she does,' I said. 'You'll have my blessing if you can make her happy again.'

Sonia didn't refuse. 'I don't have to struggle to make him like me, and that's never happened to me before,' she said with a ghostly smile. 'Will you come to the wedding please, Amy? You've been very good. I won't speak of pals since the word always made you wince, but I've felt closer to you than the rest.'

Calm contentment settled on her. I witnessed the marriage and helped to move her into her new husband's house. Then I was alone, making my occasional journeys and waiting out the last anxious months as the Allied forces advanced into Europe.

The war there came to an end. Men still fought on and died in the east. An atom bomb was dropped on Hiroshima and we felt relief at first because it brought a final peace. We didn't then realize that with the falling of the bomb the world changed terribly and for ever, and that no peace was final.

After being demobilized at the end of 1945, I felt miserably at a loose end. Claudia expected to be married in the next year and Hildegarde's executors hinted gently that it was high time I removed my bequest from her property.

Reluctantly I set out for Dorset not relishing at all the prospect of going through what still were to me my great-aunt's belongings. The furniture would have to be put into store anyway until I settled where I would live.

The day was chilled by March winds racing through the lanes. I had left home before the milk delivery. It was an unauspicious beginning for I found that the car was almost out of petrol and I had barely enough coupons to see me through the double journey. Before reaching Petersfield I stopped at a single petrol pump outside a small garage and asked the lad in charge to check the tyres.

'Is there anywhere I can get coffee or a cup of tea?' I asked. 'No breakfast this morning.'

'Round the corner in the village; the caff there'll do you a nice poached egg on toast. Leave the old bus here if you like. I'll put a drop extra in the tank and give the windscreen a wipe while I'm at it.'

He pointed to a narrow lane that had no look of going anywhere. After twenty yards or so it opened out and there lay a wide green with houses of all ages and all styles heaped higgledy-piggledy around the perimeter. In the centre a pond glinted among drifts of purple crocus. A round lady in a round hat and dufflecoat threw handfuls of bread to the ducks and geese. She waved a hand. 'Good morning. Fairish sort of day. Greedy things, birds, but I like 'em.'

I smiled and nodded though my mind was not with her. The spirit of Aunt Hildegarde stood at my

233

shoulder as I stared across to the far side of the green. I walked slowly, not quite believing what I thought I could see. Three white houses, two of them close together.

The third stood a little apart. It was square and the casement windows shone. The stucco had recently been painted as had the black wrought-iron railings in front of it. Four steps led up to the door with its semicircular fanlight. It was perfect. My heart beat strongly. Beside the gate stood a board announcing that the house, my dreamhouse, was for sale.

'In perfect order,' the estate agent said. 'A maiden lady owns it but she wanted to be nearer to her nieces in Leicestershire.'

Portia country! The young duchess kept up standards and watched morals fiercely, holding at bay the raffish Savernakes who had so badly let the side down. I smiled to myself. 'May I make an appointment to view?'

'We can go now if you like. The house is empty.'

It reached out and embraced me. 'There, buy it quickly,' whispered the disembodied Hildegarde, 'I told you not to worry.'

Two months later I moved in her furniture and myself. A long time had passed since I started my house-fund and told of my heart's desire to a genie and a caliph. The dream had come true at last.

The bell rang. I had a trainee housemaid but I got such a kick out of callers that I usually opened the door to them myself.

'Hallo, Amy,' Rudi said. 'May I take you to lunch please?'

'Would that be Dutch?'

'Not at all, my treat. I love your white house.'

'Where have you been for so long? Not a word for months. Come in and see it properly if you'd like to, but I warn you I'm house-proud to the point of tedium so say it's lovely.'

'It's lovely. Do you always wear that overall? It shows rather a lot of leg – very shapely leg admittedly. I got trapped in Burma by the Japs and picked up a germ or two.'

'Are you better? You look a little thin and pale, or is it just a bid for sympathy?'

'I'm thin and pale and dying for a cup of tea. Shall I put the kettle on?'

'Sit down. I'll do it. The range has gone out. It's temperamental and simply gobbles up the fuel-ration. Until the gas company delivers my new stove I'm managing on one gas-ring.'

Rudi followed me into the kitchen. He smiled at the maid and said, 'Can you go away and make beds or something, like a good girl, while I sell your mistress a vacuum cleaner?'

She got confused and dropped a cup. 'Sorry, Miss Savernake.'

'It's not your fault. He's not quite right in the head. We shall be lunching out so you might as well go home now.'

As we drank our tea he said, 'No title nowadays?'

'No. I've wanted to escape it for years.'

'Oh,' Rudi said, looking thoughtful. 'How old are you now, Amy?'

'What year is this, 1946? Then I'm twenty-seven.'

'I'm forty-four, isn't that disgustingly old?'

'Are you afflicted with piles and chronic rheumatics yet?'

'Almost certainly. The last time I was in England I had a mystical experience at Clapham Junction station. I hope you won't laugh.'

'Try an economy raspberry bun. They're pretty boring. I got the recipe from Grandmother.'

'Please don't try to divert me with delicacies when I'm nervous, Amy. I've adored you since you were eight and after the Dolphin I realized quite suddenly on the train that I had fallen madly in love with you. I want to marry you. Does that sound ridiculous?'

So this was what had been wrong with my life, why I had chosen relationships that led nowhere. Loving a child, allowing safe impotent Naughton to pick me up, evading strange beds, had all happened because of an old friendship that turned into love while I wasn't looking.

'Would you say that again please, Rudi, and try to do it properly.'

'You don't want me to use my look, I trust?'

'Are you beginning to wriggle? You may be sex-mad but if ever I see that look again I won't be responsible for your safety. Now don't waste time.'

He said in his most tender voice, 'I love you very, very much and what's more you fill me with lustful dreams. Will you marry me please, Amy? If you feel at all the same, that is.'

'Yes, Rudi, of course I will. I feel exactly the same and it's been an awful handicap with other men. A wasted war as far as sex was concerned. Now you can kiss me properly the way you used to kiss the trollop, Marie Dearlove.'

'Righto, Amy.'

After a while I said, 'I've been a frustrated virgin long enough. Can we go to bed now?'

'Good idea, Amy.'

A mislaid magic of twenty years ago shook off dust and began to shine again: something complete and wonderful, something understood.

THE END

After the Unicorn
Joyce Windsor

The sequel to *A Mislaid Magic*.

The Savernakes were one of Dorset's oldest and most
aristocratic families. They were also outrageous and
sometimes, just plain peculiar. The earl had finally married
Gwennie, the nursemaid, while his eldest daughter, Lady
Portia, had married the vile Coritanum and become a duchess
(and *that* marriage hadn't turned out to be a bed of roses).
Beautiful, bad-tempered, tart Claudia was *about* to get married
but was setting the family on its head with plans for her
approaching nuptials. Would Claudia make it to the altar this
time or would she be off on another mysterious and hard-
drinking carousel of her own?

And quiet, delightfully sharp and observant Amity Savernake,
knowing more of the family's strange – and sometimes sad –
secrets than anyone else, watched them all from her small
white house on a village green, hoping for a kind of happiness
but finding her own life becoming increasingly complicated,
funny, and bizarre.

0 552 99651 3

BLACK SWAN

The Golden Year
Elizabeth Falconer

One enchanted summer in Provence and its aftermath.

Summers, to Anna, had always meant the Presbytery, the mellow old stone house in Provence where her mother, the formidable Domenica, lived. Now that Anna's marriage to Jeffrey was all but over, she thought that she had herself well organized, dividing her time between her riverside home in London, her two teenage children and her career as a gilder and restorer of antiques. And then there were her summers in France – a chance to eat and drink magnificently, to sit in the sun and to recharge the batteries. She hardly realized how narrow and lonely her life had really become.

But one summer her brother Giò, an antiques dealer in Paris, brought down a new friend to the Presbytery. Patrick, a handsome television director, suddenly opened up Anna's life in a new and wonderful way, offering her a wholly unexpected chance of happiness. But she did not immediately see that others might not share her joy, and that her beloved brother Giò could have quite different ideas about Patrick and the future.

'A DELIGHTFUL EVOCATION OF THE SIGHTS, SOUNDS AND FLAVOURS OF LIFE IN PROVENCE'
Family Circle

0 552 99622 X

BLACK SWAN

Touch and Go
Elizabeth Berridge

'MISS BERRIDGE HAS AN EYE FOR THE BEAUTY OF
HUMBLE AND FAMILIAR THINGS . . . SHE HAS A QUIET,
WICKED SENSE OF HUMOUR'
Honor Tracy, *New Statesman*

When Emma Rowlands returned to Wales, to the village where
she had spent her childhood, she brought with her no more
than some favourite pieces of china, books, flowers, and her
small pregnant cat. Behind her she left a broken marriage and
an eighteen-year-old daughter who had fled to India to escape
the marital fights.

As Emma, approaching thirty-nine, stood in the solid red brick
house on top of a Welsh hill, she felt a tiny sense of happiness
displace her apprehension. Years before, as a small child, the
somewhat maverick village doctor had asked her what reward
she would like for being brave, and she had asked for the shell
house. Now, at a time of uncertainty and despondency in her
life, she discovered he had left her not the toy house she had
asked for, but his own home.

As – hesitantly – she began to renew old friendships and re-
examine her relationships with not only her daughter, but also
her mother, a widow who assuaged her loneliness by continual
travel, so gradually she began to interpret the meaning behind
the gift of the house, and with understanding came the chance
to rebuild her own future.

'ONE OF THE BEST, BUT NOT ALWAYS ADEQUATELY
APPRECIATED, OF BRITISH NOVELISTS'
Martin Seymour-Smith, *Oxford Mail*

'ELIZABETH BERRIDGE HAS THE SHARPEST OF EYES. BUT
SOMETHING RATHER MORE IMPORTANT AS WELL . . .
WHAT HER PEOPLE DO AND FEEL AND REPRESENT
MATTERS, SEEMS MORE MEMORABLE'
Isabel Quigley, *Financial Times*

0 552 99648 3

BLACK SWAN

A SELECTED LIST OF FINE WRITING
AVAILABLE FROM BLACK SWAN

☐	99629 7	SEVEN FOR A SECRET	Judy Astley	£5.99
☐	99618 1	BEHIND THE SCENES AT THE MUSEUM	Kate Atkinson	£6.99
☐	99716 1	RANGE OF MOTION	Elizabeth Berg	£6.99
☐	99648 3	TOUCH AND GO	Elizabeth Berridge	£5.99
☐	99593 2	A RIVAL CREATION	Marika Cobbold	£5.99
☐	99622 X	THE GOLDEN YEAR	Elizabeth Falconer	£5.99
☐	99589 4	RIVER OF HIDDEN DREAMS	Connie May Fowler	£5.99
☐	99656 4	THE TEN O'CLOCK HORSES	Laurie Graham	£5.99
☐	99610 6	THE SINGING HOUSE	Janette Griffiths	£5.99
☐	99681 5	A MAP OF THE WORLD	Jane Hamilton	£6.99
☐	99387 5	TIME OF GRACE	Clare Harkness	£5.99
☐	99392 1	THE GREAT DIVORCE	Valerie Martin	£6.99
☐	99649 1	WAITING TO EXHALE	Terry McMillan	£5.99
☐	99693 9	IMPOSSIBLE THINGS	Penny Perrick	£6.99
☐	99696 3	THE VISITATION	Sue Reidy	£5.99
☐	99606 8	OUTSIDE, LOOKING IN	Kathleen Rowntree	£5.99
☐	99672 6	A WING AND A PRAYER	Mary Selby	£6.99
☐	99607 6	THE DARKENING LEAF	Caroline Stickland	£5.99
☐	99650 5	A FRIEND OF THE FAMILY	Titia Sutherland	£5.99
☐	99130 9	NOAH'S ARK	Barbara Trapido	£6.99
☐	99643 2	THE BEST OF FRIENDS	Joanna Trollope	£6.99
☐	99636 X	KNOWLEDGE OF ANGELS	Jill Paton Walsh	£5.99
☐	99673 4	DINA'S BOOK	Herbjørg Wassmo	£6.99
☐	99592 4	AN IMAGINATIVE EXPERIENCE	Mary Wesley	£5.99
☐	99639 4	THE TENNIS PARTY	Madeleine Wickham	£5.99
☐	99651 3	AFTER THE UNICORN	Joyce Windsor	£6.99